I Loved You Yesterday

Book One in the Trading Heartbeats Trilogy

Julie Navickas

I Loved You Yesterday
Book One in the Trading Heartbeats Trilogy
Copyright © 2022 Julie Navickas
All rights reserved.

ISBN: (ebook) 978-1-958136-05-8
(print) 978-1-958136-06-5

Inkspell Publishing
207 Moonglow Circle #101
Murrells Inlet, SC 29576

Edited By Audrey Bobek
Cover art By Fantasia Frog Designs

DEDICATION

I Loved You Yesterday is dedicated to my husband, Tommy.
Thank you for showing me that it is indeed possible to
find your soulmate at seventeen.

You never forget your first love.
I don't have to.
I married mine.

JULIE NAVICKAS

CHAPTER ONE

Josh

The lights flickered on in the parking lot outside of Josh's office window, a gray haze creeping over the Los Angeles skyline as darkness descended on the early-December day.

Balling his hands into fists, he rubbed his aching eyes. The burn behind his lids screamed at the pressure—the long hours logged on the computer catching up with him as he sifted through the backlog of patient charts.

With a groan, Josh snapped his laptop shut and began the monotony of his pre-departure routine. His hands glided along the hard, sleek wooden surface of the desk with a sanitizing wipe. *Mental note: pick up more of these.* Lifting the metal nameplate engraved with *Dr. Joshua Templeton*, he slid the white cloth beneath it.

The vibration of his phone interrupted the stillness of the office and the preliminary shopping list running through his brain, each tremor disrupting the end-of-day calm. With a glance at the screen, Josh bit down on the inside of his cheek before accepting the call. The metallic taste of blood filled his mouth.

"What do you want, Tess?" His stomach churned as her

name left his lips.

"Lovely way to start a conversation, Joshua. Truly."

Josh shrugged. After being married to Tess for four torturous years, her shrill voice looped on repeat in the back of his mind, an instant tension headache in the making.

"Again, Tess, what do you need?" His palms tingled, and a numbness settled in his fingertips. "And don't call me that. You know I hate it." Josh dropped the wipe in the trash, put Tess on speaker, and cupped the back of his neck to knead the sore muscles. *It's already been a long day… now what?*

"I have our final divorce papers, and I would like your signature on them. Tonight."

Oh.

Josh exhaled and smashed his eyes closed. "I don't trust you. I need Austin to look over everything first. If he can come, I'll sign."

Anger seeped into the pit of his stomach, agitating the remains of a veggie burger he'd eaten for a late lunch. A wave of nausea washed over him, and a sheen of cold sweat coated his forehead. *How do you still do this to me?*

"Well… text me. I'm in the neighborhood." She snickered and ended the call.

In the neighborhood…

Josh snorted, an ironic bubble of laughter surfacing from the depths of his soul. "Give my best to Dalton Sheppard," he spit into the silent phone, each word punctured by the knife she'd rammed into his heart with her betrayal. *Homewrecking fucker.*

His knuckles cracked as he pounded out a quick, angry text to his brother. Placing his phone on the top of the desk, he rested his head on the surface. His cheek stuck to the top layer of his notepad, the pen's ink colliding with his skin, tattooing him with smeary blue.

One deep breath later, and his phone lit up.

My marriage ends tonight.

Josh turned into his driveway, the sole home on the street absent of holiday cheer. He sneered at his neighbor's ten-foot blow-up Santa and flashy light show. *Shove it, Santa! There's nothing holly and jolly about tonight.*

Shifting his Jeep into park, he killed the engine and allowed the momentary silence of the car's cabin to fill his ears. In the darkness, the living room lights on the main floor glared through the front picture window of the modern, un-festive home; the home he and Tess had bought together.

Air infiltrated his lungs, working to quell the uneasy pit growing in his stomach. He dropped his head to the cool steering wheel, breathing out the last minutes of his marriage, counting down to the finale. Five… *This will be over soon.* Four… *She'll finally be gone from my life.* Three… *The nightmare is almost over.* Two… *This is the hardest thing I'll ever have to do.* One… *No, wait, there's been one thing harder…* The sudden realization chilled his broken soul, an invisible force squeezing his heart. Josh pushed the memory—and the pain—aside, allowing ire to replace it as he slammed the car door closed.

With a twist of the doorknob, he stepped inside, each footstep falling heavier than the last as he trudged forward.

"Hey," Austin grunted, pushing a place setting aside on the dining room table.

"Yeah…" Josh nodded at his twin and dropped his backpack to the lowermost step of the staircase. With a flip of the lock on the front door, the sloshing acid in his stomach dissolved the final, minuscule shred of desire he had to save his marriage.

Tess's pale blonde curls bounced with each step as she climbed the small set of stairs, the silhouette of her lover hidden in her prized Mini Cooper on the shadowy curb.

"You're alone?" Josh held the screen door open, his scattered mind flashing back to middle school etiquette class. *Just be polite even though you know she won't.*

"Did you want an audience?" she asked, waving her

hand behind her. She'd painted each fingernail in her signature bubble gum pink color.

There it is.

Sadness peaked at the top of the emotional roller coaster. The sorrow consumed him as she swept past, joining Austin at the dining room table with the large pile of divorce papers she'd housed in a blue folder. Without a word, she handed it over.

Austin perched a pair of reading glasses on his nose and took a seat, reserving a small glare for Tess as she stalked away.

"Just give me a few minutes to look these over, Josh." He disappeared behind the folder.

Josh nodded. *I failed.*

The woman he vowed to love and cherish for a lifetime stood before him, her gum smacking the roof of her mouth as a neon-green bubble blew from her pink lips. He stared, forcing his brain to see past the woman before him—past her adultery—past her disinterest in commitment. *I don't even know who you are anymore.*

"What are you thinking?" Tess eyed him.

He grinned, his gaze dropping to the floor. "Umm... I guess where it all went wrong, when it all went wrong." Josh shrugged and stuffed his hands in his pockets. "What I did to make you feel like you wanted, err, needed someone else." A dull ache pounded in his heart, grief hammering through his bloodstream.

Josh locked eyes with her, and for the briefest of moments, the girl from their early days of college gazed back. The girl he'd fallen in love with gripped his battered heart as the memory of their blossoming romance preyed on the cloud of depression blanketing the room.

She laughed, her shrill cackle piercing the air like a needle to a balloon.

"Oh, please. It was all wrong from the start. I never should have married you when you were still in love with someone else."

Josh scrunched his nose and squinted. "What?"

"All right, Josh. This is all fine. You can sign." Austin interrupted, rising from his seat and removing his glasses. He held out a black ballpoint pen and gestured toward the chair in front of him.

Tess raised her pencil-thin eyebrows. "I told you so…"

"Can't blame me for not believing you. Honesty hasn't been your strong suit," he added with a snort.

She scoffed and Josh accepted the pen. He sat, firmly signing *Dr. Joshua Michael Templeton* in monotonous repetition on each highlighted line. Each stroke of the pen—each stain of ink—sealed the failure of a lifetime.

Laying the pen on the table, Josh picked up the pile of papers and returned them to their home in the blue folder. As he swallowed the bile rising in his throat, his attention drifted to the abstract swirl of blue and black colors in the painting on the opposite wall. *Why didn't you take that ridiculous piece with you when you moved out? You took everything else.*

"I can take these to City Hall in the morning and get them processed by the judge," Austin said softly.

Josh nodded and handed the folder over as the growing burn behind his eyes threatened to break the feeble dam.

"That would be outstanding, Austin. Saves me a trip." Tess flung her purse over her shoulder, the fringe swaying rhythmically with each click of her heels. Cracking the front door, she glanced back at the brothers. Tess opened her mouth as if to speak but bit back the words. She left in silence instead, quietly closing the door behind her.

It's over, and I never truly knew you at all, did I?

"I don't know what to say," said Austin, gripping Josh's shoulder. "I'm sure it hurts like hell right now, man, but you are *way* better off without her." He squeezed before letting go. "Want me to stay? Put a game on or something? Take your mind off it?"

Josh inhaled, the imagined squeak of sneakers on a basketball court gripping his ears with consideration.

I just want to be alone.

"No… thanks, Austin. I appreciate your help tonight and for coming over so late. But I think I'll just go to bed and bury this whole fucking nightmare." His lips attempted a smile, but the quiver of his muscles betrayed him.

"Okay. Call me if you need anything, all right?"

"Yeah, I will. Thanks, man."

Austin smiled and exited through the side door. The garage opened, then closed. His Corvette pulled out of the driveway and sped down the street, leaving the house in complete and total silence.

I'm absolutely fucking alone.

Josh forced his shaking legs to stand. With each step forward, he dragged his body to the staircase like a ball of lead had been strapped to his ankles under the confines of a prison sentence.

As he pushed the door to his bedroom open, the hinges whined. An empty bed looked back, solemn yet inviting. With the intent to face plant into the mattress, Josh entered the room. Cheerful colored snowflakes danced across the bare walls, the festive merriment from outside invading his hole of despair. He sneered and crossed the space, tugging the curtains closed to block out the holiday happiness.

Fuck you, Frosty.

Josh pushed the door open to the walk-in closet, unbuttoned his shirt, and tossed it in the hamper. His back roared, protesting the long hours spent at the computer. With a twist, the stretch lifted his line of sight to a cardboard box tucked in the back corner. And like the flaps of the cardboard, Josh's heart tore down the middle, the same cold chill from the car returning to ricochet throughout his body.

"At this point, why the hell not?" he muttered, snagging the box from the top shelf and retreating to his bed. His butt met the mattress as he lifted the flaps and stared at the variety of forgotten mementos from his youth: science medals, team photos from high school football, yearbooks… even a dried flower from senior prom.

The petals crumbled to the touch as the air escaped his lungs, rushing forward with the energy and excitement of a fugitive.

"Duchess..."

His shaking fingers glided along her photo, rousing her youthful presence from what now seemed a distant dream. Josh closed his eyes, filling his mind with the recall of her essence. A shiver erupted along his spine with the memory of tender companionship... of her soft giggle... and the way the very beat of her heart stirred his own. The girl from his youth trudged across his soul, fresh footsteps on his grave.

Her cascade of dark curls met her shoulders in the photograph, flowing wildly about like ivy on a trellis. And her big, striking green eyes smiled back at him—full of secrets. Full of mystery.

Josh touched her cheek in the photo as the first tear overpowered the dam. *Too much. It's too fucking much.* As he shoved the box aside, the contents crashed and dispersed across the floor. He waved his hand in dismissal and rubbed at his eyes as the photograph fell from his fingertips. It floated to the floor to join the trinkets of the past. With a flop onto his stomach, Josh tucked the single pillow on the bed beneath him.

One giant sigh later, he nodded off.

The thunder boomed and lightning splintered the inky sky. Disoriented by the sudden storm pulling him from sleep, Josh opened his eyes to witness the lightning show cut through the cracks of the curtains. The storm raged, pouring buckets of water over Rosewood.

"You've got to be kidding me," he groaned, flinging his legs over the side of the bed.

His feet collided with the contents of the box, each toe meeting a piece of his childhood. Josh rolled his eyes and waved the metaphorical white flag. *I fucking give up.*

With the click of the lamp, he surveyed the damage and

dropped to the floor, resigned to stuffing his past back into the depths of his locked soul.

But there it was.

An innocent crumbled-up envelope stared up at him from the floor, his name written in loopy cursive on the front. It invited him, beckoning him inside.

Agony bit into his stomach, squeezing the fleeting contentment of sleep from his gut only to be replaced with the bitter taste of solemn defeat.

You fooled me completely.

His hands toyed with the envelope. Dipping a finger beneath the lip, he flirted with the idea of revisiting the seventh circle of hell once more.

"Damn you, Mavs," he whispered and tore the letter from the envelope. It fluttered to the floor and the words of the past rippled over his body with the intensity of a rusted razor gliding across his skin.

My dearest Joshua,

By the time you read this, I'll be gone. I'm not asking you to understand, but I am asking that you let me go. Please don't try to find me.

I left because I had no other choice. If I stayed and you learned the truth, you would put your dreams aside in favor of me. I can't let you do that. I can't let my mistake be the reason you're kept from your future and the man you're meant to be.

I didn't know what else to do, Josh. I'm scared. I'm terrified. I'm stupid… And I just hope one day you'll find it in your heart to forgive me, to forgive us. Until then, my love…

I loved you yesterday, I love you today, and I'll love you tomorrow, Joshua Templeton.

Mavis

It still stung. Vomit threatened Josh's throat as he swallowed the memories erupting from the remains of his shattered soul. *Damn it, Duchess! Why did you leave me?*

"I fucking loved you," he whispered to the silent room,

all traces of thunder having subsided. Josh crinkled her letter in his fist and dropped his head to his knees. The stillness of the room beat across his brain, only the pitter-patter of soft rain meeting the window, breaking the lifeless moment.

You never forget your first love, do you? Josh snorted, grinning for the first time that day. His head lifted from the safety of his knees. "Tess, you were right…"

I've always been in love—just not with you. It's always been Mavis.

He stuffed her letter back in its envelope.

JULIE NAVICKAS

CHAPTER TWO

Mavis

Ten Years Before

"There! Do you see it?" Josh pointed to the white letters in the distance.

"Oh! Yeah, I think I can!" Mavis squinted. The iconic Hollywood sign appeared as the Ferris wheel car reached its peak in the late morning sky. She smiled, her gaze sweeping the rolling hills of the cityscape. "Ah, it's gone. I think you can really only see it at the tippy-top."

"My view still looks pretty good from here." A smirk grew along Josh's lips as the gentle springtime breeze rustled his short crop of brown hair.

Her cheeks warmed, the familiar dip in her stomach having nothing to do with the descending carnival car. "You're such a cheese, Joshua." Jabbing her fists playfully into his gut, a giggle escaped her belly as his arms encircled her, forcing her silly physical assault to cease.

"Yeah, but you love me anyway."

"Guilty, sir." Mavis grinned, lifting her gaze to meet his. The sunlight danced across his dark eyes, reflecting the simple connection her heart never questioned. As children, an invisible magnet had pulled her and Joshua together, and like the gravitational pull of the earth, the center of the world rested in the way he looked at her.

His boyish grin stole her breath, the air escaping her lungs in a wild rush. Clasping her palms to his smooth cheeks, she ran a thumb over the small scar above his upper lip.

My one and only… Joshua.

The Ferris wheel car jerked to a standstill at the base of the platform, and Josh lifted the safety rail free from their laps. Exiting the ride, they hopped down the rickety wooden staircase until Austin appeared at the landing with the twins' younger sister, Lauren.

As she approached, Austin's hand stretched outward.

"Always the gentleman, Mr. Templeton."

His cheeks flushed as his fingers squeezed her palm. "All hail the princess," he murmured, dropping his hand from hers when her feet safely met the pavement.

Mavis smiled, the warmth of his fingers gripping her palm. Her skin tingled, his touch like hot wax on a sealed letter of secrets. She pressed her hands together, interweaving her fingers as a familiar face appeared in the distance.

Mitch sauntered through the crowd, beaming proudly as he elbowed his way over to their group.

"Your brother looks way too happy," Josh whispered in her ear, wrapping his arm back around her waist.

She giggled, tearing her hands apart. "Once a show-off, always a show-off."

A stuffed purple dolphin spiraled through the air in their direction, and Lauren caught it like a star wide receiver, grinning ear-to-ear.

"And you said I couldn't shoot hoops," Mitch teased, slinging his arm around Lauren's shoulder, whopping the dolphin on the head. "You can keep him as proof of my talent, Peaches."

"I know football is your thing, but I never said you *couldn't* shoot hoops…" She giggled and stroked the stuffed toy in her hands. "I think I'll call him Finn."

"Your creativity knows no limit." Austin bonked the toy on the head and led the group away from the Ferris wheel. "I'm starving. Let's go eat lunch."

Making their way through the crowd at Pacific Park, the group of five navigated to an empty picnic table. The smell of fried carnival food and sweet, slushy lemonade wafted through the air as their feet crunched the dropped and forgotten popcorn on the pavement.

"Hungry?" Josh tucked a stray curl behind her ear as they took their seats. "What do you feel like having?"

"Funnel cake and cotton candy!"

"Why did I even ask?" Josh smiled and jumped to his feet, planting a kiss on the top of her head. "Be right back, Duchess." And with a wink, he stepped away, Austin and Mitch following on his hungry heels.

Mavis squirmed, pulling her toes free from her flip-flips. Tugging her right foot upward to rest on the seat, she ran a finger across the angry red blister where the rubber met her skin.

"Ouchie," she murmured with a frown.

"You need new shoes." Lauren squinted, eyeing the blister over the picnic table. "Wanna trade or something?" She pulled her foot into the air to reveal new strappy leather sandals.

"You're very sweet, but you don't have to do that." Mavis rammed her toes back into the offending cheap shoes and winced. "I'll tough it out. It's okay."

A shower of pebbles pelted the tops of her feet, the little fragments of stone stinging the raw wound.

"Ouch!" Mavis growled, yanking her injured foot back up to the bench.

The blonde passing by her right snickered. "Oops, sorry." Her curls bounced as she moved beyond the picnic table, giggling under her breath.

Lauren wrinkled her nose. "Oh, real nice, Tess."

"It was an accident!" she called back over her shoulder, the tips of her bubble-gum-pink fingernails covering her mouth.

"Like hell it was." Mavis dropped her foot back to the pavement as Tess fell in line behind Josh for a funnel cake. Her hands glided over his forearm, working to capture his attention. "What a bitch," whispered Mavis, swallowing the bubble of jealousy swelling in her heart.

"Hmm?" Lauren's hands stroked the stuffed dolphin, eyeing it like a new pet.

A million miles away, aren't you?

Mavis grinned and tapped the dolphin on the tail. "You like him, don't you?"

Her cheeks flushed as she quickly set the stuffed toy down. "The dolphin? Absolutely. Purple is my favorite color."

Rolling her eyes, Mavis shook her head. "My *brother*. You totally have a thing for Mitch."

Lauren tucked her head down, pretending to examine her cuticles. Crossing her legs beneath the table, she mumbled, "It's just a little crush. Not a big deal."

A smile tugged at her lips as she lifted her gaze to search for her brother. Ten feet ahead, Mitch squirted a pile of ketchup on a plate, sneaking in a quick peek at Lauren before grabbing extra napkins.

"He likes you too, you know."

"Really? You think so?" Lauren perked up but hid her growing excitement as the boys returned with mountains of fried food.

"Funnel cake with extra powdered sugar and pink cotton candy for you, Duchess." Josh kissed the top of her head as he lowered himself into the seat next to hers, leaving scarcely an inch between their bodies. He pulled a small bottle of hand sanitizer from his pocket and rubbed the clear goo on his hands. "Want some?"

Mavis snorted and extended her hand. *Always on germ*

patrol…

"Hey, have you heard from Harvard yet, Austin?" Mitch asked, a fist full of kettle corn on the way to his mouth.

Austin grinned, popping the top on a can of soda. "They accepted me yesterday," he muttered, rolling his still steaming corndog in ketchup.

"Oh, my God, Austin! That's freaking amazing!" Jumping from her seat, Mavis tossed her arms around his shoulders and squeezed. "I knew you'd get in," she whispered in his ear, planting an exaggerated kiss on his cheek. "Congratulations."

Smiling, he dragged his hands along his reddening cheeks, his fingertips lingering where her lips collided with his skin.

"Damn! Ivy League all the way for the Templetons! First Josh gets into Georgetown and now Austin at Harvard. No pressure, Lauren." Mitch jabbed his elbow into her side.

"Don't remind me. And don't stroke their egos anymore! They're unbearable to live with as it is." She popped the last bite of corndog in her mouth, dropping the empty stick to the paper plate. It landed in the pile of excess ketchup, creating a murder scene of condiments. "I know Mom and Dad have high expectations for me, but what about you? Where are you going to apply when it's our turn?"

"College? Uh-uh. That's not for me," Mitch responded, sureness rising in his voice. "I'm going to enlist in the Navy right after graduation."

"The Navy? When did you decide that?" Josh furrowed his brow.

"Eh, I'm no good in the classroom. I doubt even the community college in Rosewood would take me," Mitch answered with a crooked smile.

"I mean, shop class and a football field? They have both." Mavis shrugged, a pain in her gut blossoming. *The Navy? Really?*

"Well, Mavs, what about you? Where do you think you'll

go to school?" asked Lauren.

"Me?" she hedged. "Umm… I guess I haven't thought about it too much yet. I'll never get into Georgetown like Josh. And I couldn't pay for it anyway. I don't know. I like the snow. Maybe somewhere in the Midwest with a good journalism or creative writing program?"

"You *like* the snow?" A skeptical grin grew along Josh's lips.

"Yeah, I do. There's something magical about it. Mystifying even… yeah, I'd pick a school where it snows."

Josh wrapped his arm around her and pulled her body closer. "Sand or snow, Duchess, I'd follow you anywhere." He brushed his lips against hers, triggering a shiver to zip along her spine.

Austin rolled his eyes. "I see you two suck face enough. I'm outta here. Who's up for the West Coaster again?" he asked, pulling his legs free from the picnic table.

Mitch and Lauren jumped from their seats, seemingly ready to return to the long lines. And with a grin, Mavis rose too before Josh gripped her wrist.

"You really want to go on more roller coasters? Because I have another idea if you're interested…" Tugging her onto his lap, he ran his hand along the length of her thigh, his grip tightening at her waist.

Oh! Her stomach dropped. *No roller coaster needed.*

They drove back to Josh's home, Templeton Manor. Built in the early 1900s, the historic Victorian-inspired mansion sat on three acres of wild land in Rosewood, California, a suburb just outside the city limits of Los Angeles. As the third generation of the Templeton family, Josh, Austin, and Lauren had all grown up there. Despite the home's age, it lived on in pristine condition and the grounds were kept in immaculate form from the countless crews of landscape workers. Rolling green hills dotted the property with weeping willow trees, each pruned and perfected over time. Compared to Mavis and Mitch's foster family's bungalow fifteen minutes down the road, Templeton Manor was a fairytale come to life, a high castle in the clouds of a dream.

"My parents aren't home. Dad mentioned something about a fundraiser at the golf course. I don't think they'll be back 'til late, so we have the place to ourselves."

Oh!

Her heart pounded, the growing ring in her ears gripping her brain. She exhaled, forcing her body to expel the bout of nerves in her gut since leaving the carnival.

"What're you thinking?" he whispered. His gaze found hers in the darkened garage as he put the truck in park and cut the engine.

"Umm… probably the same as you?" Reaching for the handle, Mavis unlatched the SUV's door. Her feet stilled on the running board, every muscle in her legs resistant to move. *Jump down, Mavis. What's your problem?*

Josh appeared, his hand tugging at the door. "Something wrong?"

She searched his familiar face, taking in his sweet and silly grin. As the right side of his mouth pulled upward in a smile, the scar from a rogue Fourth of July firework tightened. The ambulance lights flashed through her memory, each squeal of the siren wreaking havoc on her heart.

"Joshua…" Reaching out to him, her hand rested over his heart, her fingertips rubbing against the soft material of his t-shirt.

He covered her hand with his own and tugged, guiding her down from the SUV and into his embrace. Peppermint greeted her nostrils as she snuggled into his chest, nuzzling her nose into his familiar scent. *Two halves of one whole…*

"You okay?" he asked, threading his fingers through her hair. "You've been quiet since we left the park."

Her stomach somersaulted, turning over the funnel cake. "Sorry… I think all the college talk got to me. I can't really picture you leaving."

Frowning, his grip tightened. "It's all months away, Duchess. Let's not worry about it yet, okay?"

Make every minute count then.

"Come on, let's go inside," he cooed. "Because I mean, nothing screams romance like a garage."

Mavis snickered into his chest, sneaking a peek at the shelving units of tools, gardening equipment, and lawn care gear beside him.

"I don't know… the way Mitch looks at that twenty-volt impact driver, you'd think no greater love existed."

Josh snorted. "You know, you're kinda right."

Tugging her backward, he led her to the small set of steps. Their feet pounded against the wooden stairs as they entered the house. And with the exception of the grandfather clock ticking away at the end of the hall, Templeton Manor stood in silence. *Tick-tock, tick-tock.*

"Can I get you something to drink?" He pointed to the kitchen.

"Umm, sure. Water please?"

With a nod, Josh disappeared, and Mavis wandered into the sunroom. Mrs. Templeton had furnished the room with white wicker furniture, accented with bright red and yellow cushions and pillows. Her butt plopped down on the loveseat, and she crossed her legs. Breathing in the fresh ocean air, the looping roller coaster in her gut slowed.

Josh plunked down into the seat beside her, dropping a chilled bottle of water into her lap. His lips brushed her forehead as he sighed.

"I know we're both thinking about it, but you know, we don't have to do anything you're not ready for, Mavs." His cheeks reddened with each breath as his chest rose and fell with a rhythmic pattern. "I never want to pressure you."

Mavis tucked a curl behind her ear, smiling at his sweet sincerity. "Joshua, I get it. You're going to be leaving for school soon. And it's not that I don't want to be with you… like that. I'm just… umm, I don't know how… or what…"

Her voice trailed away as her attention dropped to the zigzagging pattern of the gray patio carpet, its swoops and spirals mimicking the roller coaster ride in her stomach.

"And you think I do?" He snorted and shuffled his feet, tugging at the hem of his shorts. "Let's go for a walk, yeah? Get some fresh air?" With a slap of his palms to his knees, Josh hopped to his feet and extended his hand in her direction.

She giggled. "Are you saying Pacific Park didn't have fresh air?"

Biting his bottom lip, he rolled his eyes. "Come on, you know what I mean."

Mavis nodded, setting her unease aside. She stood and dropped the bottle of water to the sofa, accepting Josh's hand. Together, they walked outdoors, across the backyard, and out the gate into the overgrown brush.

Having explored the manor's property together their whole childhood, the wild land brought forth memories of an enchanted forest. Recalling Josh as the brave prince who rescued her from a fierce dragon's captivity, a smile returned to her lips as she giggled.

"Something funny?"

"What was the dragon's name again?"

Josh snorted. "Oh, come on. You don't remember Smaug? Bilbo Baggins would be disappointed in you."

She stumbled over a stray stick in their path and grinned. "Oh geez… how did I forget?"

Smiling, Josh continued leading the way as he held back low-lying branches. "Come on, Mavs, there and back again."

"I didn't think we'd be hiking to the Lonely Mountain today. I would have worn better shoes," she joked, pointing to her dirty white flip-flops and growing angry blister.

Josh scrunched his nose at her injury. "Ouch. That looks like it hurts."

She nodded.

"Well… hop on then, Duchess." He crouched in front of her.

Climbing onto his back, her soul smiled with understanding. Two halves creating a whole, stitched together with the thread of love.

He carried her through the maze of trees and vegetation until they arrived at the meadow of their childhood. The orange blossoms of the wild California poppies spread across the open field like a million burning suns.

Dropping from Josh's back, Mavis kicked the offending flip-flops from her feet and ran, euphoria spreading through her body at the sight of the poppies, all nerves and embarrassment left behind in the sunroom of the manor.

"Save me from Smaug, my prince!" she called back over her shoulder.

Josh roared with laughter, catching up with her quickly as her toes tread through the tall grass. Grabbing her waist, he lifted her from the ground, twirling her in circles, two souls united in love. In this place. In this moment in time.

Things are perfect.

Her feet met the earth as his lips found hers. Tightening his grip on her hips, he tugged her body closer.

"I love you, Mavs," he whispered. "I promise you, I always will."

Her head spun—dazed—lacking oxygen from the way his mouth moved against hers. Blood pounded through her veins, pumping through her heart as he awakened her body. Her knees buckled, each muscle falling limp until she dropped to the ground, tugging Josh with her.

A soft smile played across his lips as he plucked an orange poppy from the ground and handed it to her. The sweet floral scent pierced her nose as she brought the bulb closer. Her cheeks flushed, warmth settling in her skin.

This is it.

"Joshua?" she whispered, burying her nose in the flower.

"Hmm?" Lifting his face to the sky, he closed his eyes, basking in the sunshine.

"I… umm…" she stammered. *Just say the words!*

Pulling his face from the sun, he turned and dragged a

thumb over her lips. "What, Mavs?"

Her heart hammered, threatening to escape her ribcage as her brain forced her mouth to form words. "I... I want you to make love to me."

The tip of his finger tilted her chin upward, his eyes searching hers for the truth. "Are you sure?" he whispered. "Because I—"

Mavis nodded in rhythm with her hammering heart. "I'm sure."

Josh exhaled, releasing the air from his lungs as his fingers skimmed the fragile path of silver around her neck, a token of his love wrapped up in the small heart charm. With a slight nod, he leaned forward. His lips greeted hers, each finger interweaving with the cascade of curls that fell from her head.

"Just..." He paused, pulling away. "Tell me to stop if you change your mind, okay?" His fingers shook, tugging at the fragile zipper on her dress.

The spring air collided with her bare skin as his warm palms raked across her body. A tingle grew in her fingertips, her chest tightening with each gulp of air.

"I don't know what I'm doing." Josh tugged at his own clothes with a silly grin.

She giggled. "Together then."

He nodded and guided her body to the grassy earth. The scent of poppies penetrated her nostrils, and a bumblebee hummed near her ear. Each heartbeat in her chest hammered wildly, competing with the ragged breaths falling from their lips. Butterflies flapped in her belly as his hands explored her body, each squeeze of his fingers pulsating in rhythm with the buzzing bees.

As his lips kissed her neck, the silver chain of her necklace tickled her skin, bringing with it a sense of security—his love wrapped around her body forever.

"I love you, Mavs," he whispered.

All breath escaped her lungs when he entered her, the foreign feeling clouding her brain. With each move of his body, a new sensation built, a pressure that intensified with each passing minute until it culminated in a sense of sweet release.

His eyes found hers among the blades of grass, his gaze committing the tender moment to memory. The closeness. The vulnerability. Their bond strengthened both emotionally and physically.

He smiled. "Let's get married right here one day, okay?"

"I do."

CHAPTER THREE

Josh

Present Day

The overgrown meadow looked back as Josh stepped from the forest floor. Tall stalks of dead grass infiltrated the once beautiful open landscape that held the precious memories of his youth. As he stood amidst the weeds, his shoes sank into the wet soil beneath his feet. With each step forward, the grass tickled his bare calves and mud caked the bottoms of his tennis shoes.

What happened to this place?

Time was the enemy. Ten years had disappeared. Each day, each hour, each minute had ticked away, taking him further from Mavis and the love that blossomed among the wild California poppies in this very place so long ago. The memory crashed through his brain like a dream, as if perhaps it never really happened at all.

"Was it even real?" he whispered to the lifeless meadow. A lifetime had passed, each season bringing with it the fading edges of a memory, disintegrating at every corner.

Josh took slow deliberate steps through the overgrown

brush, his hands skimming the tops of the dying grass. Nothing looked the same, but there was no mistaking the overwhelming rush of excitement reverberating throughout his body with each step forward. She was here. Her soul lingered in the heavy, damp air. Her essence caught up in the whistle of a songbird in the treetops above. *You're still here, Mavs. We're still here.*

The sun broke through the gray clouds, each ray illuminating the thicket surrounding him. Josh raised his face to the sun, the warmth penetrating his skin. He closed his eyes and grabbed on tightly to the memory the meadow held, willing each wild orange blossom to bloom in his mind. The ghost of her laughter wrapped tightly around him in the morning breeze, the joyous sound squeezing his heart. It hammered against his ribcage, threatening to smash its bone prison. Her name escaped his lips, the taste of her on his tongue as "Mavis…" caught in the wind and disappeared.

His eyes popped open, the green and brown hues of the brush forcing his momentary exhilaration back to reality, each orange poppy from his memory fading in color one by one.

"It *was* real," he whispered to himself as he pulled her note from his pocket. Brushing his index finger across her loopy handwriting, his gaze lingered on the worn paper. Each letter—in each word—appeared choppy and disjointed, as if her hands shook while she penned her feelings.

What happened, Mavis? Why did you leave me?

The question had worn on his mind many years ago. There were nights it took on a rhythm, like a song stuck on repeat. Asking it again, today, with no more clarity, was replaying a well-worn record.

Whatever happened—whatever caused her to write these words—would forever be a mystery, the reason buried in the past.

But his soul spoke, speaking the question aloud to the

meadow. *Does it have to be though?*

A shiver of excitement ran up and down Josh's spine at the sudden thought. *Does it have to be?* Ten years had passed, but time hadn't healed all wounds. Her letter had lived on in a box in his closet, and the emotions that unraveled when her words were released from their envelope hadn't lessened in the slightest.

Blood pumped through his veins, accelerating at the prospect. *What's keeping me from trying to find you?* His gaze returned to her note, each finger touching the words, *Please don't try to find me.* Having ignored her request from the start, Josh had dragged the police into it no more than twenty-four hours after her disappearance. But she wasn't a missing person's case. The letter was evidence of her decision to leave, and the investigation turned cold with no trail to follow.

"But it's been ten years, Duchess," he mumbled to her request on the paper. *And I have absolutely nothing to lose anymore.* Josh shifted his body weight and stuffed his hands in his pockets. He breathed in a deep gulp of the fresh morning air and allowed his eyes to seek out the path where he'd entered the meadow, the start of his journey—the beginning of the road back to Mavis—and the path back to love.

He took a sure step forward, and then another, each movement more deliberate than the last until his feet carried him back into the forest. With adrenaline coursing through his body, he jogged back to Templeton Manor, Mavis's letter tucked snuggly away in his back pocket.

Within minutes, Josh reached his childhood home and entered through the sunroom. Sliding the glass door open, he tiptoed inside, catching sight of a brilliant ball of fiery orange on the dining room table. A bouquet of California poppies rested in a crystal vase, each bulb a single burning sun. Warmth spread throughout his body as a smile grew steadily on his lips. *I'm going to find you, Mavs. There's no doubt in my mind now.*

"What're you smiling at?" Mitch rounded the kitchen corner and wrinkled his nose. "And why are you here?" His dark hair on the left side of his head stuck upward, bed head at its finest. He rubbed at his right eye and stifled a yawn as the mug of coffee in his grasp released steam into the air.

"Oh, umm… sorry. I was taking a walk." Josh clasped the back of his neck, his fingers toying with his hairline.

"It's like seven-thirty in the morning, dude." Mitch brought the cup to his lips and grimaced as the scalding liquid met his tongue.

"Couldn't sleep. I needed some fresh air." Pulling a chair out from the dining room table, Josh eyed the vase of poppies as he sank into the seat. The one in the center called to him, its bulb in full bloom.

"Are you okay? I know you had a rough night, but why would you drive over here this early?" Mitch sat down in the opposite chair, setting his coffee on the table with a shaking hand. A tiny drop of brown liquid escaped, staining the sunny yellow tablecloth. Frowning, he rubbed at it with wide eyes.

"Lauren's gonna kill you for that."

"Probably." Mitch grabbed the vase of flowers and covered the stain with a weak smile. "There."

"You know that's not gonna work." A grin tugged at Josh's lips.

"Yeah well, your sister's crazy." Mitch scratched his cheek and leaned back in the chair, pulling his arms up and over his head as the sunshine streamed in through the patio doors behind him.

"Yeah, a bit, I suppose. But hey… umm… speaking of sisters." Josh hedged, lowering his gaze to his feet as he pretended to adjust his socks and retie his laces.

"You can't be serious right now, man."

The table shook as his brother-in-law stood, sloshing another drip of coffee onto the tablecloth. Mitch groaned and stomped off to the kitchen. He returned moments later with a wet cloth, ready to dab at the stain.

"You're in big trouble."

"Yeah well, so are you. Lauren said you might do this." He rubbed ferociously. "But I didn't believe her. Told her she was crazy. That there was no way you'd even consider breathing her name again."

"Look, Mitch… I was just thinking. That's all." Josh raised his palms in defense. "Mavis—"

He scowled, doubling the speed of his attempts at stain removal.

Well, you've got some deeper feelings here than I realized.

"Then that's why you're here, isn't it?" he accused. "It's because of her. You were out walking in that damn meadow, weren't you?" His hands stopped scrubbing, halting all attempts to clean the stain. Mitch's green eyes, identical to Mavis's, found his, intent on pulling the truth from his heart.

Josh sighed. "I took a walk in a place that reminded me of her. Big deal." He rose from his seat and pushed the chair back beneath the table. *This was a mistake talking to you about this.*

"She's gone, Josh. Mavis is gone."

Returning his gaze to the floor, his brother-in-law's cruel and direct words gripped his heart. The motivation fueling his system minutes before diminished, and the flood of excitement he'd felt in the meadow failed.

Mitch exhaled, returning the rag to the coffee stain. "Josh, buddy, I know you're hurting right now, but tracking down my sister isn't the answer. You're a smart guy, but your head isn't on straight yet."

Josh snorted. Everyone's pity—treating him like a child who'd lost his puppy—weighed on his mind. And the embarrassment of his failed marriage would follow him for the rest of his life, thanks to Tess.

"Mitch…" He sighed. "All I want to know is if you've heard from her. Has she ever reached out to you?" Josh straightened, but his brother-in-law's face twisted the knife in his heart before he even spoke.

"No," he said firmly. His head shook as he slumped

forward, dropping the rag to the table. "She's long gone, dude. I don't have a clue where she is. Honestly, I'd like to keep it that way."

Disappointment flooded his body, blanketing him with another cloud of sorrow.

"Josh, just go home and get some rest, okay?" Heading for the staircase, Mitch grabbed the railing as his foot met the first step. "Please. Leave my sister in the past where she belongs. Do not try to find her. It was her stupid choice to leave us all." He disappeared from view, each footfall growing fainter as he climbed to the second floor back to his bedroom.

But was it really her choice though? We don't know the truth...

With a shake of his head, Josh snagged the single poppy from the vase and walked to the front door, departing Templeton Manor. The sun met his face again as he slogged down the porch steps and followed the path around the house to his Jeep. Speeding away, his mind returned to the meadow and the memories it held as he dropped the bloom on the front passenger seat.

Maybe Mitch is right. And I'm just thinking crazy...

Several miles of highway later, Josh tapped the left turn signal and pulled into a parking lot beside the ocean. The beach was a haven, the salt water a drug of clarity when he needed to think.

His feet plowed through the wet sand as he passed picnic tables, rental tents, and lounge chairs in the early morning hour. Ducking beneath a volleyball net, the wet material skimmed the top of his head, stirring a memory from ten years prior.

*

"Heads up!" Mitch screeched as the volleyball he whacked went flying sideways toward a line of sunbathing girls.

Squeals of fear reached Josh's ears as Mitch chased the ball down to the edge of the beach, profusely apologizing over his shoulder for the stray spike. Having managed to hit a blonde square on the head, Josh snickered and elbowed Lauren until she pointed.

"Oh shit, that's Tess that he hit!"

"I'm so sorry, Tess! It was an accident!" Mitch yelled, hiking back up the beach with the ball in his hands.

"You're a total idiot, Mitch Benson!" she screamed, readjusting her ponytail.

"I'm sorry! I didn't mean it!" he called again, sidestepping her fury to return to the volleyball court. "Geez, it was an accident," he whispered, rejoining Josh and Lauren as the wrath of Tess Browning raged on behind him.

Lauren smiled and squeezed his forearm. "It's okay, we know. Josh… go over there and smooth things out for him. Tell Tess it was an accident."

Josh wrinkled his nose. "Why me?"

"Because she likes you, that's why!" Shoving him in the gut, Lauren pushed him in Tess's direction.

His stomach flip-flopped as her words pierced his brain. "What? No, she doesn't! What're you talking about?"

"Dear Lord, how oblivious are you?" Lauren squinted, pushing him forward again until he moved.

His feet plodded over the hot sand, aiming for the swarm of girls surrounding Tess. As he approached, a round of giggles greeted him.

Josh cleared his throat. "Umm… hey Tess, are you okay?" He dragged his hand through his hair, gripping the back of his neck.

"Oh! Hi, Josh!" Her scowl disappeared, replaced with an instant grin. "Yes, I'm fine. Just tell Mitch he should stick to football." An award-winning smile grew on her glossy lips as she adjusted her bikini top, untying the straps, just to retie them.

His cheeks warmed as the girls surrounding him stared, eyeing their conversation with intense interest. Turning back to the volleyball court, Josh yelled. "She says you should stick to football!"

Mitch nodded and waved, tossing the ball over to Lauren with an eye roll.

"Well, umm… I'm glad you're okay." He pointed in her direction and retreated quickly, embarrassed by the swarm of girls and their inquisitive stares. As he trudged back through the sand, giggles reached

his ears. Maybe Tess does like me? Huh…

Once he returned to his team's side of the court, Austin and Mavis ducked beneath the net to join the group.

"Is she okay?" Frowning, Mavis wrapped her arm around his waist, sneering in Tess's direction.

"Yeah, she's fine." Josh snorted and pointed at Mitch. "I guess volleyball isn't your game, dude."

"It's not really mine either," said Austin with a wink. "But come on, the score is tied. We need a winner."

Shaking her head, Mavis leaned against Josh's chest. "Uh, actually, I think I'm gonna take a break for a minute. I don't feel so great."

"When's the last time you had any water?" Leading her away from the court, he guided her back to their small beach camp as his eyes raked over her pale complexion.

"I don't remember." She sat, accepting the bottle of water he pulled out from the cooler.

Austin tilted the umbrella, blocking the sun from her path. "It is pretty hot out here today. You're probably just dehydrated. Drink that and you'll feel better."

She nodded.

"Well, I'm starving anyway, let's just eat lunch." Mitch dug into the cooler, grabbing from within a stack of sandwiches, cheese and crackers, fresh fruit, cookies, and a container of cold peach cobbler. He smiled and rested his hand over his heart with delight. "Straight to my heart, Peaches. I love your cobbler."

A smile overtook Lauren's lips as she sank to the sand beside him and pulled out plates and napkins.

"Oh! Dibs on the pineapple!" yelled Austin, sideswiping Mitch's hand on the pile of fruit.

"No way!" He playfully shoved his competition, swatting at Austin.

Frowning at the juvenile fight before them, Josh turned and dropped to the sand beside Mavis, pressing the back of his hand to her forehead. "Can I get you something to eat?"

She scrunched her nose. "Ugh, no, I'm not hungry. I'll just stick to water."

Beside them, Austin won the battle and stuffed the pineapple in his mouth, grinning with victory as he chewed the juicy fruit. Lifting his gaze to Mavis, he swallowed. "Oh, umm… sorry Mavs. I should have offered it to you. I know you like pineapple."

Shaking her head, she smiled and pressed the cold water bottle to her forehead. "It's okay. I umm… don't really have an appetite right now anyway."

Austin crawled over to the crackers and stacked some on a plate. "Well, maybe a few crackers would be a good idea anyway."

Josh nodded and accepted the plate, resting it on Mavis's lap. "He's right. You should eat something."

But she frowned and pushed the plate away, dropping her head into her palms instead.

*

"Are you okay, dude?"

The sudden question jarred Josh back to reality as a shirtless, blond teenager appeared before his eyes, holding a volleyball.

"Huh?" He shook his head, forcing his brain back to the present.

"You've been standing there like a really long time, and we need this court." The kid gestured to his friends behind him.

Josh snorted. "Wow, I'm sorry. Guess I got lost in my thoughts." He rubbed his eyes and slowly dragged his palms down his cheeks.

Why in the world did that memory just come back?

JULIE NAVICKAS

CHAPTER FOUR

Mavis

In the emergency room of Chicago's Northwestern Memorial Hospital, Mavis stared at the magazine on her lap, glossing over the words with unfocused eyes. The unease in her gut grew as her mind reeled, recalling the last forty-eight hours spent caring for her roommate. Not a thing had helped the abdominal pain—not rest, not fluids, not over-the-counter painkillers—nothing. At a total loss for what to do, she'd dragged her best friend to the emergency room. Casey had stubbornly protested right up to the triage room door.

From the corner of the room, the television blared at a nearly unbearable decibel, the Weather Channel reporter tracking the winter storm moving across the Midwest. "We can expect upwards of nine inches to hit the City of Chicago overnight, folks…"

Mavis sighed, stealing a glance out the front doors. A blizzard of white pelted the glass. "Perfect," she murmured, recrossing her legs. "Just perfect."

Her back ached. The three hours spent in the plastic waiting room chair wreaked havoc on her body. *Ugh. What the hell is taking so long? Is it appendicitis or not?* As she tapped her winter boots against the white tiled floor, the disquiet in her chest squeezed the air from her lungs, perpetuating the queasiness in her empty stomach. *Something has to be wrong.*

Her gaze drifted down to the *Cosmopolitan* on her lap. Page thirty-seven's article on how to please a man in bed still looked back at her, just as it had for the last two and a half hours. With a surge of sudden adrenaline, she stood and approached the reception desk, leaving behind the mystery of bedroom pleasure on the plastic seat.

"Excuse me?"

The receptionist rotated her chair, her fatigued stare raking over Mavis. "Can I help you?"

"Umm… I was wondering if I could get an update on my friend? She's been back there a really long time and I'm getting kinda worried."

"Name?" Her chair spun again, the ancient hardware scraping against the rusted metal.

"Casey McDaniels."

She banged on the keys with vibrant midnight-blue fingernails and perused the screen, her eyes darting back and forth absorbing information. Mavis eyed the woman's nails, distracted by the swirls and glitter, like a lava lamp from the 1970s.

"Oh. Wait here," she instructed and shuffled away as her white tennis shoes squeaked against the floor.

Unnerved, her pulse quickened. Despite the winter weather outside, a bead of sweat formed on her brow beneath the harsh fluorescent lights of the ER. Folding her arms across her middle in a self-hug, she lifted her gaze to the clock on the wall, content to watch the minute hand as it circled once… twice… three times.

Damn it. What the hell is happening back there?

The door to her right creaked open and the receptionist poked her head out, curling her finger toward her in a summons. "She'll see you," she whispered, holding the door open.

The ring in her ears grew, blocking out the updated prediction on the television of now ten inches in the forecast. Mavis stepped forward, reruns of *Grey's Anatomy* flashing through her mind as she crossed the threshold beyond the waiting room.

Blue Fingernails led her down the hall, passing several occupied rooms before stopping at 6A. The typical standard-issue, light-green hospital curtains surrounding Casey's room wafted in the breeze as they arrived. The look of their faded and stained material alone egged on the rising bout of nausea in her belly. *God, I hate hospitals.*

The woman pointed. "She's in here."

"Umm, okay… thank you." Mavis inhaled, working to replace the growing dread in her gut with courage.

"Mmm-hmm." Her shoes squeaked away back down the hall.

With a sigh, Mavis gripped the curtain and tugged. The breath caught in her throat at the sight of Casey's body on the bed, curled into the fetal position beneath a thin white blanket.

"Case?" Swallowing, she forced her feet to step into the small space and tune out the beeping machines lining the wall.

"Mavs?" Casey shifted, lifting her head from the small pillow. She sat upright, hugging her knees to her chest as tears spilled from her puffy eyes, staining the well-traveled path down her pink cheeks.

"What is it? What's wrong?" Resting the weight of her body on the edge of the narrow bed, she gripped Casey's knee and squeezed. "Tell me."

Her blonde curls bobbed with each sway of her head as she dragged the back of her hand over her eyes, blotting at the pools of tears and smeared mascara.

"I don't even know how to say it," she squeaked, dropping her face to the safety of her knees.

Mavis frowned, scooting her butt closer to her friend. "It's just me," she whispered, tucking a curl behind Casey's ear. "You know whatever it is stays between us."

She sniffled and nodded, reaching out to grasp Mavis's hand. Squeezing her palm, she sucked in a breath and opened her mouth to speak. "I... umm... didn't even know I was pregnant." Her small body quivered as the words tumbled from her lips. "How could I miscarry?"

A pressure around Mavis's heart built, squeezing at her tender heartstrings. Frail and frayed with time, the edges of a memory flitted across her brain. Mavis pulled Casey into a hug, looping her arms around the sad, shaking form of her friend. Her eyes burned as her vision clouded with the tears of the past.

I understand, Casey. God, do I understand.

Shielding her eyes from the sun's blinding rays, Mavis emerged from the emergency room exit of the hospital in the early morning hour. As she tugged her coat tighter around her body, she stepped from the curb and chartered a way through the slush to the adjoining parking garage.

The winter wind lashed at her unprotected face, whipping her already untamed hair as she trudged through a makeshift path in the snow. Her bare fingers numbed, and her eyes drooped with exhaustion as she sought the stairs to the third floor. Yanking the steel door open, the seam split in her right boot, a flood of cold air biting her unprotected toes.

"Fucking awesome," she muttered, gripping the railing and running up the concrete steps. "New boots are not in the budget this month."

At the end of the row, her rusted-over Ford Fiesta appeared, tucked behind a large SUV. Mavis jogged toward it, seeking the nominal shelter it would provide from the wind. Ramming her key in the lock, she tugged the door opened and dove into the driver's seat, quickly turning over the ignition. A blast of cold air stung her face as she cranked up the heat level to high.

Mavis groaned and closed her eyes, dropping her head back against the seat as it pounded with the beat of a bass drum. She rubbed her neck and swallowed a threatening sob, allowing the tears she'd fought back for Casey's sake to finally trickle down her wind-bitten cheeks. *The pain of the past back to haunt me.*

"It was all my fault," she choked out, admitting her truth to the empty car. The pressure in her chest returned, squeezing her heart in the private moment of weakness. Hidden from view behind the SUV, Mavis turned to the passenger seat and conjured his image beside her.

"I'm so sorry, Joshua," she whispered.

The ghost of his soul appeared as her hand reached outward, each numb tip of her fingers grazing the empty seat, seeking the long-lost part of her own soul.

A rush of childhood memories descended as peppermint scented the air and his soft brown eyes searched hers for the truth. The scar on his upper lip stretched, his silly grin consuming his boyish face. And the sweetness of his voice penetrated her ears as her name caught in the web of memories. The connection they shared hummed back to life as she pulled the corner open on Pandora's box.

Clinging to his memory, she gave in to her weakened state, recalling the last moments they shared together before her world upended.

*

"Please take it, Josh." With shaking fingers, Mavis shoved the crumpled envelope into his hand.

"What is it?"

She dragged a hand across his chest and bit her bottom lip. "It's something I need you to have. Just don't open it right now. Wait until tomorrow, okay?"

Accepting the envelope, Josh pulled her closer and trailed the sensitive skin of her neckline with his lips, triggering a tingle deep in her belly.

"*Whatever you say, Duchess,*" he whispered, stuffing the envelope in his pocket. His hands disappeared beneath the hem of her shirt, gripping her lower back.

"*Oh! Your mom is watching us!*" Mavis giggled with unease and pointed at the window over Josh's shoulder. Susan Templeton glared back through the glass, her finger wagging back and forth at her son.

"*I'm not doing anything she hasn't seen me do before.*" Josh sneered but pulled his hands free from beneath the material. "*That dorm room can't come soon enough,*" he muttered, leading Mavis over to the porch swing and away from his mother's view. It creaked as they sat down and a spider shook itself free, dropping to the wooden floor.

Rain trickled from the sky, beating against the tin roof of the porch. The wind picked up, blowing through the grass and rustling the long branches of the willows dotting the driveway.

When the storm breaks, I'll do it.

Josh slung his arm around her shoulder, his body's warmth colliding with her skin. His breath fell on the top of her head as his lips pressed into her hair. Mavis snuggled into his chest, eyeing his right front pocket where her letter now lived.

"*What am I gonna do without you, Joshua?*" Her eyes closed as her fingers sought the silver chain around her neck. Toying with the little heart charm, she sighed.

"*I'll be home all the time, Mavs. You know that.*"

She snorted.

"*Georgetown is far… you won't be home as often as you think.*"

He squeezed her thigh, rocking the porch swing with his feet back and forth, back and forth.

"*Well, fall break is in November. And I'll head home on some weekends. Plus, you can visit me too.*"

She scrunched her nose and peered into his eyes. "*Oh, yes, Mrs. Randle, please forgive me. I can't turn in my chemistry homework or participate in lab this week. I need to visit my boyfriend across the country at college.*" She grinned. "*I'm not going to be able to visit, and you know it.*"

"*Screw chemistry.*" He smiled and looped a curl around his finger, tugging gently. "*You won't need it for the books you'll write. That last short story you wrote about Mamelda and her cats… absolutely hysterical.*"

With a small grin, she pulled away from him, leaving the warmth of his body and the comfort his words exuded. A tear broke through the dam behind her eyes. Swiping at it, she stood and walked the short distance to the porch railing. As she gazed out over the immaculately manicured front lawn, now wet from the steady rain, reality rocked her core.

I'll miss this place.

"Mavs, I don't have the right words. And I don't have all the answers." *His gaze dropped to his lap. "I know things are going to change, but it doesn't mean things have to change between us."*

She nodded, his words absorbing into her heart. But everything's gonna change anyway. You just don't know it yet. *Turning to face him, she crossed her arms over her stomach in a self-hug. "I'm not trying to take anything away from you, Joshua. I know how much you want to be a doctor."* *Tears leaked through her lids, sliding along her cheeks. "I'm just really going to miss you while you're at school. I'm going to miss us."*

Josh stood, closing the distance between their bodies. Pulling her into his chest, his fingers threaded through her hair. "Please don't cry, Duchess. It breaks my heart with every tear."

"I can't help it," she sobbed, pressing her face harder into his chest.

"I love you." *His lips brushed her forehead. "I love you so goddamn much," he whispered.*

The swift summer storm dissipated, the last of the raindrops kissing the grass. In the distance, the branches of the willows hung heavy, the weight of the moment wrapped up in their weeping state. My time's up.

Running a hand over Josh's pocket, she summoned the courage she'd found to pen the letter. "I love you too, Joshua." She sighed. "But I should go. It's getting late."

Josh nodded, scooping her hands into his own. His lips pressed against her knuckles. "I loved you yesterday, I love you today, and I'll love you tomorrow, Mavis Benson."

His words hammered into her heart, the tip of a jagged dagger piercing the tender center. Her hand rose, skimming his cheek before her lips found his for a final time.

He moaned against her mouth as she pulled away, her feet pounding against the wood as she shot down the steps.

His eyes followed her retreating figure as her feet padded through the wet grass, each step carrying her further away from the only true home she'd ever known, the only safe place in the world. And Josh would never know that when she rounded the corner, she had no intention of ever turning back.

*

A blast of hot air brought her back to reality. The little Ford had finally warmed up enough to heat the cabin. *What am I doing?*

Wiping the evidence of tears from her face, Mavis fastened her seat belt and adjusted the gear shaft. The little blue car puttered out of the space, down the parking garage ramp, and over to the entrance of the hospital where Casey stood, ready to depart and leave the memories this place held far behind.

Tears leaked from Casey's eyes the full ride home. Burying her face in her jacket collar, she slumped in her seat and sniffled, hiding beneath the hood of her jacket.

"Can I get you anything, Case?"

Her hood shook back and forth.

I'll take that as a no.

Mavis steered into the first open space in the apartment complex parking deck and put the car in park. The engine lurched and quieted. Cold air infiltrated the cabin as Casey yanked on the door handle, her feet dropping to the pavement. Shaking her head, she padded off toward the elevator. "I'm sorry, Mavs…" she choked out over her shoulder, disappearing through the doors.

You never need to apologize to me.

With a gulp of frigid air, Mavis grabbed her purse from the backseat and followed from a distance, silently tailing

Casey's steps directly to their third-story apartment door. Dropping her bag to the dining room table, the click of Casey's closed door met her ears.

Mavis sighed and dragged her hands over her cheeks, exhaustion catching up with her. "My heart hurts for you, Case," she whispered, closing the door to her own bedroom. A dull ache in her temples throbbed, each hour in the emergency room culminating in an emotional windstorm. Collapsing on her mattress, she closed her eyes and yawned, tugging the blankets up to her neck. "Sleep," she murmured. "I just need sleep…"

But the roar of the city disagreed with her wish. Even three floors up, the angry traffic below collided with the quiet of her bedroom and the red line slid along the tracks with the grace of a bulldozer.

Oh, come on…

Mavis rolled her eyes and stuffed her head beneath the pillow. The city sounds muffled, but the ringing in her ears left nothing but the reminders of fatigue and heartache. Swallowing the distaste rising in her throat, she fought with the guilt that reared its ugly head no more than an hour ago.

"Goddamn it," she murmured, dragging her body from the bed. She tiptoed out the door and back into the kitchen. "If I can't sleep, then I need food." *And I have a date with both Ben and Jerry.*

Grasping the full pint of ice cream from beneath a frozen pizza and bag of French fries, Mavis cozied up on the living room sofa, spoon in hand and carton in lap. She reached for the blanket on the backside of the couch. Yanking it free from the weight of Casey's iPad, the sleek black device slid down onto the seat beside her. Mavis pushed it aside, wrapping the blanket around her shoulders while digging into the cold delicious treat.

In the calm of the living room, her mind wandered, divulging from the path of reality onto the rocky shores of memory lane. The waves of the ocean crashed into her mind, pulling from the depths of memory the day she learned she was pregnant herself.

She groaned, recollecting the beach, the volleyball game, Tess Browning battling with Mitch, and Austin's crackers in her lap. A carefree beach day turned tear-ridden evening on the bathroom floor.

The recall soured her stomach on the ice cream treat. "And there goes my appetite…" Marching it back to its home in the freezer, she chucked the carton inside. *Ben and Jerry, you betrayed me.*

Mavis returned to the couch and tucked her legs beneath her, huffing out a breath and dragging her fingers through her long hair. She tightened the blanket around her shoulders, dropping her gaze to the iPad on the seat beside her. Its blank screen looked back as a shiver snaked along her spine, planting the seed of an idea in her brain. *Do I dare?* Her pulse quickened, a rush of adrenaline coursing through her veins. The device rested innocently, withholding answers to the questions burning in her gut.

"Mavis Benson… what are you thinking?" she asked the empty room. But her fingers grasped the iPad anyway, pulling it toward her until it rested in her lap. Her index finger tapped away until a blank search box appeared on Google's homepage.

Her hands ignored what her mind cautioned, and she tapped in *Joshua Michael Templeton.* The enter button taunted, teasing and toying with her self-control. *But what do I have to lose?* Curiosity won, and she selected the green button with a twinge of anticipation.

Her breath caught in her throat as his face—older, but still boyishly handsome—appeared on the screen. The caption below the photo read *Southern California Hospital at Hollywood welcomes Dr. Joshua Templeton, OB-GYN…*

"An obstetrician, huh?" *Wow, irony is morbid.*

But despite the air of surprise still held prisoner in her lungs, a sense of vindication washed over her, a small release of pressure disappearing from her heart. He'd become what he always wanted to be. *A doctor.* But the long-held guilt residing at the bottom of her soul crept to the surface. *At what cost though?* Actions had consequences, and while hers may have allowed Josh to pursue his dream career, the truth remained hidden, buried beneath the grave of their relationship.

Mavis swallowed and scrolled past his photo as the blue link to his Facebook profile appeared. Conflicted with the idea of snooping further, her gaze lifted from the screen. Her small and tired apartment stared back. The edges of the faded curtains, no longer white, danced against the stains on the carpet beneath the window. To her left, the second-hand table balanced precariously on the toe of a tennis shoe and the arm of the sofa beneath her butt. *Ten years apart, and this is what I have to show for myself. A drab apartment, a paycheck earned behind a bar, no high school diploma, and nothing more than a pit of guilt tied up in a bow around my belly.*

"At least one of us found success," she whispered.

The tips of her fingers tingled as she shrugged and clicked the link, waiting for his profile to appear. His photo popped up first, and Mavis pulled the iPad closer to her face. His lips twisted in a grin, but the smile didn't touch his eyes like the boy in her memory—like the boy in her heart.

"What happened to you, Joshua? Where'd your smile go?"

An unknown object dropped to the floor in the apartment upstairs. Mavis jumped as the silence shattered, cutting into the memories blossoming in her heart. The bowling ball—or whatever else could have made the noise—rolled down memory lane and collided with the questions growing in her mind. *Can I? Should I?*

A fire burned within her, hope threading through her heart with the stitch of a needle. Her finger hovered over *direct message*, and one impulsive tap later, a blank note opened, ready to write, cursor blinking in anticipation.

"But how can I message you after what I did?" The secret pregnancy and miscarriage were just part of the story. And Austin Templeton definitely made up the other half.

JULIE NAVICKAS

CHAPTER FIVE

Josh

Sipping from a cup of black coffee, Josh leaned back in his chair beside Austin at the local coffeehouse, Java Jane's.

"And then he quit! Just up and walked off mid-shift!" From across the table, Lauren frowned, her arms stretching high in the air. Her cup met her lips, silencing her story for a fraction of a second. "Leaving me completely short-staffed! I almost had to grab an apron myself!"

Josh raised a brow. "All part of owning a restaurant, right?"

"That's just it, I *own* Pier Ninety-two. I shouldn't be managing it too. Or waiting tables for that matter!"

Josh nodded, sneaking a peek at Austin. But his brother scrolled through his phone, grinning at something likely far more entertaining than their sister's managerial conundrums. *Real nice. Leave me flying solo. Thanks, dude.*

Propping his elbows on the table, Josh dropped his chin into his palms, resigning himself to the next twenty minutes of sporadically interjecting the words "Really?" and "Mmm-hmm" into the one-sided conversation. Lauren chit-chatted away and Josh's mind wandered.

Where are you right now, Duchess? Are you thinking about me too?

Rediscovering her goodbye note had lit a fire in his belly. With each passing day since finding it, he'd turned over each individual letter in his mind as he scoured her lost soul, analyzing every word she'd penned in her goodbye.

What was your secret? Why did you leave me?

In spite of himself, he found his mind back in the meadow again. Wild orange poppies filled his head as he lost himself in the memory, recalling the way their souls had intertwined…

But Lauren's voice yanked him from the meadow—and the memory.

"So? Have you heard from her?" she asked, tapping the table. "Josh? Earth to Josh." She snapped her fingers, her voice swimming in irritation.

Beside him, Austin barked out a laugh as his leg banged into his under the table.

Ouch! When the hell did you change topics?

"I'm sorry, Lauren, what? Have I heard from who?" His cheeks flushed as he squinted at his sister.

"Tess, of course. Have you heard from her?"

Ugh. Why are you asking me about her?

"Ahh, no." He wrinkled his nose and frowned. "And I hope I don't." Josh leaned back against the wicker chair and adjusted the sunglasses on his nose. His eyes glossed over the crowded patio and the coffee-goers sipping fancy drinks, chatting the morning away. He took a big gulp of coffee as Lauren's eyes zeroed in on his from across the table.

"Josh, are you okay? You've barely said two words since we sat down."

"That's because you say enough words for all three of us." Austin smirked and tipped his head, pulling his Dodgers baseball cap down to shield his face.

The table jerked as Lauren aimed a kick in his direction. Austin's coffee toppled over, black liquid coating the tabletop. It dripped down the side, pooling on the concrete patio floor.

Lauren's cheeks turned bright pink. "Oh, shit… Damn it, Austin! Look what you made me do!" She grinned with humiliation but mopped up the mess with the few paper napkins available.

"Smooth, Lauren. Keep your feet to yourself next time." Austin rose from his seat and tossed his napkin on the soggy mess for good measure.

Josh snorted and rolled his eyes. "Kettle. Black." Rising to his feet too, he elbowed his brother in the gut. "And on that note, let's stop embarrassing ourselves." Josh reached into the back pocket of his jeans for his wallet. His fingers dipped inside, brushing against Mavis's letter in search of cash. *A piece of you in my back pocket.*

"Tell me that's not what I think it is." Austin's smile vanished, his blue eyes icing over as he peered over his brother's shoulder, all color draining from his face.

Josh snapped his wallet shut. "Mind your own business. Please." A twenty-dollar bill floated to the table as Josh stalked away, navigating the zigzag of coffee patrons.

Well, shit.

Lauren's hurried whispers followed him through the maze. "You have got to be kidding me, Joshua Michael!"

The trio stepped through the gate and onto the sidewalk, winding their way back to the parking lot.

"Can you guys please just leave it alone?" Josh begged. "It's nothing," he added, shuffling away toward his Jeep. His fingers grasped the door handle as Austin's hand gripped and squeezed his upper arm.

"Why do you still have that thing?" His eyes bore into him, his brow furrowing in question.

"Damnit, Josh! Mitch told me you were acting all weird the other morning, and now you've got that terrible note of hers back in your wallet!" Lauren smacked her palm to her forehead. "I know you're hurting, but you have got to be reasonable! Mavis Benson is not the answer to your divorce!"

"Come on." Austin's grip tightened. "She's right. Mavs is…" He shook his head, dropping his wide eyes to stare at the pavement.

Yanking his arm free, Josh pulled away from his siblings' attack. Embarrassment snaked under his skin, their unsupportive words darkening his desires with defeat.

"Look, it means nothing. *She* means nothing." He raised his palms in defense. "I tossed it in my wallet by mistake."

Lies. All lies.

"You're a shit terrible liar, Josh. You've always been. Why the hell would you carry that thing around with you?" She readjusted her purse strap on her shoulder and stepped back. "You know Mitch is going to murder you, right?" she whispered under her breath, shaking her head.

Josh sighed as he yanked the door open. "Please, just let it go. It's really nothing. Mavis is nothing." *More lies.* After hopping into the driver's seat, he slammed the Jeep's door.

Lauren stepped forward and tapped the glass with the tips of her fingernails, her gaze blazing with intensity.

Fuck.

Josh rolled down the window.

"We're not done with this. We can't be." She backed away, yanking open the door of Austin's Corvette. "Manor. Now," she threatened, dropping into the passenger seat.

Austin frowned, wiping the sweat from his brow beneath his hat. He hopped in beside her, their stares of horror darkened by the tint of the windshield. Speeding away, the tires of the Corvette squealed across the parking lot.

Josh pulled the letter from his wallet, his finger tracing the cursive swirl of his name. "You're about to get me in a lot of trouble, Duchess," he whispered, putting his Jeep in gear.

Lauren's anger whirled in his mind and Austin's unease twinged his gut. *The question is… just how much?*

"Dude, haven't we had this conversation already?" Mitch's gaze jumped to the yellow tablecloth and the vase of flowers hiding his coffee stain. He rubbed his neck with both hands, interlacing his fingers in his dark, shoulder-length hair. "And just to be clear on this, because I think you've lost your mind—my sister, the same girl that disappeared in the middle of the night, shattered your heart with a stupid letter, and never came home again—*that's* the girl you want to track down?" Mitch exhaled and dropped into his seat. "How can you even begin to think about wanting her back? When she left, I swear she took half of you with her."

Josh sighed and leaned back in his chair, stuffing his hands in his pockets. "She did." He shrugged. "And I know it sounds crazy, but I just can't shake this feeling that I'm meant to find her again." He sucked in a breath and stared at the orange poppies on the table.

Because I am meant to find you again, Duchess.

His gaze surveyed the room of jurors. Austin, Mitch, and Lauren stared back, placing him on a figurative trial for loss of sanity. Ironically, the true lawyer in the room sat in silence, leaving Mitch to fill the role of prosecution. And while Josh willed Lauren to play the role of a defense attorney on his behalf, her arm draped over her husband's shoulder in solidarity.

I don't stand a chance.

Mitch frowned, crossing his arms over his chest. The displeasure on his face rivaled Tess at any Templeton family gathering.

Josh shook his head, pushing away the lack of enthusiasm radiating from their bodies.

"It's not just crazy. It's honestly just really stupid. None of us know what happened to Mavis, why she left, or where she is now." Mitch cleared his throat. "I can't and I won't forgive her for what she blindly did to us all. She *destroyed* you, Josh. We all witnessed it," he said as he gestured around the table. "It was selfish and stupid of her, and we'll never know the truth behind it. And I for one, have no interest anymore. It's been too long. Wherever she is, she needs to stay there. I told you this already."

But she's your sister, asshole!

Austin shifted in his seat, gripping his beer with white knuckles. Pulling his baseball cap from his head, he tossed it to the table. It thumped against the stack of magazines.

Why're you so goddamn quiet, huh? You usually have an opinion about everything.

Josh huffed out a breath and leaned onto the table, clenching his jaw. "Mitch, my marriage blew up in my face. Tess humiliated me. Thanks to Dalton, I know why she left , but after all this time, I still can't help but wonder *why* Mavis did too. I'm taking my divorce as a sign to say *fuck it.*" Josh pulled the letter from his pocket and chucked it across the table in his brother-in-law's direction. "This letter… her letter… turned up a week ago. It's been ten years now since she disappeared. I'm done wondering. I'm owed the truth after all this time, and I've got absolutely nothing to lose. I'm going to find her."

Lauren groaned and huffed out a breath. "What're you going to do, huh? Show up at her home with no warning? What if she's married, Josh? Do you think her husband would appreciate her newly single high-school sweetheart showing up unannounced on her front porch? What if she has children?" She reached forward and clasped his hands in her own. "Think this through. Please!"

Ugh.

Slumping backward, Josh tugged his hands free from Lauren's grasp. With a roll of his eyes, he grabbed the top magazine from the stack on the dining room table. The words *The Funny Part* stared back in chunky font. Flipping through the pages without care, he let the magazine fall open at will. A cat's squishy face consumed three-quarters of a feature story and Josh read the title: *Fancy Fish? A Cat Lover's Guide to Extreme Shopping* by E. Banks.

Josh scrunched his nose and read the first sentence. *Mamelda peered through the glass doors of the grocery store.* Déjà vu clouded his brain. *Mamelda?*

"Josh! Are you even listening to us?" Lauren's fist pounded the table, shaking the poppies.

He shook his head, ridding the prickly sensation from his body. "I am, Lauren. I really am. I know everything you just said is probably true, but I have to know." He rolled up the magazine and tucked it beneath his arm. "I just have to try."

Mitch dragged his palms over his cheeks and exhaled. "How are you even going to start? Ten years is a long, hard, cold trail to follow."

Well, duh...

"I'll hire a private investigator." Josh turned to Austin. "You work with the police sometimes, right? Do you have a contact I can use?"

Sweat glistened on Austin's forehead as he stared down the neck of his empty beer bottle. With an exaggerated exhale, he lifted his gaze to the ceiling. "You don't need a private investigator. Mavis is in Chicago." He licked his lips and covered his eyes with his hands. "She's been there for the last eight years."

JULIE NAVICKAS

CHAPTER SIX

Mavis

Mavis opened her eyes. The creaky flooring in the kitchen called to her subconscious in sleep. She shifted, pulling her arm from beneath her body on the crappy living room couch. Her fingertips were numb, paralyzed with lack of blood flow.

Ugh, that hurts.

Casey slammed a cabinet door in the kitchen. Through a sleepy haze, Mavis eyed her barefoot movements across the tile floor. Plugging in the coffee pot, Casey licked the tip of her finger and peeled the top filter from the stack. Within seconds, the rich scent of her signature dark roast from the grocery store clearance shelf wafted through the tiny apartment.

A sad smile crept along Mavis's lips, silently observing her best friend as she stared at the trickle of brown liquid collecting in her favorite Chicago Cubs mug. *I'm so sorry this happened to you, Casey.* With a sigh, she lifted her head from the couch cushion. The forgotten iPad on her lap tumbled to the floor.

"Oh, shit, I'm sorry, Mavs! I didn't know you were in

there." Casey rounded the corner with her mug of coffee, brown liquid sloshing over the rim in her haste.

"You're okay, Case." Mavis brushed the hair away from her face, shifting to sit.

"Still…" Casey squatted and retrieved the iPad. "I'm sorry. I didn't mean to wake you. I just needed some caffeine." She brought the mug to her lips and grimaced. "But we need more creamer."

"I'll go to the store today." Mavis yawned, taking in Casey's lopsided ponytail, wrinkled tank top, and neon-yellow shorts. "Did you sleep okay? Feel all right?" She patted the seat on the couch beside her and scooted to the left. "Maybe you should sit down."

Casey hedged, clutching the iPad to her chest. "I, umm… don't really know what to say, or where to even start." She sighed, pressing her hand to her forehead. "But thank you for, you know, everything you did for me yesterday." Wrinkling her nose, she shuffled her bare feet across the carpet. Her big toe rubbed in the coffee she'd just dribbled. "I'm so embarrassed. I don't know where I'd be if—"

Mavis shook her head. "Don't. I'm umm, just sorry to see you experience it." Her stomach plummeted, churning with each word that left her lips. "The pain is just…" Her eyes widened. "Nothing you can really describe."

The late afternoon sun streamed in through the window, bringing an orange glow to the otherwise small, tired apartment. Mavis squinted, dropping back on the couch to avoid the blinding rays streaking through the faded curtains, and the look of growing confusion on Casey's face.

"What time is it?" Mavis lifted her arms to shield her eyes as the couch sank beneath Casey's weight.

Her fingernails tapped the iPad.

Oh, shit.

"Who is Dr. Joshua Templeton?" Casey grinned, pushing the iPad toward Mavis. "He's really hot, but umm, I don't think I need his services."

"Oh, Casey. That was tasteless." Rolling her eyes, she pushed the iPad away, forcing it back into her roommate's lap.

Casey shrugged. "Maybe, but still. Who is he? Why were you Googling him?" She perused the search results with a practiced flip of her index finger. "A doctor in Southern California... trust fund baby... joint heir to the Templeton fortune... divorced..."

Mavis snatched the iPad back. "Divorced? Where did you see that?" Her heart pounded, intrigue twisting along her spine. *How did I miss that before?* With a tap of her finger, the link Casey found brought her to *The Rosewood Register*, the local newspaper back home. Her eyes skimmed for an accompanying article to the headline, but nothing populated.

"What's the date on it?"

Scrolling to the bottom of the screen, her stomach lurched. "This was published a week ago. Joshua is *recently* divorced." Mavis sucked in a breath, the new information gouging a fresh hole in her heart. *He's single.*

"Well, spill it. Who is this guy? Ex-boyfriend or something?" She tucked her feet beneath her on the couch, sipping her coffee with the expectant eyes of a child ready for a bedtime story.

Mavis studied her, the past eight years of her own life reflecting back. From coworker, to roommate, to best friend, Casey had unknowingly been along for the ride as Mavis fought to reclaim her life beyond the fallout of Rosewood. Tugging at a stray thread on the bottom of her t-shirt, Mavis looped it around her finger, cutting off circulation to the nail bed. She breathed out a slow exhale.

"Come on, Mavs. You know I won't say anything to anyone." Casey sipped her coffee, nudging Mavis with her toes. "Whatever it is stays with me."

She swallowed, battling Casey's request with her instinct to hide. "It's hard for me to talk about him. I've never really told anyone..."

Except for you, Austin—my savior and forever source of guilt—the sole keeper of all my dirty little secrets.

Mavis shivered, quickly hurling Austin's sweet grin from her mind.

"Well, I'm a good secret keeper. I swear." Casey dragged a finger in the shape of an *X* over her heart. "Cross my heart and hope to die."

I'm not sure it's the right time for me to tell this story. "You know, Case, you went through something pretty traumatic yesterday. The focus shouldn't be on me right now."

She stared at the coffee in her hands, blowing on the hot liquid. Pressing a palm to her tummy, she gulped. "Distract me then."

It all hits too close to home.

Mavis eyed Casey's fingers as they dragged along the material of her tank top. The simple gesture forced the memories to overflow, the vision of her own hospital room reappearing before her eyes. "I don't think my story can," she whispered.

Looking up from her mug, Casey furrowed her brow. "I don't understand."

Then I guess… let me help you.

The ringing in her ears returned as hurt and anger swelled in her heart. Parting her lips to speak, the pain of the past spilled out. "The loss of a life, even a life that was created unintentionally, never truly leaves." Mavis shook her head, tucking her hair behind her ears. "It becomes a part of you, a phantom soul tied to your own. At least… that's what I think of when I remember the child I lost."

The revelation hung in the stale air, met only by the honk of a horn as it blasted through the city streets below.

Casey drew in a breath, sloshing coffee on her shorts. "Wait, are you saying… you too?" She rubbed at the new blemish on the neon.

The familiar burn behind her eyes roared, threatening to smash the floodgate. Mavis nodded, dropping her gaze to the iPad in Casey's lap. Josh's photo returned her stare as a pool of guilt swelled around her heart. *And you never knew the truth. Because of me.*

Curly blonde hair fell into her lap as Casey lowered her head to rest against her legs. "I don't know what to say," she murmured.

Brushing at her matted curls, Mavis pulled a stray piece of hair from her friend's face. "It's more common than I think people realize. Something like one in every four pregnancies end in…"

Casey heaved out a sigh, her warm breath beating against Mavis's bare skin. "It was so early I didn't even know I was pregnant. Mavs, was it my fault? Did I do something wrong?" She sniffled, wiping a tear from her cheek.

"Don't do it. Don't blame yourself." *Because that's exactly what I did too.*

"How can I not?"

Mavis squeezed her shoulder as Casey returned to a sitting position.

"And geez, Mavs—the father—it could have been Ryan… but it also could have been David. How awful is that?" She wiped her nose with the back of her hand. "God, what is wrong with me?"

"Nothing, Case. These things happen. It's not always someone's fault."

"Is that what you told him too?" As she pressed the iPad back in Mavis's hands, Josh looked up from the screen. "It's him. Right? The father?"

Mavis turned the device off and set it aside. Enough guilt had already settled in her heart. "Yeah."

"Will you tell me what happened?"

Wrapping Casey in a hug, Mavis sighed. And as if the words spoke directly from her heart, the ghosts of the past peeked forth from her soul.

*

A big fat plus sign appeared, carving its way through the little plastic stick. It glared, clear as day, the little pink lines etching a dagger through life as she knew it.

"Pregnant?"

Her knees gave out, dropping her body to the floor as the contents of her stomach lurched. A cold sweat broke out across her forehead as a searing headache set in.

"This can't be happening…" Her feeble voice echoed in the quiet bathroom, her cries meeting the blue-tiled floor as tears welled behind her lids and cascaded down her cheeks. "Joshua," she moaned. Her head met the ground as she cradled her stomach in her shaking hands.

His face swirled in her mind, his eyes wide with panic and confusion. Picturing him dragging his hands through his hair, he pressed his eyes closed in disbelief as she broke the news to him in her imagination.

"Oh my God, this is all my fault…" The image of the meadow— making love in the field of poppies—danced across the image of Josh. His sweet voice in her memory quickly drowned with the ring in her ears, colliding with the fog clouding her brain.

Sobs overpowered her body, and shivers attacked her spine, drilling holes through her skin to pierce her heart.

"What're we going to do, Joshua?"

And from deep within her soul, a protective, powerful voice spoke forth from her heart.

"We" aren't going to do anything, but you are.

*

"Mavis, you didn't!" Casey interrupted, tears streaking down her face as she swiped at them. Rising from the couch, she stomped away toward the kitchen.

"I never said what I did was right!" she yelled.

Returning with a roll of paper towels, Casey tore off a sheet and blew her nose, sinking her butt back into her seat on the couch. "Want one?" she asked, dropping the large roll in her lap.

Mavis snorted. *I share the most vulnerable moment of my life with you, and you hand me a paper towel.* Nonetheless, her fingers unraveled a fresh piece. She dabbed at her eyes, ignoring the scratchy sensation on her cheeks.

"Well, keep going…"

*

The light of the moon funneled through the tiny window above the shower stall. Mavis pressed her cheek against the hard surface of the tub, her body curled into a ball on the bathroom floor. From the moment the pink positive sign had appeared, the world had stilled— motionless, paralyzed.

Mitch's strong snores from the adjacent room bit into the stillness, the sounds of his slumber speeding time forward. The shock now settled in her stomach, truth seeping into the core of her heart.

"We can't have a baby, Joshua…" she murmured into the quiet. Mavis forced herself to stand, steadying her wobbling legs on the bathroom rug. Gripping the porcelain sink, she turned on the faucet. Cold water collided with her face, an unwelcomed return to reality. The water trickled down her cheeks, calming the red droves of tears and cooling the warmth of her skin.

Terror reflected back as her gaze lifted to the mirror. Mavis tipped her head forward to meet the glass, its hard surface steadying her shaking body. Josh's necklace pulled free from beneath her shirt, the little heart charm hammering into the mirror. She cupped the charm in her palm, squeezing it tight as she tore herself away from the sink, and away from the reflection piqued with panic.

Down the hall, she tiptoed, closing her bedroom quietly. She sank to her bed, reaching for the small teddy bear propped on her pillow. Clad in a navy-blue Georgetown sweater, the small token from Josh's most recent campus trip smiled through the threads of his mouth.

His little eyes met hers, both black beads boring into her soul. And in the quiet of the bedroom, his little inanimate voice spoke the words that had settled in her heart the moment the test turned positive. Josh won't go to Georgetown if you're pregnant with his child.

The bear dropped to the floor as Mavis buried her face beneath the pillow. She screamed, muffling her shriek into the mattress.

*

"Oh, geez, Mavs…" Casey tugged a hand through her ponytail, gripping the tips of the little blonde curls.

"I really thought I was doing the right thing! I didn't want to keep him from school. Since he was like six years old, Josh wanted to be a doctor!" Mavis slapped her hands against her knees and huffed out a breath. "I was seventeen. I was stupid. And scared. I did the only thing I could think of."

"Which was?"

"Run." Mavis shook her head, her eyes widening at the simplicity of the word.

"You just left?"

Mavis stood, wrapping her arms around herself in a hug. The light of the room dimmed; the sun's afternoon rays blocked by the apartment complex across the street. She paced, each toe dragging across the carpet of the living room.

Her stomach churned, the actions of her past stirring the turmoil of retelling her truth. She dropped her hands to her hips and shrugged. "I mean, yeah… eventually. I stayed until Josh was ready to leave for school." The image of a pen scratching across paper settled in her brain, the words *my dearest Joshua* stealing the air from her lungs. "I wrote him a letter."

"But you didn't tell him about the baby?" Casey scrunched her nose.

"God no." She snorted. "Case, it was my fault we got pregnant. My fault!" Her index finger rammed into her chest.

"You climbed on top of yourself? Come on, Mavs! All you ever do is take the blame for someone else." She sighed, unraveling another paper towel to blow her nose.

"You don't understand. You weren't there." Mavis shook her head. "I just… I just couldn't take his dream away."

"And what about your dreams, huh?"

"Oh, Case... I'm living them." Her sarcasm cut through the silence of the room as her feet carried her body down the hallway and into her bedroom.

Casey followed and dropped her butt to Mavis's mattress. She tugged her knees up to meet her chest. "Well, keep going, Mamelda. You can't stop the story there, and your dreams can't end with *The Funny Part*."

"Case, just lay off, all right? It's hard enough having to live with my regrets, let alone be reprimanded for them." Mavis tugged a black uniform from her closet, the words *The Broken Shaker* emblazed in gold across the chest.

"I'm not reprimanding you! I'm just trying to understand! Everything you did was so *selfless*. I don't get it!" Her head rested against the wall as her arms flopped to her sides.

"How can you say that? Everything I did was completely *selfish*! I left town and took Josh's child with me! I never told him the truth!" Tears trickled from her eyes as she dragged her uniform over her head. The pit in her gut grew, spewing forth the sadness that had collected for a decade. "And I broke both our hearts in the process..."

Casey sighed. "Where'd you go?"

"Boston."

"Why?"

"I had a cousin who lived in the city."

"And no one looked for you there?"

Mavis tossed her dirty clothes in the laundry basket. They landed with a thud, spilling over the rim. "After my parents died, we all lost touch. My foster parents didn't know Angie even existed."

"What about your brother?"

Mavis laughed. "Mitch? No way."

Casey nodded. "So, you're hidden away in Boston. Then what?"

Mavis swallowed. A hard lump in her throat formed as she struggled to choke down a gulp of air. She sank to the floor, ramming black flats on her feet. "I miscarried," she whispered, averting her gaze.

"Mavs…"

She shrugged, sucking in a breath. "All in the past, right?"

"I mean, maybe not. Clearly you still have feelings for this Josh guy."

Mavis pulled her hair back in a low ponytail, securing it with a black ribbon. "Doesn't matter. I can't ever see him again." Her heart sank, the truth of her words stomping through the glimmer of hope that allowed her heart to beat again when she read the word *divorced* no more than thirty minutes ago.

"Why not?" Her nose crinkled as her shoulders rose.

"Because of his brother!" Mavis cringed. *Why did I just say that? Dammit, Casey!*

"Huh? Who? Why?" Casey shook her head, rubbing her temples.

"You want to talk about selfless versus selfish? Well, here we go…"

*

Her fist pounded on the door of Suite 283A. Tears stained her cheeks as they traveled down her face. Mavis pulled the hem of her sweatshirt up to wipe away the evidence, swiping away the sadness spilling from her eyes.

"Hi," a boy answered, a headset covering his ears and chip crumbs clinging to the outer corner of his mouth. "Can I help you?" He crunched as he spoke.

"Austin," she choked out, swallowing a sob. "Does Austin Templeton live here?"

The boy furrowed his brow. "Umm yeah, hang on." He disappeared behind the door, his voice shouting behind him. "Hey! Austin! There's some chick crying out here for you!"

Footsteps pounded against the floor inside the suite before Austin's blue eyes peeked around the door frame.

"Fuck. Mavis!"

The door swung open as Austin's body slammed into hers. His arms encircled her, pulling her tightly into his chest. He squeezed, each muscle holding her prisoner against him.

"Austin..." She exhaled into him, collapsing into his embrace, reveling in the warmth projecting from his skin.

"Where the fuck have you been?" His words pummeled into her ear, the harsh tenor of his voice betraying the comfort his arms provided. Austin squeezed her upper arms, pushing her away to pierce her with his icy blue stare. "My God, Mavis. Do you have any clue what you've put us all through? Josh is a fucking mess!" He shook her, willing the truth to shake free from her body. "Jesus, are you okay? Are you hurt?"

"I'm so sorry." She stifled a sob, pressing her face back into his chest. Sandalwood scented his t-shirt, and she breathed it in, inhaling the comfort of home as her fingers glided along the Harvard letters stitched to the front.

He tugged her inside, pulling her behind him until they entered the quiet of his bedroom. The door closed with a soft click as Austin guided her to his bed and hopped onto the mattress beside her.

"Should I be calling the police or something? What happened? Where have you been?" He gripped her hands, pressing his lips to her knuckles.

She shook her head, burying her face in her palms. "I didn't know where else to go, Austin. I'm so sorry for barging in here like this."

Austin pulled her hands down, brushing his thumb along her cheek. "You are always safe with me, Mavs. Don't apologize. Just tell me what the hell happened."

The truth bubbled to the surface, pulling from the depths of her soul. The months of turmoil and hardship culminating in a single spill of the truth. The words tumbled from her lips, ready to fall into Austin's lap for safekeeping.

"I was pregnant."

His arms tightened, his hand cupping her head, pulling her back into his chest. He blew out a slow exhale and swallowed.

"Josh didn't know," she murmured. "I couldn't tell him."

He nodded, threading his fingers through her curls. "Princess..."

he whispered. His breath beat down on the top of her head. "Princess…"

"I'm so sorry, Austin." She peeled her face from him, tears spilling from her eyes as the words seeped outward from her heart. "I'm so sorry. I didn't know what to do!"

Austin's palm dragged along her stomach. Her breath hitched at his touch.

"Did you say was?"

The ground beneath her feet shook, rattling the truth from the fresh confines of the grave. A pit in her stomach unlocked, the portal to hell opening with an invitation tied up in a bow. And the two words that hurt more than anything in the world left her lips, ready to deposit the secret of a lifetime into the man beside her.

"I miscarried."

His eyes glossed over as his grip tightened, lifting her body until she curled onto his lap. His hands shook as he cradled her, drawing her into him until their bodies melded together.

A weight fell from her heart—the secret truth no longer just her own—split down the center, equally divided between her soul and Austin's. Her eyes closed, her body resting for the first true time in weeks as the tension dissolved.

As the minutes ticked away, their bodies lowered together to the bed, pressed together.

"Stay here with me tonight, Princess," he whispered in her ear.

She nodded, opening her eyes to find his. In the comfort of his arms, she breathed, breathed into the safety, into the comfort.

"You can't tell Josh I'm here. He'll never forgive me."

"Your secret is safe with me. Always."

Her heart pounded, ramming into her ribcage—her bloodstream fueled with the sense of unbreakable trust. Fog clouded her brain, exhaustion stealing all thought. And in a moment of connection, of safety, of truth, and of pure vulnerability, his lips found hers.

*

"Oh, my God. The hot blond guy that came into The Broken Shaker that one time! That was this same dude?"

"You remember that?" Mavis dragged her hands along her cheeks, feeling the heat of embarrassment radiate through her hands, her dirtiest secrets aired to another soul.

"I mean, yeah! You were like shaking when he walked up to the bar!" Casey's eyes widened as she scootched to the edge of the bed. "Plus, he was sexy as hell!"

"Sexy yes, but the biggest mistake of my life." She shook her head, dropping to the mattress next to Casey. "I don't know what the hell was wrong with me that night."

"The night he came into Shaker?"

Mavis snorted. "Maybe I should have said night*s*, plural." The tips of her ears turned pink. *He has always been the piece of home I needed.*

Casey giggled. "At least now I know you're human. Wasn't too sure before." She slung her arm around Mavis's shoulder and squeezed. "Have you kept in contact with him? That was like what, five years ago?"

"Six. And no… I ran out of that hotel room the morning after. Haven't heard from him since. He's probably pissed he woke up hungover, naked, and alone."

Casey giggled. "Well, you write the script and I'll cast the actors. This story is meant for the *Hallmark* channel."

"Thanks, Case." She snorted and stood, scooping up her phone. "My shift starts at seven, but I'll swing by the store on the way home, okay? Text me anything else you need."

She stepped toward the doorway, slinging her bag over her shoulder. With a glance down at her phone, she stopped. The blood in her veins froze, paralyzed. The beat of her heart paused—completely still.

Austin's name appeared on her screen, the words written below stirring her soul from sleep after a decade of hibernation.

Josh wants you back.

The ring in her ears overpowered her brain as the dizziness took control. And she dropped to the floor.

CHAPTER SEVEN

Josh

The rain pounded against the window, each drop falling from the pane in predictable patterns. *Drip. Drip. Drip.*

Josh ran a hand through his hair as he stared out into the darkening parking lot, the storm gaining momentum. Exhaling, he leaned back in his chair and rubbed his eyes. The rain poured, triggering memories to flood his brain in the quiet of the still office. The past swirled around him as his teenage self, stood on the porch of his childhood home, the rain tapping against the tin roof above his head. And through a cloud of heartbreak, Mavis appeared, leaning her back into the railing in their final moments together. The tears slid down her face, each second ticking away as she secretly prepared to flee.

His skin prickled, tingling with the knowledge that now lived in his heart. *If I just would have reached out and grabbed you... or refused to take your stupid letter... maybe you'd still be here with me today.*

Josh gripped the edge of his desk, grounding his body in place, in the memory of her. But like day fades into night, the vision floated away on the disintegrating corners of a dream. He shook his head, allowing a rush of simmering anger to bubble to the surface. *Austin.*

"You know why she left too, don't you?" His question penetrated the silence of the office, his words voicing the steadily growing unease in his heart over the last several days.

Josh tossed his pen to the surface of the desk. It collided with his laptop and rolled to the floor. "Goddamn it." Sighing, he bent forward to scoop it up, whacking his head on the underside of the wood.

Ouch!

Rubbing at the soon-to-be bruise, he furrowed his brow at the chaos in front of him. What normally would have been organized and sanitized was now scattered and in disarray, like the aftermath of the rainstorm outside.

Josh put his hands to his notes, shuffling the papers until they aligned in a neat pile. Dropping them into a file folder, his heart stopped. *Wait, where is it?* Panic erupted, tingling along his spine. *Mavs, your letter. Where'd it go?*

The air escaped his lungs as Josh pushed his files aside and upended his notebook. A cup of pens toppled over, and he brushed the writing utensils out of his way as the contents in his stomach churned.

A knock on the door interrupted his search, his gaze drawn from his desk with minor intrigue.

"Excuse me, Dr. Templeton?"

"Hi, Sandra." His hands rifled through the stack of mail. *Dammit! How could I lose it?*

"Dr. Emmet is on line two for a patient consult. Are you available?"

Josh's elbow banged into his office phone, sending the clunky plastic device sailing to the floor. Sandra stepped forward and kneeled, picking up the phone and replacing it on his desk. "Line two, Dr. Templeton."

"Hmm?" Josh shoved a medical journal to the side, assaulting the printer in his frenzied search. The machine whined and beeped before spitting out a blank piece of paper.

"Are you okay?" Sandra squinted, crinkling her nose as she placed her tiny red-rimmed glasses on her face.

"I'm just looking…" He slammed his laptop shut, pushing his bottle of hand sanitizer to the side. Beneath his nameplate, a crinkled envelope appeared. "Aha!" Josh grinned and snagged the letter, pressing it against his chest.

"Got what you need?" Her brow furrowed and she balanced her hands on her hips.

"I do now." He smiled, tucking Mavis's letter back in his pocket. "Oh, umm… did you need something?"

She backed away until her hand rested on the doorknob. "You know, sweetie, you should get out of here for lunch. Step away for a little bit or something. You look pale." She smiled, but concern blazed behind her eyes.

Josh snorted and dragged his palms along his cheeks. "It's been a weird few days," he admitted.

"I can tell." Her head tilted, the familiar look of pity growing on her face. "Maybe a few days off wouldn't hurt you either?"

I could fly to Chicago.

His heartbeat accelerated, the sudden idea blossoming in his chest. Josh nodded, grinning at her suggestion. "Actually… yeah. That's a great idea."

"Let me poke around your schedule. Get some appointments rescheduled, okay, honey?"

Thankful for the motherly affection, Josh nodded. "Thanks, Sandra."

She grinned. "Oh, and Dr. Templeton?"

"Yeah?"

"Line two." She winked and left the room, snapping the door shut behind her.

Josh looked down at the phone as the red light on line two disappeared.

Oh well. She'll call back.

He gathered his things, straightening his desk until it returned to its usual state of organization. Pulling his laptop toward him, he opened a web browser, ready to follow his sudden heartfelt idea and book a flight to the Windy City.

His mouse hovered over the search tools as Lauren's voice wracked his brain. *What if she's married? What if she has children?*

"What am I thinking? I can't just fly to Chicago..." He slammed his laptop shut and groaned, picking up his phone to dial Lauren instead.

"Hey, Josh. What's up? Everything okay?"

"Do you want to go get lunch? I need to talk to you."

"Umm, yeah, sure! When? Where?"

"Now? Mary-Anne's Diner?"

"Meet you there!"

Josh yanked open the double doors to the diner, the water droplets rolling from his jacket as the storm outside persisted. He spotted Lauren in the corner booth, and his shoes squeaked across the floor in her direction.

"Thanks for meeting me." Josh shrugged into the seat opposite her, grinning at the coffee she'd already ordered for him. "And for the boost of caffeine."

"Hey, I needed the pick-me-up too." She brought her mug to her lips and sipped. "Mitch has had us up late watching *The Lord of the Rings*—extended versions—every night this week." She yawned as she set the cup down.

"In the Land of Mordor where the shadows lie—"

"Oh, my God! Stop!" She cringed with a giggle. "You guys are such nerds!"

Josh laughed and let his shoulders sink back into the booth. "Guilty."

She picked up her menu, the smile on her face disappearing behind the pancake options. "Well, all right, Frodo Baggins, why did you want to have second breakfast with me?"

He snorted. "Straight to business."

"Yeah, well, my business is falling apart, so let's focus on yours." She slapped her menu shut.

"Huh?"

"Oh, never mind. It's fine. I'm just complaining." Lauren shook her head and sneaked a peek at her phone.

"Really?"

She grinned. "Really. I'm just salty today. Mitch…"

The waitress stepped to the edge of their table, pulling a pen from her ear. She blew a bubble of gum before speaking. "What can I get you kids?"

Josh pointed to Lauren, snagging a menu from the table. "Ladies first."

"Two pecan pancakes, no whipped cream please."

The waitress scratched a note onto her pad of paper. "No whipped cream," she repeated. "And for you?" Her eyes brightened, turning to Josh.

"Umm… same please." He stuffed the menu back in the holder.

"Make it two," she said. Her feet squeaked away from the table, her perfume holding strong in the air.

Lauren waved her hand in front of her nose. "Pungent."

Josh snorted and took a sip of his coffee.

"For real though, Josh. What's up?"

He inhaled, summoning the courage to answer her, to seek her support in finding Mavis. Turning his attention to his coffee, his hands swirled the cup to stir the sugar.

"This is about Mavis again, isn't it?"

Josh grinned, his gaze lifting to meet hers. "I have to find her."

"Is this because of Tess?" Her eyes narrowed.

"Screw Tess."

"She's done enough screwing for the both of you." Lauren winked and dropped back in her seat. "But Josh, seriously, the timing is kind of coincidental. I haven't heard Mavis's name in years, and now all of a sudden she's all you can think about again?"

"I love her." Josh shrugged, fidgeting with the stuffing oozing from the ripped seat cushion. *Gross. Why did I just touch that?*

"Look, I get it. I know you loved her. And she loved you too. But that was *teenage* love." She leaned forward and grasped his fingers in hers. "It was never meant to last forever."

He squeezed her hand before pulling away, dropping back into his seat with a sigh. *I disagree.* His gaze lifted to the portrait above Lauren's head. A silhouette of a man wrapped his arms around a woman on the beach at sunset. Happy, complacent, in love.

"Well, you married Mitch."

She flinched. "Yeah… but maybe not my best move."

"What's that supposed to mean?" Josh scrunched his nose.

"Two pecan pancakes with extra whipped cream." The waitress shoved the warm plates across the table. The tower of whipped cream slid, melting into a pool of white goo. "Can I get you kids anything else?"

Josh shook his head. "No, this looks great. Thank you."

She winked and marched away, smacking her gum to the roof of her mouth again.

Lauren giggled, scooping the melting cream onto a spare plate. "Close enough I suppose."

"What did you mean, Lauren? Maybe you shouldn't have married Mitch?" Josh shoved the soggy cream to the side too, slicing his pancake with a fork.

"Forget I said that, okay?" She raised her brow, widening her eyes. "It was stupid."

"Are you guys okay?"

She shook her head, stuffing a bite of pancake in her mouth. "These are good."

He nodded. "So, you can comment on my love life, but I can't comment on yours?"

"Hey, you invited me to lunch, not the other way around."

Josh grinned and sipped his coffee, stuffing Lauren's comment about Mitch into the *keep an eye on this* folder in his brain.

"You know I miss her too, right?" She dragged her fork over the slowly sogging cake, spreading the syrup evenly across each bite. "She was my best friend."

Josh smiled. "Don't you want to know what happened to her too then?"

"It's not like I haven't considered it, but Mitch—"

"Hope ya'll have a nice day. Come back soon." The waitress dropped the receipt on the table as Josh stuffed the last bite of pancake into his mouth. She stepped away to welcome the next group of customers.

"Look, Josh... Mavis hurt me when she left, and she *destroyed* you. But she also stole this tiny little piece of Mitch's heart that he never got back. If you're going to find her and drag her back into all of our lives... just think for a minute about what that means for the rest of us, okay?" She stuffed the last of her pancake in her mouth and chewed, wiping her lips with a napkin.

"You're right. It's not just me here." He nodded as a text came through from Austin. He glared at the invitation to join him for a beer after work. "She hurt all of us, except perhaps our brother." He pushed the phone across the table.

Lauren read the message and shoved it back. "He knows more than he's admitting."

"He knows more than he's admitting," Josh repeated and pocketed the phone, pulling his credit card from his wallet.

JULIE NAVICKAS

CHAPTER EIGHT

Austin

Austin hammered on Josh's front door, each rap of his fist a cry of unease. Having received no response to his text about a beer, the restlessness in his gut redoubled and he drove over, ready to force a conversation.

But the door didn't budge. *Not home yet, huh?* With a frown, Austin punched in the code on the keypad and let himself in with a six-pack of beer. Stepping inside, he flipped the hallway light on. The empty space sank his heart as he gazed around his brother's barren bachelor pad. *God, it's depressing in here.* Josh needed new furniture. And a hammer and nails to hang something—anything—on the walls.

Austin ran his hands along the banister as he kicked off his shoes and headed into the living room. Dropping into the single remaining chair, he sighed.

"W-h-y, Mavis?" he whined, dragging his fingers through his hair. The silence of the house met his ears, and Austin rolled his eyes. "Anyone but her…" Snagging a beer, he opened the Goose Island with his keys. The label crinkled in his hand as he examined it closer. *Made in Chicago.*

He snorted and slapped a hand onto the armrest, knocking an open magazine to his lap.

A huge glossy-paged cat face stared back at him.

"*Fancy Fish? A Cat Lover's Guide to Extreme Shopping* by E. Banks. What the hell is this?" He flipped to the cover and read *The Funny Part*, recognizing it as a regular mail subscription Mitch enjoyed. "He's got you reading this crap now too?"

Austin skimmed the story, laughing into his beer at the delightful antics of the main character and her questionable senior-citizen shopping habits for her beloved cats. A shiver ran down his spine, a swirl of déjà vu settling into his psyche. *Have I read this before?* He flipped to the page with the cat face.

"E. Banks... no idea."

Shrugging, he closed the magazine and peeked at the darkening sky. His mind wandered, the chatter of a crowded Chicago bar bringing forth a memory. Mavis appeared, her bright smile growing as she turned to greet him, the green glow of her eyes intent on his own.

The beat of his heart accelerated, the recall of the moment coating his forehead in a light sheen of sweat. Austin exhaled, expelling the rising unease erupting in the pit of his stomach. He shifted, dragging a hand across his chin. *What the hell did I do?*

Draining his beer, he set the empty bottle on the floor and grimaced at the parallel it drew in his mind with the last time he'd seen her. "I'm in so much fucking trouble." In spite of himself, Austin grinned at her memory, the long-ago childhood days of the Lonely Mountain consuming his brain.

The right corner of his lips tugged upward as his former alter-ego Smaug, the princess-capturing dragon roared, locking Mavis amidst his scattered treasures in a makeshift tree-fort.

"Princess." The name on his lips pierced the memory, melting his heart into a gooey puddle of mush. *Shit.*

Austin closed his eyes, inhaling the imagined scent of coconuts in her hair, feeling the rake of her fingernails as they dragged across his skin, tasting her lips as they met his own. A shiver sizzled down his body, triggering a tightening sensation in his groin.

"Oh, I'm so fucked."

Snapping his eyes open, he yanked his body from the chair and shook his head, forcing the feelings rebounding in his heart away.

The neighbor's holiday display flickered on, and Santa's larger-than-life body filled with air until his belly swelled with Christmas cheer. Austin rested his forehead against the glass of the picture window, the red and green lights flashing along his face as the holiday town across the street came to life. The windowpane, cold to the touch, calmed him, soothing the guilt ricocheting in his soul. But Santa stared back, his black eyes speaking of nothing but gifts of coal.

A surge of jealousy tugged at his heart, a sense of territorialism erupting in his gut. He pressed a hand to his chest and stepped back from the window. *Mavs, you were never mine to begin with, but...*

Dropping back into the chair, he cracked open another beer, unrest settling into the pit of his stomach as he gulped the golden liquid. "And what about you, huh, Princess? What're you gonna do when Josh finds you? How much are you willing to keep hidden?" He bit his bottom lip as fear gripped him. *What secrets will you spill?*

A blurred vision drifted to the forefront of his thoughts, his brother's stricken face materializing into focus as he learned the truth about their time between the sheets over the years.

"Shit! I can't let that happen. Josh can't know what we did." Austin dug his hands into his pocket and pulled out his phone. With a few taps of his fingers, he opened a new text message. *What do I even say to you? It's been six years...*

His thumbs tapped out her name as a concoction of confusion and angst collided with his heart. He stumbled, typing out words, only to quickly delete them. *Ugh*. At last, he settled on: *Mavis, it's Austin Templeton. I'm sorry to contact you this way after so long, but you need to know that Josh wants you back. Don't tell him anything about us.*

Headlights flashed through the front window as Austin hit *send*. He jammed his phone back into his pocket and stood, ready to face Josh.

"Just like a courtroom," he muttered to himself, pulling a beer from the carton and readying it for his brother. "Dodge and evade."

Josh entered through the side door, backpack in hand and a look on his face that declared brotherly war.

"Before you say anything, just hear me out." Austin stretched his arm out and jiggled the beer, like coaxing a toddler with candy.

Josh waved his hand, shooing it away. "I just can't understand why you would keep a secret like this from me. You're supposed to be my best friend here." He shook his head and dropped his backpack to the floor, pulling his hands upward to rub at the muscles in his neck.

Austin nodded and fell into a chair at the dining room table. Pushing the beer toward the seat opposite him, he gestured for his brother to sit.

With a roll of his eyes, Josh followed and slumped into the chair, scooping up the beer and bringing it to his lips. He wiped his mouth with the back of his hand. "Explain it to me, please."

Here goes nothing.

"Mavs begged me not to tell you anything." Austin's eyes widened, bracing his body for the impending outburst.

Josh shook his head and snorted. "And why would she do that?" He raised his shoulders. "She was *my* girlfriend, not yours. Why would she come to you?"

Heaving out a heavy sigh, Austin dragged his hands along his cheeks. Pulling his gaze to the ceiling, each word on his lips filtered through the prerequisite question: *what's okay for me to tell you?* He exhaled. "Look, Josh... I can't answer those questions. But what I can tell you is this. She showed up at my door at Harvard, about a month or two after we started school freshmen year. She was alone, and crying, and honestly, I think just desperate for a familiar face." He shrugged.

"Harvard? Why the hell was she there?"

Austin blanched. "She was in Boston."

"Boston? Why?"

"I can't tell you that."

"What the hell use are you then?"

Austin rolled his eyes. "Josh, I swear to you, I am telling you everything I can. But the full truth is not mine to share. That's on Mavis."

"So, you know…" Josh cocked his head. "You know it all, don't you? Why she left, what her secret was?" He squinted and leaned forward, his stare hardening.

"Yeah, I do." Austin hung his head, staring into his lap. "I swear, Josh, I'm telling you everything I can. But I did make a promise to her, and I won't go back on that."

Josh smirked and flicked the bottle cap across the table. It rolled, finding a new home on the dining room floor. "Fine. Keep going." He sneered. "So, she showed up at your room at Harvard. What happened then?"

A twinge in Austin's gut grew, oozing throughout his body until it squeezed the air from his lungs. He swallowed, shoving down the guilt creeping upward through his throat.

"I let her stay with me." *Not a total lie, just avoiding the details.*

"How long?"

"Just the night." Austin downed the remaining third of his beer.

"Okay… so that's the night you learned the truth? She told you why she left town? Why she left me?" Josh groaned, his shoulders sinking as the words fell from his lips.

"Yeah, she told me everything."

"Was she hurt? Was it something I did?" Josh's eyes

glistened, each corner filling with tears from the past.

I mean, technically?

"Josh, that's really something she needs to tell you. I can't do it…" He rose from his seat and stepped into the kitchen, dropping his empty bottle into the recycle bin. "Do you want another?"

He nodded as Austin returned and pushed another beer in his direction.

"Did you tell her…?" he whispered. Josh raked his hands over his head, cupping the back of his neck. He stared down the neck of the bottle. "Did you tell her how much it hurt? How bad it broke me for her to disappear like that?"

"I did! And she knew it, Josh. Mavs didn't leave to hurt you. I swear, she left to *protect* you." His chest tightened, the air moving through his lungs challenged by the weight—by the gravity of the conversation.

"*Protect* me?" Josh frowned and tugged at his ears, his cheeks flushing pink. "Damn it, Austin! I would have driven all night to see her! I could have been at your door before she even woke up. Why didn't you call me?" A tear trickled from his eye, rolling down his cheek. He swiped at it before bringing the new bottle to his lips.

"She begged me not to," he whispered, slouching back into the chair.

A vein bulged in his forehead as Josh snapped his knuckles beneath the table. "A letter. That's all I got. One stupid letter with some elusive truth buried behind words with no meaning." He shook his head. "I would have married that girl at eighteen I loved her so fucking much."

"Yeah, and then you married Tess instead." Austin cringed, crinkling his nose.

Josh snorted, the ghost of a smile tugging at his mouth. "Not my best decision."

"Really not your best decision." A small grin crept along his lips as the vibration in his front pocket twisted his stomach. *Mavs…*

Josh ran his hand along the table, brushing his fingers

through the condensation of the beer bottle. "Why Chicago, though? You said Boston before." He glanced up, locking Austin in an inescapable question.

"Umm… the law firm." Austin cleared his throat. "I was there a few years back, meeting with a new client. She invited me to dinner at this place called The Broken Shaker. Mavis happened to be standing at the bar, serving drinks. Total coincidence."

"A bartender?" Josh squinted.

"Yeah, but she was good! Happy, built a life for herself there. She wasn't the same girl who showed up in tears at my door."

Mavis's smile flashed in Austin's mind as she turned to face him again in his memory. At her grin, a rush of longing settled back into his heart, swelling with desire.

"Was she married?" Josh's cheeks reddened as his gaze fell to the floor.

"Not when I saw her." *And if you were, Mavs, I would be in even more trouble than I'm currently in.*

Josh toyed with the skin around his ring finger, squeezing the space that used to bear a wedding ring. "Why didn't you tell me you saw her after you came back from that trip?"

"You were engaged to Tess. What good would it have done? You'd moved on, she'd moved on… It only would have stirred up old feelings and memories." Austin stood and collected the empty beer bottles from the table. "I'm sorry that I hurt you by keeping it a secret. But Josh, I really thought it was *better* that you didn't know. You seemed happy with Tess. I didn't want to fuck with it."

Austin stepped away and tossed the bottles in the recycle bin.

"Do you think she's still there?" Josh smirked.

Austin bit down on the inside of his cheek as his gaze followed the path of the deepening smile on his brother's lips. The pit in his stomach widened, a surge of jealousy boiling forth. *Stay away from her. Josh, please stay away from her.*

But he plastered a returning grin on his face and opened his mouth. "I guess there's only one way to find out."

Shit. I'm in so much trouble.

CHAPTER NINE

Mavis

Shooting stars burst before her eyes. Sweat glistened along her brow as the cold and clammy feeling of illness wracked her shaken body. When the light show dispersed, Casey's face swam into view.

"Oh, my God, Mavs, are you okay?" She gripped her shoulders, guiding Mavis to a sitting position. "Don't stand. Just lean back against the wall and don't move."

"My phone, Case. Where's my phone?" She searched around her, patting the floor. *I had to have been hallucinating!*

"Don't worry about your phone. Geez, you just dropped like a pile of bricks. Are you bleeding? Did you hit your head?" Casey dug through the thick mop of curls, removing the ponytail and black ribbon. As she pulled away, her fingers caked with blood. "Shit! You are definitely bleeding! Hang on, don't move." She jumped; her bare feet pounded away down the hall.

Mavis lifted her hand to the back of her head. Slick, sticky red wetness coated her fingers. She pushed against the wound, regretting the pressure almost immediately as her stomach lurched. Closing her eyes, she rested her head against her knees.

Ouch.

Casey returned with a roll of paper towels and dropped back to the floor. Despite the pounding in her head, the nausea in her gut, and the anxiety gripping her heart, Mavis grinned at Casey's EMT skills—or lack thereof.

"Hold still, okay?" She dabbed a paper towel against the back of Mavis's head, initiating the thick metallic scent of blood to fill the air. Crumpling the towel, she grabbed a new sheet. "It's not that bad," she insisted, repeating the process.

Mavis took over the press-and-pat procedure, her stomach churning with each fresh sheet until the bleeding lessened.

"Thanks, Case," she murmured, wadding up the used paper towels into a ball.

"Can I help you to the shower or something?" She squeezed Mavis's knee and cringed. "Your hair…"

"Oh! My phone! Help me find my phone." Mavis pushed her body forward and forced her eyes to focus on the tile flooring.

"Umm… I mean, that's probably not like the biggest priority right now." But Casey's gaze zeroed in on the floor around them.

"You don't understand." Mavis willed her body to search the space. "He just texted me."

"Who?" Casey's eyes widened. She crawled down the hallway and grabbed the elusive device, returning it to Mavis's outstretched palms.

"Austin," she sighed, taking in the shattered screen.

"Are you kidding? The guy you just told me about? That's fucking really weird timing! What does he want?"

Mavis drew in a deep breath and opened his message, rereading the text: *Mavis, it's Austin Templeton. I'm sorry to contact you this way after so long, but you need to know that Josh wants you back. Don't tell him anything about us.*

Casey leaned over her shoulder. Her warm breath collided with Mavis's damp skin, sending shivers throughout her body. "What does it say?" She angled herself, hovering overhead to read the screen.

Mavis turned, her gaze unfocused. The inkling of embarrassment crept back to the surface of her psyche, and she let the phone fall to her lap.

"Case, can I have a minute to think?" Mavis rubbed the back of her head again and shifted, crawling into her bedroom on all fours.

"Should I call Shaker and tell them you can't come in tonight?"

"Oh, geez... I almost forgot." Mavis climbed onto the mattress and tossed a pillow to her lap, resting her head against the wall.

"Actually, why don't you just let me take your shift?"

"No." Mavis shook her head, swallowing the bile rising in her throat. "That's ridiculous. You should be resting, not covering for me." The air escaped her lungs as another dizzy spell fogged her vision. "I'll just go—"

Casey raised her hand. "Mavs, listen. You've done way more for me these last few days than I can ever repay you for. And holy hell, you're still bleeding!" Casey pointed to the smear of blood on the white wall. "I mean, maybe we should go back to the ER?"

"No... no, I'm fine. Really. It's just a bump." Mavis frowned at the red stain. *There goes the security deposit.*

"Are you sure? I feel like head wounds are one of those things they tell you to see a doctor for." Her hand rested on the doorknob as she toyed with the lock.

"I'm fine, Case. I think I just need a few minutes to rest. Maybe just tell Shaker I'll be late—"

Casey pulled her hand from the door and threaded her fingers through her hair. "Nope. I'm going. You're staying.

Mavis looked down at the text message. Her stomach dipped seeing Austin's name again. "I don't know, Case."

"Decision made." She sighed and pointed to the phone. "Look, Mavs. I know what you're thinking. But your head is bleeding. And you're like the color of those bedsheets.

Please, just let me do this for you, okay?"

Guilt settled in her gut. The thought of Casey covering her shift so she could play games with her past fueled the ache in her heart.

"I feel like I'm being a selfish asshat right now." Her face dropped into her hands.

Casey giggled. "You've never once been a selfish asshat in your life, girl. Lie down and get some rest. I'll see you in a few hours."

"Case…"

"Seriously. I need the normalcy. I need the distraction," she pleaded.

Now that, I can understand. Mavis nodded and watched Casey back out the door. It snapped closed with a soft click.

A wave of adrenaline surged through her bloodstream as she turned her attention back to the phone. Her eyes glossed over Austin's name. *What the hell is going on? Why would Josh want me back?* Panic gripped her, the words *don't tell him anything about us* consuming her attention on the shattered screen. *How much does Josh know?*

Her fingers hovered over the *reply* icon, shaking and sweaty. *I guess there's only one way to find out.* She summoned the courage, settling on the simple words: *Please call me, Austin* and hit *send.*

Nothing happened.

Mavis stretched her legs until her feet dangled off the edge of the bed. She closed her eyes, allowing her heart to pull forth the memories of Joshua she'd long ago buried and locked away.

Have you forgiven me for leaving? Why now?

A swell of longing crashed along her body at the prospect of being near him once again. Having held his memory at arm's length for so long, the floodgate threatened to burst. His sweet smile pulled at her heartstrings, stirring irrevocable feelings of love in her broken soul. The recall sent a wave of yearning hammering through her system. *I still love you.*

She tossed her phone aside and leaned over the bed to grip the nightstand drawer. Her fingers tugged at the broken, dangling handle, and she sifted through the contents within. *Where is it?* A tarnished silver necklace peeked out from beneath a stack of old journals filled with short stories. The little charm had rusted with age, but the solid outline of a single heart still lingered.

A smile broke free, spreading along her lips as she recalled when Josh gave it to her for an eighth-birthday present. "We didn't even know what love was…" she murmured to the necklace, toying with the charm.

She squeezed it between her thumb and index finger, looping the necklace around her palm like she used to wear it around her neck—a token of loyalty—and a symbol of the relationship they'd built together as they grew. Ten years may have passed, but beyond any doubt, Josh still held his place firmly in her heart, as strong as the day she'd left him.

The necklace swayed in the air as she examined the charm. A gouge in the bottom right corner drew her eye, a crack in the otherwise full heart. Mavis frowned, rubbing her thumb along the imperfection. *When did that happen?* Her gaze lifted from the charm and fell to the phone beside her. "Probably when I fucked your brother."

She closed her eyes as embarrassment descended on her body, recalling the moment she'd appeared at his dorm room, a blubbering mess.

He'd been understanding and tender in her moment of vulnerability. But nothing short of regret lingered in her soul after the night they shared as teenagers. Then he'd strolled into The Broken Shaker four years later with his charming grin, heart of forgiveness, and shared love for gin and tonic. A shiver ran down her spine as a warmth stirred in her groin.

What the hell is wrong with me?

Rolling her eyes, her mind drifted back to the last time she'd seen Austin, before their evening ended in a hotel bed.

*

"*Mavs?*"

The voice behind her raised the hairs on the back of her neck, eerily recognizable and absolutely unforgettable. Her body stilled with her hand wedged firmly inside a glass behind the bar at The Broken Shaker. A ghost from the past whispered in her ear after a four-year hiatus.

Her chest tightened, and the tips of her fingers tingled. What are you doing here? *Mavis squared her shoulders and lifted her gaze from the sink. With all the courage in her heart, she plastered a smile of false confidence on her lips and turned her body to face Austin Templeton.*

"*It is you.*" *A silly grin consumed his face as he released a long-held breath. His eyes met hers, and for a moment, the noise of the crowded bar faded. Time stood still as she soaked in the details of his presence. The boy from her youth standing before her in the present.*

Where guilt should have peaked, happiness washed over her heart instead. For the first time since arriving in Chicago, a pull to Rosewood encouraged a smile.

"*Austin.*" *Her feet moved with little direction. They carried her body from behind the bar until they stopped before him. His arms—always a source of comfort—embraced her immediately, no different than memory. The scent of sandalwood clung to his shirt, impaling her nose as she pressed her face firmly into his chest. His grip tightened, and a sense of security unfelt in years consumed her.*

"*What're you doing here?*" *His hands rested on her upper arms as his eyes searched hers for answers.*

"*I work here.*" Duh. *She gestured to the bar.*

"*You work with her?*" *His head tilted, eyes widening as he stared over her shoulder.*

Mavis turned, locking eyes with her coworker, Brandy. Her brow furrowed; one hand placed precariously on her hip as her fingers tapped against her apron with annoyance.

"*Oh, shit. Hang on a second. Let me catch up. I'll be right back.*" *She patted a barstool, and Austin sat down, wearing a grin that matched her own.*

His gaze followed her every move behind the bar as she mixed and poured. The smell of the alcohol churned her stomach as beads of sweat formed on her brow. Mavis wiped her forehead with the back of her hand and motioned to Brandy.

"Who's the hottie?" she asked, approaching the counter.

"A ghost from my past come to haunt me." Mavis widened her eyes and exhaled at the ironic accuracy of her words.

"Well, if you don't want him, I'll take him." She winked.

Mavis shoved her hair away from her damp face, cringing from the momentary pain in her jaw as she clamped her teeth together.

With a tray in hand, Brandy marched away to table eight. Swallowing the surge of jealousy, Mavis mixed two gin and tonics before returning to Austin. Each step in his direction doubled the beats of her heart, agitating the nerves in the pit of her stomach.

His eyes sought hers as he reached for the drink she set down. "These are my favorite." He gripped the glass and winked.

"Mine too. But, umm… well… cheers to an awkward reunion." She clinked his glass and brought the drink to her lips. The liquid courage slid down her throat.

Austin smiled but dropped his gaze to his lap. "It doesn't have to be awkward, Princess."

She nodded, pressing her lips together in a thin line. "What're you doing here?"

His eyes returned to hers. "Meeting a new client. I flew into town for the weekend, and she suggested meeting here for dinner. I saw you about an hour ago," he added as he gestured to a table across the room near the window. "Took every ounce of my willpower to focus on Mrs. Randolph's divorce and not come running over here the second I saw you."

"I'm surprised you came over at all." She set her drink down and glanced at the clock. Twenty more minutes before I can ditch this apron.

"You're kidding, right? Nothing could have stopped me." He frowned. "Do you even realize how much we all still think about you, how much we miss you?"

Her breath caught in her throat. Did he say 'we'?

"Ancient history though, you know?" The blood rushed to her head as her cheeks flushed with embarrassment.

Austin raised his shoulders and tilted his head. "I don't know about ancient…"

"Mavs! Come on! Another round for table six!" Brandy's voice screeched over the music.

"Hold that thought. I'll be right back." Mavis shuffled away, her head in a fog.

Every nerve in her body awakened, tingling beneath her skin. Her hands shook, pouring pineapple juice where it should have been orange juice and whiskey where it should have been rum.

"Mavs, what are you doing?" Brandy scrunched her nose, frowning at the wrong mix of liquor pouring into the glass on the counter.

"Ugh! I don't even know!" Mavis dumped the drink down the sink and released a dramatic sigh. "I'm sorry. I'm completely distracted."

"Hey, are you okay?" A gentle squeeze on her shoulder had her body turning to greet the restaurant's manager, Jim.

"Umm, yeah… I'm sorry, just a bit on edge." Mavis lifted her hands to her temples, rubbing the skin until the ache in her brain lessened.

"Why don't you take off early. Casey's already here for the next shift. We got you covered." The right side of his mouth tugged upward in a grin. "You're okay, right?"

She laughed at the simple question, dropping her hands to her hips. Okay? Yeah right!

"No idea," she answered truthfully.

"Who's the guy?" He nodded in Austin's direction.

"Ghost from her past. Now come on, we have thirsty men at table eight who need another round of tequila!" Brandy grinned and rubbed her index finger and thumb together. "And mama needs the tips they're gonna dish out."

Mavis snorted, unwinding the tie of her apron at the back. "Thanks, guys. I owe you one."

"He's cool, right? Not a weirdo?" His right eyebrow lifted.

"Probably the sweetest guy you'll ever meet. Which is why I'm in trouble." She squeezed Jim's forearm before turning and walking away.

The ice clanked in Austin's empty glass as he swirled the cup in his hands. He shifted in his seat as she approached, tugging at the tight *knot on his tie.*

"All right, I'm off the clock now. Want to grab a table?" Mavis pointed behind the bar. Grasping his hand, she tugged him away from the audience of curious coworkers and headed toward an empty two-person table at the back of the restaurant. The noise level dropped, and Casey delivered two gin and tonics with a wink.

"Thanks, Casey."

Austin grinned, nodding his head in her direction as she stepped away.

"I don't really know what to say, Austin."

Even in the dim lighting, his baby-blue eyes sparkled, the white lashes in the corner of his right eye paramount as he stared at her. You haven't changed, have you?

"You don't have to say anything. It's honestly just a relief to see you, to talk to you again. To know that you're doing okay after..." He leaned back in his chair and drained the gin like a pro.

Whoa.

"That was a long time ago. And I'm sorry for..."

His hand squeezed her bare knee beneath the table, and her stomach dropped to the sticky floor.

"I'm not."

Mavis blew out a breath, reveling in the warmth flushing her skin. She grinned, dropping her hand on top of his.

"You're different. You're still you... but... I don't know." Austin shook his head.

"I've worked hard to change. I don't know the girl you remember anymore."

He smiled. "No, I guess not. But I'd like to know who you are now, Princess."

Mavis drained her glass and smiled.

*

Her ringtone disrupted the silent bedroom, and Mavis lunged from her past to her phone. Austin's name appeared on her shattered screen, along with his face. *Fuck. FaceTime?* With a roll of her eyes, she tucked her blood-stained hair behind her ears. The pounding in her chest intensified, and every nerve in her body prickled with anxiety as she pressed accept.

Austin appeared on the screen, staring back at her, a handsome grin on his beautiful face.

"Hey, Mavs." His cheeks reddened.

"Austin... uh, how are you?" She eyed his sweet, shy smile and cringed at the dip in her stomach, recalling the walk of shame from his hotel room door.

"I'm okay. Umm... I'm sorry, I probably scared you with that text, huh?"

"I'll admit to some confusion." She giggled. "Should I be expecting a visitor or something here?" Her necklace dangled in her lap, tickling her thigh as it dragged across her skin.

"I sent you that text before I talked to Josh tonight." He raised his right arm and scratched behind his neck. "He's been super weird these last few days talking about trying to find you... and honestly, the thought just scared me. He can never know what you and I did together, right?" Austin raised a brow.

"Why would you think I'd tell him?" Her stomach churned. "Those aren't exactly the first words I'd want to share after walking out on him. *Hey, Josh, it's been ten years. By the way, I fucked your brother a few times.* Not the first thing I'd start with, Austin." Shame flooded her body.

"The point is, Mavs, it may not be the *first* thing you say to him, but it can never be *anything* you share with him." He flipped a switch beside him, the new lighting highlighting the contours of his face.

"I mean, what's another lie? What's another secret at this point?" She shifted in her seat and wrapped her arms around herself, propping the phone between her knees.

Austin squinted. "Where are you? What's on the wall?"

Mavis turned, her heart sputtering at the blood smear. Angling the phone away, she shifted. "My bed. And, umm... just marker."

He snorted. "Do you color in bed often?"

A belly laugh burst free from her gut, and she doubled over at the stupid question. The ripple of laughter had her head throbbing and the wound on her head pulsating. "Only on the weekends," she answered, pressing her fingers to the growing bump.

"My kind of weekend. Maybe I should move to Chicago," he joked.

She smiled and looked down, eyeing the stray thread on the hem of her uniform. "I miss you." *Did I really just say that?*

"I miss you too." His fingers ran through his hair. "But, umm... so does my brother." His gaze fell from the screen.

The breath hitched in her throat. "Tell me more?"

Austin nodded and drew in a deep breath. "He got divorced a couple of weeks ago. I don't know. It kind of rattled him." He scratched his right ear and yawned. "He keeps saying he's ready to move on, which is great because he needs to. But the problem is, he keeps moving backward instead. He found the letter you wrote to him."

Mavis shuddered. *The worst letter I've ever written in my life.* The thought of Josh still staring at it ripped new holes in her already battered heart.

"What do I do, Austin?"

He shrugged. "I don't know, Mavs. Do you want to see him?"

The ring in her ears grew, each pump of blood through her veins sending bouts of anxiety rippling through her body. She blinked, working to overcome the fog in her vision.

"I mean, yeah. Without a doubt."

Austin bit his lower lip and nodded, his gaze returning to his lap. "Then I guess, let him call you."

"Sure." Mavis snorted. "And then what, huh? Tell him why I left? I've spent the last ten years of my life living with those consequences." She pushed her hair back, a sudden burn behind her eyes triggering an imminent burst of tears.

"The truth hasn't changed just because time has passed."

His silence sent chills zipping down her spine. *Wait...*

"Oh, my God. You told him, didn't you?"

Austin shook his head and frowned. "You think I'd do that?"

Guilt wracked her. *Of course, you didn't say anything. Why'd I ask that?*

Mavis dropped her head, shame resetting in her heart. "I'm sorry, Austin. I know you didn't. I don't know why I said that."

"It's fine, Mavs. You and I have our own secrets to hide. I'm not in the business to air the dirty laundry from the bottom of your basket."

"The start of it all, wasn't it?" Her eyes widened.

"Team effort." He grinned, but his smile didn't meet his eyes. "I gave him your phone number. Don't be mad, okay?"

Mavis rolled her eyes. "I could never be mad at you, Austin."

He pursed his lips. "Wish I could say the same, but waking up alone kind of sucked."

She cringed, a deep pinch in her stomach inciting a wave of nausea. "Austin..." She shook her head resting her hand over her mouth.

He grinned. "Sorry," he said, shrugging. "Couldn't help it."

"I was really embarrassed, all right?" The nausea lessened, but the pain in her heart swelled.

Resting his hand over his heart, he tilted his head. "Just another notch on my bedpost, Ms. Benson."

What number was I?

"Well, can Ms. Benson come stay with you for a few days?" Rosewood—Templeton Manor—and the friends and family she'd left behind so long ago filled her mind with a renewed hope in her heart. If Josh wanted to see her and revisit their past, she'd be on her own terms to do it.

"I hear Chicago is known for their red-eye flights."

She nodded with a grin. "See you soon, Mr. Templeton."

He smiled.

"Oh. And Austin?"

"Yeah?"

"No more gin and tonics."

He snorted, his cheeks reddening as the seconds ticked by. "No deal, Princess," he answered with a wink, then ended the call.

JULIE NAVICKAS

CHAPTER TEN

Josh

Josh opened his eyes, unjumbling the tangle of satin bedsheets from his legs. He kicked his feet, tossing the covers from his body as he rolled to the side. Mavis's letter stared back from the bedside table. But instead of the sinking dread that had emitted from the envelope for the last ten years, today it offered hope. *Today's the day, Duchess…*

Beside her letter rested her teenage photo, uncovered in the treasures from the cardboard box time capsule. With lingering sleep in his eyes, Josh admired her smile, bathing in the youthful happiness radiating from her lips. The memory of her voice echoed in his ears, calling his name, giggling with sweet love and the sense of ease found in a soulmate.

"Ten years, Mavs…"

Tearing his eyes from her green-eyed gaze, Josh dragged his hands along his cheeks, sighed, and stretched his arms. The ghost of her laughter settled in his heart, and his lips tugged upward in a smile. *What the hell am I even going to say to you when I see you again?*

His mind raced, parading through the last decade of his

life without her. Endless days and long hours filtering through his brain… His head in a book studying at school, twenty-four-hour shifts at the hospital, an ill-fated marriage dripping with deceit… Josh exhaled, revisiting his past, inhaling again only when his thoughts turned to consider the last ten years of Mavis's life instead. Skyscrapers erupted in his mind, snowfall covering the famed Midwestern city. And there she stood… in a crowded restaurant, behind a bar, gripping a glass. She smiled at him in the vision, but the green glow of her eyes had diminished.

Why Chicago, Mavis? The photos Tess returned with after a girl's trip to the city several years ago flashed before his eyes. Josh pushed his ex-wife from the still images, focusing on the landmarks, on the people, on the atmosphere. "Chicago…" he muttered.

With a snap of his knuckles, he pulled his body from the bed. His feet met the morning sunshine on the carpet, and Josh rubbed his big toe over the small pink nail polish stain beside the nightstand. His eye caught Mavis's again in the photo, and his heartbeat accelerated at the prospect of contacting her. The possibility of reconnecting with the girl who captured his heart so long ago triggered a flood of adrenaline.

Josh shuffled to his feet and dragged a pair of gym shorts over his legs. "So, you were protecting me, huh…" A twinge of unease squeezed his stomach as he pulled his eyes away from her photo and exited the bedroom. "What the hell from?" he whispered.

His feet carried him down the stairs and into the kitchen. He powered on the coffeepot, allowing the rich scent of his standard medium roast to fill the empty space. The brown liquid trickled, plop-by-plop and drip-by-drip, into his mug, each drop a physical representation of the moments lost to time, of the moments lost with Mavis.

The machine screeched, and Josh dumped a spoonful of sugar into the brew before returning to his bedroom. Setting the steaming coffee down on the nightstand, Josh climbed back into bed and rested his head on the single pillow.

The bedsheets fell lightly on his bare legs, stirring an unexpected tingle on his skin. His pulse quickened, a rush of warmth spreading through his body. *How long has it been?* "Too long," he mumbled, rolling his eyes. *Geez... it's a fucking sheet!* But as his body caved, his right hand dipped beneath the covers with a sense of urgency.

Coconuts filled his nose, the scent of her hair familiar and unchanged. Josh grinned, the memory of her lips covering his as her breathing labored in his mind, whispering his name.

Surrender sizzled along his spine as his hand found an exciting rhythm, the escalating motion sending sharp pangs of pleasure to each nerve in his body. Pressure built in his groin, the sensation reaching the tip of each finger and toe in a wave of coveted desire. With a gasp of anticipation, he climaxed with her name on his lips. His muscles relaxed, and Josh relished in the slow glow of release.

One deep breath later, he opened his eyes to peek at the photo beside him. The coffee in front of the photograph still steamed. And her smile hadn't faded.

Josh emerged from a deliberately cold shower, dressed in comfortable sweatpants, and headed downstairs. Embarrassment followed him as he descended to the living room.

As he collapsed in his chair, the worn material scratched against his bare back as he snuggled in. *The Funny Part* slid from its home on the armrest and dropped to the floor as Josh tucked his feet beneath him and ran a hand through his wet hair. A flush appeared on his cheeks as he stared at his phone and pulled up the number Austin had given him. *Am I really going to call you after what I just did upstairs in front of your photo?* His fingers grazed the prickly stubble on his chin as his stomach churned with a twinge of humiliation. Josh shook his head, willing the last thirty minutes of his life into the void. *Embarrassing.*

His gaze raked over the living room as his breathing calmed, and the mortification melted away. The memory of Tess hiring professional painters and interior decorators wafted to the forefront of his brain. A shiver rolled through his body, cringing at the price tag and final product. *I never liked any of it.* The paint color clashed with the impressionism artwork they'd hung on every square inch of the house. The now bare walls glared back at him, sans Monet—a true blank canvas.

A true fresh start.

Disgust bit into the moment of contentment as Tess's name appeared on his phone screen. With a frown, Josh swallowed and declined the call, silencing the will of his ex-wife. *No thank you, crazy woman. There is not one thing left in the world we have to talk about.*

He snorted and rolled his eyes, navigating again to Mavis's number. The letters of her name peaked and swirled, morphing in his mind into the looping print she'd penned in her letter. Josh wiggled his toes beneath the weight of his body, working to shake free the nerves in the pit of his stomach that had taken up residence ever since Austin had opened his big mouth.

A mounting unease crashed through him, the truth of his brother's level of involvement driving a knife through his heart. *You've known all this time... every secret... every detail. And you had her number.* "Did you warn her I'd call too?" He whispered the suspicion as he eyed the call icon. With one last glance around the empty living room, Josh tapped the green button and brought the device to his ear. *Only one way to find out.*

One ring. His heart hammered in his chest, each beat a rap on a bass drum. Two rings. The butterflies in his stomach battled with his morning coffee, flapping their manic wings in a sea of caffeine. Three rings. Josh's vision fogged, his blood pulsating through his veins. A fourth ring sounded in his ear, and as if a ghost had answered the phone, Mavis's distantly familiar voice gripped his heartstrings.

He drew in a sharp intake of breath, burning his lungs with the sudden squeeze around his throat. The broken remnants of his soul roused from the living dead, stirring in the depths of his heart, awakening from the ten-year nightmare.

"Mavs... it's me. It's Josh."

The words hung in the ether as he imagined her response, hoping her heart raced in pace and rhythm alongside his own, beat for beat. The image of a detective discovering the evidence of a phantom erupted in his brain. *Love's fugitive found.*

A feminine squeak met his ear as a silly grin consumed his face. "Is it really you, Joshua?"

Her voice soothed his soul, the sound of his name settling into his long-term memory. *You were the only one who could ever call me that.*

"Yeah, it is." His eyes burned, and a tear escaped the confines of his lids as he pressed his free hand to his forehead. "I... umm... I don't even know where to start. I never thought I'd talk to you again."

"Why do you want to?"

Her breath hitched as her question sank into his soul. *Why do I want to talk to you again? Did you really just ask me that?* With a tap of his phone, her voice transitioned to speaker as he slouched deeper into the chair.

"Why do I want to?" he repeated. "How can you even ask me that?" An invisible force squeezed his heart at the pain in his words.

"I assumed you still hated me." A sob penetrated his eardrum.

You think I hate you? "Mavis Benson, are you kidding me? There's not one piece of me that hates you." The excitement that started the conversation soured into heartbreak. His soul called to hers, each thump of his heartbeat radiating from his body, like a love letter sent in morse code.

"I swear to you, Joshua, I didn't leave to hurt you…"

"I know," he answered, the words spilling from his lips in a rush as another rogue tear escaped. Josh wiped it away, trying and failing to control the melting pot of emotions ripping through his body. *Tell her everything. Tell her why I really called.* "Duchess… it's been ten years. I know you left because you thought you were protecting me." A grin blossomed on his lips, disbelief still consuming his heart. "But right now, I don't need the reason, or the truth. I just… want my best friend back."

She hiccuped, and Josh swallowed, pain descending on his heart as he pictured her with tears streaming down her cheeks, the image far too easy to imagine.

"How can you say that?" She sniffled into the phone.

The sun peeked in through the living room window, and Josh squinted at the glare infiltrating the glass. He shook his head, his brain too deep in his imagination. His gaze raked over the barren living room, and he pulled his feet from beneath him, forcing his body to stand. Josh's tingling feet carried him to the kitchen, and his eyes caught sight of the single orange poppy perched on the windowsill.

"Easy—" A rush of background noise on her end interrupted. "Umm… where are you?"

"I'm actually… well, I just landed in Los Angeles," she answered. "Baggage claim."

The air escaped his lungs. *You're here! You're in California!* "How?"

"Austin called and kind of filled me in." She snorted. "He, ah… well… next thing I knew I was booking a red-eye out of Chicago."

Josh grinned, a wild jolt of euphoria descending on his body. He shifted his weight and leaned forward on the kitchen counter. *That's my girl.* Resting his forehead in his hands, he squeezed his eyes shut.

"You're my same girl, impulsive as they come."

She sighed. "I'm not the same, Joshua. But I do want to see you… if you're going to give me a chance to explain, then I need to try."

Her words set his heart on fire, thawing the deep freeze he'd endured over the last decade. The tips of his fingers tingled, and he tapped them against the countertop, each rap a second ticking away until the moment she'd ring the doorbell. After ten years apart…

You'll be mine again by tonight.

CHAPTER ELEVEN

Mavis

The cab traveled the familiar streets of L.A. Having not stepped foot on California soil in over a decade, Mavis searched the skyline, ready to take in the new sights and landmarks, but the city and interstate 105 hadn't changed. The driver of the cab traversed the bumper-to-bumper traffic with ease and a well-practiced hand, navigating the four-lane highway that would take them into the elite neighboring town of Rosewood.

Mavis bumped along in the back seat with the car's worn-out shocks, her mind hovering between the realms of disbelief and denial. *Joshua actually wants to see me again. What the hell am I even going to say to him when he opens the door?* She dragged her fingers through her curls, kneading the muscles at the base of her neck. Tension mounted in her shoulders, the aftereffects of the four-hour flight settling into her overtired body. Tugging her face upward, she ogled the small TV, squinting at the infomercial. QVC's finest salesman rubbed his belly at the delicious chicken he'd fried in the incredible set of non-stick pans.

Mavis shook her head, hurling the image of the far too

enthusiastic man with a pan from the cab. Her mind reeled. The last twenty-four hours hadn't just reminded her of the past. The hours had literally carried her to confrontation's front door. She sighed, clutching the silver chain that now hung from her neck again for the hundredth time since Austin's text, stroking the heart charm with newfound appreciation and memory. Today, the trinket would—for better or worse—blend memories of the past with the present.

The ancient GPS on the dashboard broke the silence, its frayed cord drumming against the plastic meter with each bump of the road. According to the little screen, seven minutes separated her from Josh's embrace. The seconds passed, and the pit in her stomach deepened with each turn of the wheel. Vomit threatened her throat, and she swallowed hard, wiping the sweat from her forehead. The wet sheen coated her hands, and she rubbed her thumb and index finger together in disgust. Frowning, Mavis pulled at the zipper on her purse and rummaged inside for her compact.

The bloodshot eyes of a sleepless night reflected in the small mirror. *Impulsive as they come…* She snorted and rubbed below her eyes, swiping at yesterday's melted makeup. *Well, you're not wrong, Josh.*

The cab jolted, jarring her body against the seatbelt. Mavis caught the eye of the driver in the rearview mirror and grinned.

"Sorry," he murmured. "Damn city doesn't care about potholes."

She widened her eyes. "You should drive in Chicago."

With a snort, he tapped the GPS. "You're a long way from home, aren't you?"

Four minutes.

Snapping her compact closed, Mavis nodded and grinned at the irony. Another pothole had her crossing her legs at the ankles and grabbing the seat for safety.

The driver exited the highway, cruising past a little

coffeehouse with a green roof emblazoned with the name Java Jane's across the front of the building. *That's new.* But as the cab turned left onto Montgomery Street, déjà vu gripped her gut as familiarity settled in her heart. *Josh lives near Templeton Manor.*

A shiver snaked down her spine. Her homecoming meant more than just seeing Josh. "Austin…" she murmured, clutching her heart. "God, I'm in so much trouble."

Her bag pinged, pulling her attention away from impending doom. Stuffing her hand in the purse, she searched until her fingers grasped the elusive device. Casey's name flashed across the screen. *Did you land safely? Have you seen Austin? What about Josh? You have to tell me what's happening!*

Mavis bit her bottom lip and pounded out a quick reply, pushing Chicago and Casey's questions a thousand miles away.

Two minutes.

She chewed her fingernails, bouncing her right knee up and down and willing the nerves in her belly away. *What the hell am I even going to say?* Panic consumed her chest, riddled with fear. *The truth hasn't changed.*

The driver left the familiarity of Montgomery Street, turning left into a new neighborhood. Her inner monologue of panic halted, the sizes of the houses distracting her from the impossible to answer questions in her heart.

"Shit. I think my whole apartment could fit into any one of these house's foyers."

The driver smirked. "Same." He turned left onto Rainy Cloud Road and the GPS announced their imminent arrival. The wheels met the driveway of a modern, whitewashed two-story brick home that read *Templeton* on the intricate black metal mailbox. The car stopped, and Mavis's heart stopped with it.

Her hands shook. Her body quivered. For a brief moment, a vision of desperate escape raced through her mind. She bolted, running down the street in her imagination. *I don't have to do this!* Shaking her head and ridding herself of the stupid image, Mavis handed the cab driver the overpriced fare and yanked at the door handle. Tossing her feet to the pavement, she tested her legs' ability to hold her weight before standing.

The driver exited and popped the trunk, pulling out her suitcase. He set her luggage down and tugged at the adjustable handle, angling it toward her. "Miss."

"Thank you." Her hushed appreciation caught in the gentle breeze.

The wind ruffled her hair, sending a mop of curls cascading on her face. She pulled a hand through the mess, smoothing the wild mane. Her limbs had turned to noodles, but her feet shuffled away from the car, dragging the suitcase with battered wheels behind her.

The cab left the driveway as her toes met the bottom of the small porch. Three stairs stood between her and the front door. *Three stairs and ten years, Joshua.*

Mavis placed her sandaled foot on the first step. A paralyzing fear gripped her, numbing her body to the windstorm of emotions swirling in her gut, a needle of Novocaine to her mind.

Her toes touched the second step, and the flutter of a single butterfly trapped in her stomach morphed into Godzilla's larger-than-life companion, Mothra, slapping her elongated wings against the prison walls.

One… more… step. Her gaze swept over the intricate mahogany front door. The edges of her vision blurred with tears as a force beyond her control stretched her hand outward for the doorbell. Her fingers, eerily unrecognizable at the moment, trembled as they collided with the tiny button. *Ding-dong.* The tone sounded inside, level and calm, before footsteps pounded on the opposite side of the door. Mavis inhaled, the rush of air settling in her throat, unable to enter her lungs.

The weary soul at the bottom of her heart roused, tilting its head with interest as its other half whispered from the other side. Her heartbeat faltered as the knob twisted and the door creaked open.

His brown eyes smiled. Josh's body collided with hers as the instant burn behind her lids expelled the built-up tears of a lifetime. They trickled down her cheeks, crashing into Josh's chest as his arms engulfed her. Heat radiated from his body, and Mavis pressed her face into his soft skin, inhaling the faint fragrance of peppermint. The scent transported her back to her teenage youth, nostalgia gripping her weightless body. A sigh escaped her lips, breathing out the stale horror of the last ten years.

The porch beneath her feet floated away. Time and space became irrelevant, the reunion only fantasized of unfolding before her in the pale mist of a dream. Josh tightened his embrace and nestled his face in her hair, his breath warm against her scalp. He clung to her. *I've never been held tighter in my entire life. Don't ever let go again, Joshua.*

He whispered her name, each breath from his lips a stitch in her broken heart. The tips of her fingers tingled as she raised her hand from his chest to rest against his scratchy, unshaven cheek. Her thumb trailed along his bottom lip as her eyes searched for the scar above his mouth. *It's still there.*

"Damn it, Mavis," he whispered before his mouth rained down on hers. His lips crushed her, a decade of longing deepening his kiss. Tasting different from memory, his lips still greeted hers with utter familiarity.

Captivated in the moment and bathed in reunion, Mavis lost herself in the rake of his greedy hands against her waist. His grip tightened, each squeeze of his fingers a return to the safety and comfort that his presence had always offered. A sense of feeling wanted—and loved—overpowered her, nearly unfelt for a decade.

Her cheeks flushed, and a wave of dizziness descended as the nip of his teeth snagged her bottom lip. Desire flared in her heart as Josh tugged her backward into the house. Her feet left the porch, stepping from the dream and back into reality.

"Joshua… I'm so sorry." The words vomited from her lips as she crossed the threshold, spilling from the depths of her broken heart.

He frowned, searching her soul as he rammed his hands in his pockets. Pulling a crinkled envelope from his right side, he forced it into her grasp.

"Take it back, Mavis." His eyes swam with intensity, the dark brown of his irises deepening in a pool of emotion.

She looked down, examining his name scrawled across the cover. The paper—faded with time—burned her fingers with the fire of regret. She crumpled the envelope into a ball and swiped at the river of tears trailing down her face, sucking in a deep breath with a sniffle.

Josh pushed the door closed, the latch clicking with a resounding snap. Silence filled the space between them, interrupted only by ragged breaths, expelling into the air.

Mavis dropped the paper ball to the floor and kicked it aside. It rolled, colliding into the banister with a soft thud.

"I'm sor—"

He kissed her again, slicing into the apology. Josh's hands gripped the base of her neck, pulling her body closer to his while begging for more, spreading warmth across her skin. His lips… his passion. Desire deepened with each tender touch as a grin tugged at her mouth, the wild ride of emotions peaking with elation.

"Duchess…" He sighed. "You're *home*. You're finally fucking *home*." Josh angled his head, pressing his forehead to her own.

Home.

"Yeah," she breathed out. "I'm home." *Am I though?*

Mavis searched his eyes, seeking the boy from her childhood. She'd know his soul anywhere, able to recognize it in any parallel universe or lifetime. The boy from her past, the boy from the meadow didn't smile back, but the man he'd become stood before her instead. His youthful essence tugged at her heartstrings, repairing the soul she'd ripped to pieces a decade ago.

His grip loosened as he pulled her hands to cover his heart, squeezing her palms as he traced the length of each finger; his lips tickled, kissing the top of each hand lightly.

"Come on, come in," he urged, pulling her further inside his home. He reopened the front door and dragged her suitcase inside the foyer. After propping the bag against the wall, Josh tugged her hand and led her to the dining room table. She took a seat in the wooden chair as Josh sank into the space opposite her.

Her gaze settled on the whirl of black and blue behind him, the sole picture hanging in the entire space. The colors popped, a dramatic statement against the white wall. The swirl of the color and brush strokes... *well, that's...unsettling?*

"Can I get you anything? Water? Tea? Coffee?"

She tore her gaze from the painting and shook her head, ridding the unease from her system. "Umm, yeah, coffee would be good. Thanks."

Josh stood and pointed to the artwork. "I never liked it either," he said before stepping away into the kitchen.

Her gaze followed him, watching as he silently opened a cabinet and selected two plain white ceramic mugs. The muscles in his arms flexed as he closed the door.

Still boyish and handsome, Josh moved with a bit more grace than memory afforded, his motions fluid and purposeful.

"Sugar or cream, Mavs?" He snapped the cartridge down and pressed start on the machine. The aroma of the roast wafted from the kitchen.

"Both, please." She snorted. "But umm... Josh, aren't you going to scream at me or something?"

Josh turned his attention back to the coffee pot and brewed a second cup. He furrowed his brow, seemingly considering her question before adding cream and sugar to her mug. The V-shape creasing his forehead stirred the past as Mavis recalled his intentionality behind each selection of words, a characteristic both irritating and admirable. *I guess*

I forgot that. He exhaled, pausing only to add sugar to his cup before returning to the dining room table.

He shrugged before sitting. "I gave you back the letter. That's really all I've ever wanted to do. I should never have taken it in the first place." He winked. "So, no, no screaming."

Mavis tore her gaze from him and stared at the paper ball in the foyer. "That's it?"

"Look, Mavs. It's not that I don't want to know the truth. I've had ten years to think about it. But whatever the reason…" He sipped his coffee. "I know you. And you'll tell me when you're ready. You're here, and that's what matters to me most right now."

Josh reached across the table and rested his palm atop her hand. Heat radiated from his skin, warmed from the steaming mug.

Mavis examined his fingers as they ran along her own. His sun-kissed skin accentuated his recent divorce as her eyes raked over the lighter skin tone of his left ring finger. Jealousy erupted in her heart, imagining the woman who'd placed the ring there.

"But I owe you an explanation, Joshua."

With a sigh, Josh pushed the mug in her direction. "Maybe, but that's not what I care about right now."

His phone sounded in his pocket, and Josh quickly pulled it out and rejected the call.

"If you need to get that don't let me stop you. You're like a fancy doctor now, right?" She grinned and swirled the coffee in her mug. *Doctor Templeton… you did it, my sweet Joshua!*

"I'm not on call." He snorted. "And that was my ex-wife, not the hospital. Trust me. I have no desire to speak to her ever again," he added with a defiant tap of his phone on the surface of the table.

"I'd like to meet her." She brought the mug to her lips. The steam tickled her face, soothing her tired eyes.

"Why?" His eyes widened and his lips tugged upward in

a grin.

"Call me curious. What woman let *you* walk away?" She placed the mug back down on the table, wincing at the burn on her tongue.

Josh released a long breath. "You've already met her."

Mavis scrunched her nose. "I have?"

He nodded. "Tess wasn't always, you know, terrible?"

You didn't just say… Mavis bit her tongue, knocking her knee against the table's leg.

"Tess?" She squinted. "You don't mean…?"

"Guilty." He smirked.

"Oh no. Josh, just no! You *married* Tess Browning?" She jerked her hand away from his in jest. *She was like my mortal enemy!* Jealousy rebounded in her gut. *What the hell did you see in her?*

"Like I said, she wasn't always *terrible.*"

"I doubt that." A disbelieving smirk grew on her face. "She was awful in high school. I can't imagine the adult version being much better."

His lips smashed into a thin line. "She helped me through some really tough years." He shrugged and leaned back in his chair. "I'm embarrassed to admit this, to you especially, but I umm, went a little crazy after you disappeared. Did absolutely terrible my first year at Georgetown. I honestly considered dropping out, but she helped me keep going."

Mavis swallowed. Guilt settled in the pit of her stomach. *Tess picked up the pieces of your heart, the heart that I shattered.*

"Can I tell you something?" he asked, tugging her hands back into his grasp.

"Umm… yeah," she answered, sorting through the layers of guilt in her heart.

"On the night we signed our divorce papers, she said something to me. It's actually kind of the reason you're here today."

"What did she tell you?"

Josh rubbed against her bare ring finger, stroking the

117

skin. "She told me that I had always been in love, just not with her. She may have lied and cheated on me for a year, but that statement—complete, sincere truth. I just never saw it."

Mavis lowered her gaze to her lap. *What the hell do I say to that?* "Josh, I… umm…"

"I'm not trying to make you uncomfortable." He grinned. "I just want, no, I need you to know that everything we shared, it never went away for me, Duchess."

His phone rang again, biting into the sweet words escaping his lips. With a frown, he declined the call once more and muttered a small apology.

"Joshua, tell me what I'm doing here." Her anxiety peaked. *Lay your cards on the table, Mavis.* "Austin called, and the next thing I knew, I was on a red-eye to L.A. chasing my teenage life. Why am I here?"

Without hesitation, the words tumbled from his lips. "I want you back. I still love you. I never stopped."

Her hands tugged from his grasp and clasped her mug, sucking the warmth it offered into her palms. Her heart faltered in pace and rhythm, skipping a beat completely.

Josh leaned forward and cupped her hands. Her breath caught in her throat as he moved closer.

"You think you do, but you don't love me, Joshua. You love the ghost of me, the ghost of us." Her gaze challenged him. *And when you learn the truth? What then?*

He tightened his grip and searched her eyes. "No, that's not true," he whispered. "Because I know your soul, Mavis Benson. Mine bound itself to yours when we were just kids. You can say you've changed, but to your core, I know who you are. The very fact that you impulsively flew across the country in the middle of the night tells me that we have a second chance. You still feel the same way I do. It's *not* a ghost." He moved his hands upward, securing her forearms in his grasp.

"I flew here, Joshua, because I wronged you in a way I can't ever right. And after so much time, I jumped at the chance to see you, to talk to you, to try to somehow explain myself to you. It's just—I'm not the girl you used to love. That girl was gone the second I stepped off your parents' porch ten years ago." She looked down, losing the challenge she initiated. *Here come the tears…*

Josh tipped her chin up, and with his thumb, he brushed away the first tear escaping her eye, starting down her cheek.

"And I'm not the boy you remember or used to love. Like you, I've grown. Lived. Loved. And lost everything in between. But it doesn't matter. We don't need to be the same people we were. But we can give the people we've become a second chance."

Always so goddamn profound and poetic.

She scrunched her nose and pursed her lips. "You're honestly not going to yell at me and tell me how stupid I was for leaving? After all this time, that's not something you want to do?"

"I'm never going to yell or call you stupid. I won't do it, Mavis. And I mean that. The only thing I ask is that when you're ready to share, you'll tell me. I promise, no matter the reason, it won't change the way I felt about you, or the way I feel right now." He rubbed her arms and squeezed. "Just give us a chance. Let us find each other again."

The fire in her heart ignited, burning with desire and intensity for the first time in a decade. The words falling from his beautiful lips seeped into her soul after a lifetime of longing. He dangled the fairytale in her face, the dream of a lifetime within her grasp.

It can't be that easy though, can it? There's still so much you don't know.

Despite the disquiet in her brain, her mouth opened and betrayed all sense of reason. "Okay."

Josh smiled, and her soul knitted back to his, securely fastened with needle and thread. *Don't forget to tie the end.*

CHAPTER TWELVE

Josh

The water in the master bathroom whirled overhead through the pipes as Josh stood in the kitchen. He washed and dried their coffee mugs, a weight slowly lifting from his body for the first time in ten years as Mavis stood a floor above him, safe and finally accounted for. The gnawing guilt over her disappearance evaporated as his heart rebooted, rebounding to his teenage years before dread and worry blanketed his soul with the unknown.

After wiping his hands on a dish towel, Josh pulled out his phone and opened a text to Austin. If it hadn't been for his call to Mavis last night, she wouldn't be in his arms today. He tapped out a thank you and clicked *send* as Tess's name lit up his phone screen. *Again with you?* He sighed and accepted the call with a roll of his eyes.

"You could barely wait two weeks!" She screeched like an angry owl in the night.

How the fuck do you even know?

"Are you watching my house?" Josh squinted and scrunched his nose, peeking out the kitchen window. His gaze skimmed the roof of Dalton Sheppard's house, his fancy solar panels glaring in the sunshine. "Actually, why do you even care? You divorced me."

"Damn right, I did." Tess laughed. "But go ahead, Josh… fuck your weird girlfriend from high school. You've been pining for her for the last decade. Lord knows you probably need a release after all this time." She giggled and smacked her signature piece of gum against the roof of her mouth. "Maybe call Austin first though… He can give you some pointers or something."

"Why the hell would Austin—" Josh closed his eyes and folded the top half of his body over the kitchen counter. *What are you even talking about?* He sighed. "You know, never mind. Just never mind. Why are you calling? Whoever's in my bed shouldn't matter to you."

She snorted. "No, it doesn't, you're just proving me right." She snickered. "But Josh, don't forget what she did to you. She ripped your heart into a million pieces. And she's capable of doing it again with the right provocation."

His stomach dropped as his gaze snaked along the floor to spy the crumped envelope near the front door.

"She left Rosewood with one secret… Who knows how many she came back with?" Tess ended the call.

Josh stared at the silent phone, setting it on the surface of the counter with a resolute tap. *What the fuck was that? Dalton Sheppard must be waning in the bedroom or something.* He snorted and ran a hand through his hair, casting Tess's weird threats aside.

"What's so funny?" Mavis's bare toes padded onto the tile as she entered the kitchen, leaning her body against the countertop beside him. Her eyes glowed in the soft lighting as she rested her hand over his own. Longing stirred in his heart as her fingers glided across his skin.

Her damp hair dripped onto his fingers and despite the cold droplets, a warmth raced through his body.

"Sorry," she whispered, wiping a droplet of water away. "I didn't bring my hairdryer."

Josh snagged a wet curl, looping it around his fingers.

His gaze followed the trail of moisture down his hand as it dripped into a pool on the counter. He grinned, moving his gaze to her mouth. The twinge in his groin grew as she bit her bottom lip.

"Err… I think I lent mine to Mitch." He chuckled and pulled his hand from her wet head, dragging his thumb along her lip until her teeth released their grip. "More hair than me, you know?" He ran a hand across the top of his head through the short crop of dark-brown hair.

Her eyes widened. "Wait. Mitch? My brother lives here? Still in Rosewood?" Her hand pressed against her heart.

"You mean you didn't know?" Josh frowned, regret over the dumb joke rising in his throat. Mitch's words pounded in his ear. *Leave my sister in the past where she belongs.* An invisible squeeze on his heart soured their conversation's sudden turn in direction.

"Geez, no… I had no idea." Mavis pulled the wet strands of her hair away from her face, tucking the curls behind her ears. Her gaze fell to the floor as she stuffed her hands in the pockets of her navy-blue sundress. "How is he?"

Josh shuffled his feet, shifting his weight to rest against the counter again. "Umm… good. Married to my sister actually. They live at the manor." He tilted his head, sadness seeping into the crevices of his heart. *Whatever your secret, it forced you to leave him behind too, didn't it?*

Mavis nodded, a grin tugging at her pretty pink lips. "That's ahh… that's really sweet. I didn't know what happened to him. Or where he ended up." She pulled her hands from her pockets and pointed to the fridge. "Do you think I can grab a glass of water?"

"Oh, yeah, of course." Josh pulled a glass down from the cabinet above his head and handed it to her as she stepped away. He eyed her as she moved. She carried herself differently than recall retained, her posture more rigid, a heavy weight in her shoulders uncaptured by memory. But the sweet smile blossoming on her lips—and the glow of her green eyes—hadn't changed. She wrapped her arms around her body in a self-hug, pulling the glass of water to her lips as she closed the fridge door. *You can say what you want, Duchess, but you're still the same. You're still my Mavis.*

Her gaze skimmed the refrigerator's surface, presumably examining the array of items clinging to the exterior. She choked, coughing on the water.

Josh squinted. Unless a coupon for a free meatball sub offended her—or the reminder post-it note to pick up dish soap and hand sanitizer—the only other item on the fridge was a photo of him and Austin at a beer festival the previous summer. *Are you a vegetarian now or something?*

"You okay?" he asked, dragging his hand along her back.

She coughed. "Yeah, wrong pipe." A tear rolled down her reddening cheeks, and she swiped at it, dabbing at her eyes. "Sorry…"

Josh smiled and kissed her forehead, coconuts invading his nostrils as his lips met her skin. He pulled her body closer and sighed. "You know, you apologize an awful lot."

She sighed into his chest, the tickle of her breath colliding with his bare skin. Her arms snaked around his body, squeezing, tugging him closer until her lips pressed against the inside of his neck. A shiver brought goosebumps to his body, blazing a trail of excitement along his skin.

"Don't ever go again, okay?" he whispered. His eyes closed; his body bathed in contentment—all the desire held in his heart wrapped around the woman snuggled beside him.

"I never wanted to leave in the first place." She hiccupped, tightening her grip. "I just can't believe after all this time…" Her hands traveled up his back, winding behind his head to cup the back of his neck. Her nails grazed his hairline.

"You think that little of me, Duchess?"

She whimpered. "I guess I ju—"

He pressed his lips to hers, a deepening desire stirring in his heart. Each beat thumping in his chest was a cry for more, a cry for the time they'd lost together. A moan escaped her lips. "Joshua," she whispered against his mouth. Her voice pulled his mind to the meadow, to the beginnings of new love. The start of their journey before the world turned dark.

The tips of his fingers tingled, awakening his body from a dormant sleep. He'd dreamt of her for a decade and longed for a reunion of souls. And here she appeared, ready to superglue their two halves into one whole once more.

His grip tensed on her hips, weaving his hands around her curves, ready to cling to the fabric of her dress before she disappeared and slipped through his fingers again. "I loved you yesterday," he murmured in her ear.

Her palms dragged across his chest, catching his nipple on the trail downward. A blast of hot fire erupted in his belly, rerouting his blood flow to his middle. He groaned, pushing his hips into hers.

"I love you today," he whispered, dipping his hand beneath the bottom of her dress. He squeezed her butt cheek, eliciting a giggle to tumble from her lips. "Fuck, I missed you." He groaned, nipping the bottom of her earlobe.

She laughed, tipping her head back with a wide smile. "That's not how it goes!"

Josh tugged her hair, pulling her face back to his. Their eyes met as the doorbell rang, and a heavy weight of disappointment crushed his chest at the interruption.

I will murder whoever is on the opposite side of that door.

"Shh, they'll go away." He snickered, grinning ear to ear as he pressed his lips back onto hers.

"Josh, open up! I know she's in there!" Mitch's voice rang out as his fists pummeled the front door. *How many people are watching my damn house?*

"Is that my brother?" Mavis pushed against his chest, freeing her body from his affectionate grasp. She raced out of the kitchen, her bare feet pounding against the wood flooring in the foyer.

Disappointment pooled in his gut. *This can't be happening.* With heavy, reluctant steps, Josh followed her retreat, grazing his hands along the banister of the railing. His butt sank to the second step of the staircase, propping his knees up to disguise his now swiftly diminishing arousal. *Impeccable timing, Mitch. You asshole.*

Mavis twisted the lock and yanked the front door open. A rush of warm air blew in as Mitch stepped inside. The green-eyed, soul-piercing gaze of his brother-in-law raked over Mavis, his line of sight moving over her from head to toe.

Unease settled in the pit of Josh's stomach as fear shot through him.

Mitch—rarely at a loss for words—uttered none. His cheeks reddened and his face hardened, sweeping his eyes over his long-lost sister.

Uh-oh.

Josh rose from his seat, stretching a hand outward. "Mitch, please don't."

"Stay out of it, Josh." He stepped forward and gently folded Mavis into a bear hug. His arms wrapped around her small body as a sigh escaped his lips.

Thank God.

Josh stuffed his hands in his pockets, the nerves in his gut disintegrating. Mitch talked a big game, but in the end, he missed her in his own way too.

"Hey, your laundry is done. I pulled it out of the dryer for you," said Mitch, concluding the hug. He pushed Mavis an arm's length away, eyeing her with intensity.

She scrunched her nose and stumbled. "What?"

"That's what I was coming to tell you. But I never got to. Your room was empty." Mitch pulled away from her, tucking his shoulder-length dark hair behind his ears.

Mavis hung her head, her gaze meeting the wood floor. "I'm sorry," she whispered, wrapping her arms back around her body.

"Why, Mavis? W-h-y?" he pleaded. "What the hell were

you thinking?"

Josh stepped forward, looping his arms around her waist. She caved, snuggling back into him. "Mitch, come on, man. Please don't do this. Not now."

She exhaled, her warm breath beating against his skin. "No… no, Josh, it's okay. You don't have to defend me. I owe him—and you—an explanation." She pulled her face upward, all glow from her eyes melting away.

Mitch pointed at Josh. "Wait, even you don't know?"

Josh frowned and shook his head. "Now's not the time."

"The hell it isn't!" His gaze darted back and forth. "Come on, Mavs, maybe a bit of truth before you go running out of here again?" He shrugged, raising his palms before smacking them to his sides.

"Dude, knock it off." Josh cradled her head, tucking her body deeper into the safety of his arms. *You will absolutely under no circumstance scare her away from here—or me.*

She stirred, pulling away to eye Mitch. "I can explain some of it—"

"Some of it?" He sidestepped the duo and marched toward the kitchen, his work boots squeaking across the hardwood.

Mavis sighed and rubbed the back of her head, slowly pulling away. Her gaze met the floor. "Josh, I really need to tell you something before…" She sniffled and swiped at the tears in the corners of her eyes.

He smashed his lips into a thin line and nodded. A lump formed in his throat as he swallowed the sorrow emitting from her soul. Josh gripped her hand and tugged. "I'll love you tomorrow," he whispered.

The grin on her lips softened his heart as he led her back toward the kitchen and yanked out a barstool from beneath the counter. He patted the cushion as he pulled out its twin and took a seat. "Beer is in the door."

Mitch snapped the door shut, three beers in hand. He banged them on the counter and shoved two in their direction. "Mavs, I'll take whatever I can get right now."

The bottle met his lips as he gulped.

Josh gripped a beer and twisted the cap, pushing it in front of Mavis. He sighed, opening the other before glaring at his brother-in-law.

"Mitch, we haven't talked yet. Mavs just got here. And I know you want answers, but——"

Mitch shook his head, a grin spreading across his lips. "Ten years, dude. She doesn't owe me half the explanation she owes you, but she damn well owes me something." He frowned, dragging his fingers along the countertop.

Tears spilled from her eyes, flowing down her cheeks in a well-traveled trail. "I'm sorry, okay?" She sniffled, swiping at the flow. "I made a really big mistake that I couldn't fix."

"A big mistake, and your solution was to just run away?" Mitch squinted and shook his head. "Why didn't you come to me? I would have helped you! With anything!"

"You couldn't. No one could." She brought the bottle to her mouth and sipped. "I thought I was doing the right thing, leaving before anyone could get hurt."

"*Before?* Mavis Benson, do you even realize how much you hurt *all* of us?" He set his beer on the counter and scratched the back of his neck. "I literally showed up at your door with a basket of laundry, dumped it on your bed like any other day. But you never came back. You disappeared, just as quick as Mom and Dad."

A sob caught in her throat as she buried her face in her hands. "Mitch, I'm so sorry."

Josh's heart shattered as he stood, pulling her sad, shrunken form upright and back into his embrace. He rested his chin on top of her head, threading his fingers through her hair. She shook in his arms.

"Look, Mitch, I get that you're mad." Josh glowered, sizing him up. "But I can't let you do this." He shook his head, tightening his grasp. "Now isn't the time. Please." Every piece of him longed to protect her, ready to meld her body right into his own for safekeeping.

Her muffled voice spoke into his chest. "I didn't leave

because I wanted to. I was trapped."

"Whatever the reason, Mavs, you made a choice. You *left*," answered Mitch, draining his bottle of beer. "Without one fucking word…"

And you're being a fucking jerk right now.

"You know what, do I need to remind you that you did the exact same thing?" Josh raised his brow, squeezing the back of Mavis's neck.

"Huh?" She pulled her face from the safety of his grasp, wiping below her nose with the back of her hand. "What did you say?"

Mitch rolled his eyes. "It's not the same, like, at all. I didn't disappear in the middle of the fucking night."

Josh sighed, his gaze raking over Mavis as she mopped her face free of tears. "Maybe not. But you still left, dude."

"I left to join the Navy! Come on! Absolutely no comparison." He tossed his empty beer bottle into the recycle bin and glowered.

"You turned eighteen and took off without a look back. You didn't even wait until graduation. You hardly said goodbye, and you broke my sister's heart in the process."

"Don't drag Lauren into this. I gave her what she wanted. I married her and moved into your ridiculous family mansion. She got what she always wanted."

"Wow, and you're obviously really happy about all that too. Damn…" Josh rolled his eyes and dropped back onto the barstool.

Mitch waved his hand, brushing the accusation aside. "Fine. Whatever. I'll stop for now," he conceded. "But this isn't over. It can't be." He dragged his palms across his cheeks and exhaled. His gaze rolled over Mavis as she stood beside Josh, wrapping her body in her arms with a self-hug. He groaned and moved out from around the counter, stopping in front of her. Squeezing her elbow, he pulled her back into his body. "I need more answers," he whispered. "But, God, I'm glad you're home." He kissed the top of her head and nodded at Josh.

Mitch left the kitchen, his feet pounding against the floor before halting abruptly. "Oh, and I'm supposed to invite you over for a family dinner tomorrow. Lauren said she'd text you the time."

Well, that'll be fun. A true family reunion.

The fresh air freed him from the confines of the impending truth as he drove down the highway, heading for the beach. His stomach twisted into a knot. *That didn't go very well.*

Josh swallowed, recalling the basket of laundry Mitch referenced. Always wrapped up in his own feelings over Mavis and how she'd left *him*, he'd rarely considered the damage done to Mitch.

With a sigh, Josh tore his gaze from the road to peek at her. She'd covered her eyes with black-rimmed sunglasses. One hand restrained her wild hair as it whipped in the wind, and the other danced out the window. A smile played across her lips as the sun bounced off her pale skin. His Jeep stopped at a red light, and Josh turned to admire her.

"You know, right now it's about twenty degrees back home." She snorted and pulled her face upward to meet the sun.

The light turned green, and Josh hit the gas, forcing his eyes back on the road. "Why Chicago?"

"Nothing specific, really." She shrugged. "It was the first bus leaving the station, so I hopped on, but it's been good to me. No complaints but the weather." She rested her hand on his knee and squeezed, a grin growing on her lips. "Turns out the snow isn't as magical as I once thought."

Josh snorted, flipping the left turn signal on before veering off the road and into a parking lot. He navigated to an empty space and put the Jeep in park.

"Ready?"

"Absolutely." Her eyes narrowed as she stared into the distance at the ocean.

Josh hopped from the car and waited for her hand to drop into his own as they marched across the sand. At her touch, his heart fell back into the familiar sense of security. Each step forward was like an echo of their past, the sand beneath their toes as the moments they'd spent together replayed in his mind.

She ripped her flip-flops from her feet and a smile broke free on her face.

"You can pretend Chicago is your home, but you'll always be a California girl."

She grinned. "Oh, come on, Lake Michigan is like the same thing."

Josh laughed and squeezed her hand. "Now you really sound like a Midwesterner." He pulled her farther onto the beach, every step bringing them closer to the waves. When they reached the wet sand, Josh yanked his sandals off too and tossed them aside. The freezing rush of the water raced over their feet as the tide crashed forward, leaving them ankle-deep in the ocean.

Shit, that's cold!

Like the water rushing over their toes, a wave of contentment blanked him. A gull screeched above, and Josh peered at the bird as it soared overhead, its wings flapping in the wind, wild and free. Having not felt wild and free in a decade—always boxed into an inescapable set of career expectations and hardened by a crumbling marriage—the new sense of resilience fueled him.

The sun disappeared behind a cloud, and Mavis lifted the glasses from her face, balancing them on top of her head. She bent forward and ran her fingers along the swell of the tide, scrunching her nose at a piece of seaweed clinging to her shin.

"You should move home, Mavs." His mouth betrayed him, speaking his heart's desire.

Mavis froze, her fingertips still in the water. "I've been back here for like three hours." She straightened, wiping the water from her hands on her dress.

He sighed and stuffed his hands in his pockets, grinning at his own bold suggestion. "Sorry, I know I sound ridiculous." *Stop saying stupid shit!*

"You're not ridiculous, Joshua," she answered, wrapping her arms around his middle. "I won't deny that I feel it too."

She rested her head against his chest, and the simple connection jumpstarted the invisible magnet from their past to reactivate. His body quivered, holding her in his arms again. The waves lapped at his ankles, each rush of the water a repair of his long-ago ripped and frayed heartstrings.

He pressed his hand against her head, toying with her hair. "You're a survivor," he whispered in her ear. "You've always been so strong." The tip of his finger rubbed against a small bump at the base of her head, and he scrunched his nose. "What's this? Did you hurt yourself?"

She pulled her face from his chest and placed her hand over his own. "It's nothing," she said. "Damn door frame…" Her eyes widened.

He exhaled, brushing her comment aside. "How'd you do it, Mavs?" he asked, grasping his hands around her forearms. "Not why, but how? You were seventeen, and alone…" His eyes searched hers before pressing his lips to her forehead.

"I wasn't alone."

The wind whipped, confusing her faint admission.

"What?"

"Joshua, I was pregnant."

The words hung in the salty air, holding the weight of the entire ocean.

CHAPTER THIRTEEN

Austin

Austin snapped his laptop shut and glanced around the hotel lobby. His gaze landed on his newest client's retreating figure as she marched toward the revolving doors and exited the building into the late afternoon sun. With a sigh, he leaned back into his chair, focusing on the sounds of the water feature behind him. Each drop rhythmically fell into the fountain and soothed his slowly building tension headache. He rubbed his temples and tugged at the constraining tie around his neck.

His mind reeled, combing through the notes he'd just taken and the steadily lengthening to-do list he needed to start on for Mrs. Felton. She'd made her preference known. She needed quick action on her divorce, and she would pay top dollar for Austin to move with speed and discretion.

Austin snagged his phone from his pocket with the intent to open his calendar, but a missed call from Mitch distracted him.

With a tap of the call button, Austin held the phone to his ear.

"Hey," said Mitch on the third ring.

"What's up? Everything okay?"

"Mavis is back."

His heart stilled. The blood drained from his face as nausea wracked his body, paralyzing the headache in his brain. *Damn, you're quick, Princess.* He'd joked about a red-eye flight, but her impulsiveness shouldn't have surprised him; it only confirmed her feelings. She couldn't wait to be back in his brother's arms.

Austin cleared his throat, pushing aside the jealousy and disappointment swirling in his gut. "You saw her?"

"Yeah, she's with Josh."

"Wow. I umm, didn't think she'd get here so fast." A layer of sweat beaded along his forehead, and Austin dragged the back of his hand across the sheen.

"You knew she was coming home?"

"I guess. It's kind of a long story. I don't even know where to start." He sighed, slumping in his seat.

"Let's start with a beer then. Meet you at Highside in twenty?"

Austin looked down at his laptop and Mrs. Felton's to-do list. He rolled his eyes. *Who am I even kidding?* Mavis was back, and her presence would without a doubt stir up emotions for everyone. It had already started. *Mrs. Felton, you're going to have to wait.*

"Meet you there."

Austin entered through the side door of Highside and shrugged into a booth across from his brother-in-law. Mitch had picked their usual table beneath a sixty-inch TV with a view of the Lakers game. A beer already waited for him.

"Cheers," said Austin as he tapped Mitch's bottle and brought the brew to his lips.

Mitch sipped, his eyes expectant. "You said it was a long story. I guess you better start," he directed as he shifted in his seat.

Austin pressed his lips together in a thin line. *Where do I even begin? What can I even share?* Everything overlapped. Everything compounded, linked and twisted with no end to pull from. *Just be careful…*

He cringed and opened his mouth. "I went over to Josh's place last night to apologize. He's been pissed at me all week."

"He's not the only one, dude. Why'd you keep her from us?" Mitch toyed with the label on the bottle.

Austin slumped back into the cushy booth, willing his heart to return to a normal beat as it pounded against his ribcage. "I, ah… I didn't want to stir things up." *Or have to admit my colossal mistakes.* "Josh was engaged to Tess at the time I bumped into Mavis in Chicago. I made a choice and decided he was better off not knowing."

Mitch nodded. "Well, all right, maybe that was best *for Josh.* But Austin, what about me? In the years I've been back in Rosewood, didn't you consider that I'd like to know too? She's my sister, the only piece I have left of my family."

Austin hesitated. "I did, Mitch," he lied. *I was never going to tell anyone I found her.* "But come on, you know how it is. Mavis's name is like taboo in our family. No one's said her name in years, terrified of how Josh would react."

"No one said Josh had to be in the room when you told me." Mitch's gaze dropped to his lap as he tugged at the drawstrings on his sweatshirt.

"I'm sorry, Mitch." Austin's gaze fell to the sticky floor. "You're right, you're the one person I should have told." *And now I look like a huge dick.*

Mitch nodded. "I don't really know what to think. I've been so mad at her for so long. I pushed her away, hoping to forget. It was really weird seeing her again this morning. She's different now."

"She's been through a lot." Austin blew out a breath and turned his attention out the window. A happy couple strolled down the sidewalk, hand in hand, with a small fluffy white dog on a blue leash. "So much…" he added under his breath.

Mitch furrowed his brow, a deep V creasing his forehead as he squinted. "Oh my, God. You know, don't you? You know why she left."

Austin pulled his gaze back inside, his cheeks reddening as warmth showered him. He cupped the back of his neck with both hands and tipped his face upward to avoid his brother-in-law's piercing stare. *Oh, shit...*

Mitch bobbed his head up and down before downing the rest of his beer. "You're a sly son-of-a-bitch, you know that, right? All this time you've kept your trap shut, and you've known *everything* about her all along." He moved to slide out of the booth.

"Come on, Mitch, please wait a second! Let me try to explain, all right?"

Mitch stilled, his eyes wide with eager anticipation. He glowered, radiating anger through his glare.

"It's the same thing I told Josh last night. *Yes,* I know why she left Rosewood. I know her reason. But that's just it. It's *her* secret to share, not mine. And when I talked to her last night—"

"Hang on. Last night?" Mitch interrupted with a wave of his hand.

"Well, yeah, I had to warn her about Josh."

"You have her phone number, man? Like, you can just pick up your phone right now and call her? You're *that* friendly?" He grinned.

I hate that grin. When Mitch grinned, he was angry.

"All this time, I've wondered, worried that she was out there on her own. Austin, I didn't even know if she was still alive. And here you are with a piece of her in your pocket, just a call or text away."

Mitch shuffled out of the booth and tossed a twenty-dollar bill on the table. "No wonder you make such a good lawyer. You're a damn fine liar, Austin Templeton." He slapped his hand on the tabletop in dismissal and stalked away.

"Damn it, Mitch! Come on!"

He earned the stares from the nearby booths' occupants, but it didn't matter. Mitch had gone, and he left with anger in his heart.

I was just trying to keep our secrets buried.

Austin finished his beer and ordered another one. *There's no point in following him.* When Mitch was angry, it was in everyone's best interest to let him cool down. Austin replayed in his mind the one time in his life he'd pushed Mitch beyond breaking point after a loss to a rival high school football team. He squinted, remembering the bruise that swelled his left eye shut after Mitch's fist pummeled him.

"Shoulda caught the damn ball," he murmured into the neck of his bottle.

Austin sighed and slumped backward, twisting the conversation in his brain. Mitch did deserve to know where Mavis was all these years. After all, they'd shared a rough childhood together, leaning on one another after their parents perished in an accidental car crash. They navigated the foster system as wards of the State of California. If anyone deserved to know the truth about her whereabouts, he did. *He's right to be angry with me.*

He dropped his head in his hands, dragging his palms over his cheeks. Mitch's empty seat stared back, the look of his hardened brother-in-law's glare ricocheting in his brain. Austin sipped his beer, resolving to let Mitch cool off before he apologized. He turned his gaze back to the Lakers game, but nothing registered, even the three-point basket that spurred cheers from the crowd. *Mavis.* If she was back— and in Josh's arms again—it was just a matter of time before his brother would learn the truth about her pregnancy. His heart hurt considering the ten-year reveal and the sequence of events that put everything in motion.

His memory brought forth a vision of her teary-eyed face when she'd knocked on his door at Harvard. *You chose me to confide in, no one else.* "You sought me after the fallout, not Josh," he whispered, tapping his bottle against the table.

A pressure in his chest intensified, and the nerves in his bloodstream seared into his sweaty palms. More than just physical, an emotional connection had been made that night, and that connection had never truly severed.

All I want is for you to be happy, Princess. But from the pit of his stomach, another voice darkened the surface of his consciousness. *You may want her to be happy, but deep down, you want her in your own bed.*

His elbow knocked the bottle of beer over as understanding blossomed in his heart for the first time, clarity gripping his brain. *It's not just jealousy I feel... is it love too?*

Austin's heart stalled, a rush of realization squeezing his chest, robbing his lungs of air. He pulled his gaze back to the TV, mindlessly watching a cat food commercial as he processed the sudden knowledge buried beneath his heart. His brain ran rampant, toying with the revelation as an orange tabby cat smashed its ugly face into a can of food and glared into the camera. The past slammed into him, a freight train to his gut.

"Mamelda," he whispered with a laugh. "*The Funny Part.* E. Banks is Mavis."

He grinned. The quirky girl with the pen held his heart. *And I think you always have, Princess.*

CHAPTER FOURTEEN

Mavis

For over a decade, the secret of a lifetime had been hidden beneath lock and key, but now, the truth belonged to both of them.

Just breathe.

Josh didn't move. His body stood, frozen in place as the waves crashed into his shins with the rolling tide. Mavis searched his eyes to find what his mouth could not speak; they darted back and forth as he presumably pieced together every detail of the past.

"Josh, I can explain everything, but maybe let's get out of the water first." Tugging his arm, she coaxed him toward the beach and back to the warmth of the sand.

He moved on command with a stilted nod, dropping to the seat of an empty picnic table. His hands fell to the bench, dragging over a jagged gouge in the wood. *That's probably what your heart looks like right now.*

The blood drained from his face; his pale complexion accentuated in the dwindling afternoon sunlight. Mavis sank to the sand and knelt between his legs, peering into his eyes as she rested her hands on his thighs. She squeezed his skin, the tender connection pulling him back to the present. Moving his hands on top of hers, he furrowed his brow and leaned forward.

"Pregnant?" he repeated.

His voice broke her. The ten-year secret sailing from his lips squeezed the strings around her heart, sucking the life from her body. Her vision clouded in a pool of tears, blurring his sweet face. *This is it, a new beginning or the final farewell.*

She nodded and pressed a kiss to the top of his hand. "Can I please try to explain why I did what I did?" she begged. A tear trickled down her cheek, and she swiped at it furiously. His face regained focus, but the eruption of anger staring back paralyzed any further explanation on her lips.

He shook his head, disbelief spewing from his soul. His grip on her fingers lessened as he nudged her away, resentment overriding any affection he'd shown since their reunion.

"How could you hide that from me?" Squinting, a crease formed across his forehead. "You were fucking *pregnant?*" Releasing a breath, Josh pulled his body from the bench and stepped away, scattering sand with angry stomps. His hands clasped the back of his head as his feet mindlessly shuffled, his eyes gazing out at the vast ocean.

"Joshua! Please, will you let me try and explain?" Her body convulsed as her muscles weakened, and Mavis folded her body over the picnic table seat. A curl caught in the rough wood, and she yanked it free with fury, an angry burn prickling her scalp.

Final farewell it is then.

Sand tickled her bare legs as Josh returned, dropping his body on the beach beside her.

Oh!

Leaning against the bench, he dragged his palms across his face, scratching the stubble on his cheeks and chin. "Pregnant," he huffed out again. "Damn it, Duchess, I don't even know where to start." His eyes softened until her very tears reflected in his own. The anger drained from his face like the tide rolled back into the ocean.

"I was so scared—so stupid. I didn't know what to do!" A shiver raked along her spine, a cold chill raising goosebumps on her flesh. Her body shook as she sank lower into the sand. "I thought I was doing the right thing. I thought I was helping you."

Pulling her body to his, Josh wrapped his arms around her and sighed. His strong embrace was a lifeline, his connection the sole reason to draw breath at the moment. Hope blossomed in her heart at his shift in disposition, and she gripped his body, clinging to the fabric of his t-shirt. *A new beginning?*

"I think I understand," he whispered. "You were *protecting* me."

His words unraveled the small shred of composure still clinging to her broken soul. She gave in to the emotion— gave in to the moment—and her body trembled, sobs escaping from the years of pent-up stress and uncertainty spilling over the precipice.

"Take a deep breath, Mavs." His palms glided over her back, his fingertips rubbing small circles into her skin. "That's it," he added. He breathed in deeply, each breath a cathartic, rhythmic presence; it grounded her.

Time drifted away, irrelevant in the softening sun, as Josh stroked her hair. His heartbeat hammered in her ear, pounding deep within his chest.

Sweet Joshua. You'll sit here all night if I let you.

Closing her eyes, Mavis inhaled the ocean air. *One… two…three.* She saw her hand write the letter, her pen swirling across the paper as tears marked the message. *Four… five… six.* Blood stained her skin, a heavy pain cramping in her gut beneath the bedsheets. *Seven… eight… nine.* She fell into Austin's arms at his dorm room door. *Ten.* Her eyes snapped open, a swell of guilt and resentment bubbling to the surface.

Mavis pulled away from his body, ready to double over at the nausea stirring in her stomach. She hurled her memories and poor choices aside and forced her eyes to meet Josh's. Filled to the brim with tears, he blinked hard, releasing the heart-wrenching sadness down his cheeks.

She swallowed the emotion and gulped down the guilt. "Please say something, Joshua," she choked out.

"The baby?" he asked, the burning question spilling from his lips.

Her gaze met the sand, and she pressed her palm to her stomach. *It's all my fault.*

"Mavs?"

She shook her head, the ring in her ears returning. "I miscarried," she whispered.

Drawing her back into his embrace, the breath caught in his throat.

The air cooled, and the sun tucked itself behind the last cloud of the afternoon, falling into the depths of the ocean. Mavis shivered and pressed her face deeper into his chest.

All. My. Fault.

Her words bit into the wind. "I'm sor—"

"Don't. Don't you ever apologize to me, Mavis."

"But it was m-m-my fault," she stammered as a fresh wave of tears burned the backs of her lids.

"A miscarriage is no one's fault." He gripped her forearms, pinning her hands in her lap. His eyes bore into her own, the deep brown of his irises set ablaze in the light of the fading sun. "Not. Your. Fault," he repeated. "Please hear me when I say that."

Exhaustion consumed her, each muscle weakening as her head dizzied from the flood of emotions swirling in her body. Lack of sleep caught up with her and her body trembled.

"Let's get you back to the car, okay?"

I must look the way I feel.

Josh gripped her hand and stood, tugging her body up alongside him. Each step forward weighed heavier than the last, dumbbells strapped to her ankles as her feet trudged forward.

"Hop on then, Duchess," he whispered, crouching in front of her.

His words—as sweet and innocent as childhood— patched the holes in her heart as she climbed on his back with their shoes in hand. Mavis closed her eyes, her memory reaching into the depths of the meadow where their relationship blossomed among the poppies so long ago. The honied scent of their bloom mixed with the salty ocean air swirling around them in the present, and Mavis exhaled, the weight of life's consequence left back on the beach. *I hope it stays buried in the sand forever.*

At the sand's edge, Josh opened the Jeep's door and lowered her into the passenger seat, buckling her in like a child. Her eyes closed as the engine hummed to life. The cathartic release of the truth had been like the culmination of a ten-year surgery on her soul. And Josh's steady hand had stitched her up, breathing new life into her depths.

Peeking through a slit in her lids, she eyed Josh as his hands clasped the steering wheel. *It's over. He finally knows the truth.* And sleep took her before Josh pulled out of the parking lot.

Mavis woke to the sound of a closing garage door. Startled, her gaze flew to the empty driver's seat. *Joshua?* Panic stalled her heart before the door opened and she turned to see his outstretched hand.

"You fell asleep."

Unlatching her seatbelt, she sighed. "I'm sor—"

"Don't." He shook his head. "You've been through a lot today. A catnap is fine."

A smile tugged at her lips as she dropped her hand in his and left the Jeep. His grip tightened on her palm, and warmth flooded her body. Guiding her inside the dark house, Josh fumbled for the hallway light switch. One lamp popped on, illuminating the empty foyer.

Surveying the space, her eyes caught sight of her reflection in the powder room mirror. The girl staring back—windblown hair, streaky mascara, and blotchy eyes—appeared as though a pack of seagulls had mauled her on the beach.

"I, ah, need a moment."

Josh nodded and released her hand. Tiptoeing into the powder room, the lock clicked behind her as she turned on the faucet. Mavis splashed water on her face and rubbed at the trail of makeup cemented to her cheeks. "This was supposed to be waterproof," she murmured, wrinkling her nose. But the cool water rejuvenated her aching eyes and she reined in her wild hair into a manageable ponytail.

The girl in the mirror sighed, a heavy weight having been pulled from her soul. The truth—now released into the ether— was no longer confined to the prison walls of her heart. Mavis blinked, her green eyes reflecting back, and for just a moment, the carefree version of her teenage self, smiled, the ghost of the girl from her youth. *It's been a long time since I've seen you.* She stepped from the sink and wrapped her arms around herself. *One secret down – one (technically two) to still hide.*

Releasing a sigh, Mavis exited the small space and turned the corner to find Josh pouring two glasses of wine in the kitchen. He pushed a glass in her direction as she entered.

"All I have is red. Is that okay? I don't know what you like." Ramming the cork back in the bottle, he frowned. "I used to know everything you liked," he added, returning the bottle opener to the drawer. It slid closed with a small click.

"Red is perfect." She pushed her fingers through a small spill of liquid on the counter and lifted her gaze to him. "Are you sure you want me to stay though, Joshua?"

He crinkled his nose. "I'd do anything to keep you here." Taking a sip, he swirled the wine in his glass. "What kept us apart for so long doesn't need to anymore now, right?"

Mavis swallowed, his simple truth resonating in her core.

She nodded as her cheeks reddened.

"Come on." Josh motioned to the living room, and she followed his lead, her footsteps echoing behind his until his feet stalled at the edge of the living room carpet. He grinned and scratched his chin as she eyed the single chair in the space.

"Snuggle time?" he asked, his gaze landing on the sole chair in the room.

Mavis snorted. "You know, Josh, I'm not really into the whole interior design thing, but I think you have room for a couch or something."

He laughed and rolled his eyes. "Tess took most of the furniture in the divorce. But she always hated this chair, so I got to keep it." He fluffed the back of the cushion and crawled in.

"Well, I like it. Looks comfy."

Josh patted his lap and smiled. "Come test it out, Duchess."

She snuggled into him, turning her body inward to rest the side of her head purposefully on his chest. Her ear caught the rhythm of his steady heartbeat, his chest rising and falling with each breath. His fingers threaded her hair, tugging a curl free from her ponytail.

"Mavs?"

"Hmm?"

"Thank you for telling me the truth." He sighed. "I just need you to know that I'm thankful you chose to confide in me today. I'm sure it wasn't easy after so much time."

As she tilted her head, his brown eyes met hers, full of sympathy—full of pain.

"Austin told me you left to protect me," he continued. "And I think I know why. You were protecting my career—you were protecting my dream, weren't you?"

Mavis inhaled and shook her head, pressing her face back into his chest. "You would never have left for Georgetown, Joshua," she muttered. "I know you."

His chest rose, sucking in a deep breath of air. "You're

right. I wouldn't have." He raised his brow and took a sip from his glass. "But you didn't need to make that decision for me." His hand gripped her ponytail, wrapping the wild curls around his fingers. "I know it doesn't matter anymore, but you need to hear me say it just this once. We could have figured it out … *together*," he continued. "That's all I'll say on it, okay?"

Mavis nodded, swallowing the last of her wine. "I'm so sorry, Joshua," she squeaked with a hiccup. "If I could do it ov—"

"I told you. Please don't ever apologize to me." He gulped down the last of his wine and trailed his fingers down her arm. "You carried the weight of my mistake. You don't owe me anything."

"That's not true." Mavis pulled her cheek from his chest again and locked her eyes with his. "I asked you to make love to me that day. It was *my* fault it happened."

Josh squinted, his body straightening. "Wait, are you saying?"

She nodded and shrugged. "I don't know for sure. But the timing adds up, and we didn't, you know… use anything." Heat radiated from her cheeks, the wine raising her body temperature.

His eyes widened. "Wow. That first time…" He raked a hand through his hair and cupped the back of his neck, kneading the muscles at his hairline. "What're the fucking chances?"

"You tell me, Dr. Templeton," she quipped.

Snorting, he squeezed her elbow.

"So… if it was *the meadow*… that means you must have known you were pregnant for a while, almost all of that summer?"

The wine sloshed in her empty stomach, fogging her tired brain. *Of course, you want to do the math.*

Nodding, she scratched the tip of her nose. "Do you remember that day at the beach when Mitch hit Tess on the head with a volleyball?"

"Yeah, I do." He chuckled. "I don't feel so bad for her anymore," he said with a grin.

"No, she earned it for sure," she answered, giggling into his body.

"Why do you bring it up?" He pressed his lips to her forehead, his mouth stilling on her skin. "Wait," he whispered. "Didn't you feel sick that day?

Mavis nodded, twirling the empty glass.

Oh…" His hand brushed against her waist, and a shiver zigzagged up her spine.

"That's the day I umm, found out."

"And you didn't want to tell anyone?"

A sigh escaped her lips with an eye roll. "Who was I gonna tell, Josh?"

"I don't know, your foster mom maybe?"

She laughed. "Oh God, Carol?" Her eyes widened.

"I mean, well, yeah."

"Joshua, come on. She would have disowned me on the spot if she knew I was pregnant. I couldn't do that to Mitch. I didn't want to risk him losing his home. Carol *wasn't* an option."

His lips pressed to her forehead again, a rush of warm breath colliding with her skin. "I just wish you didn't think you had to do it alone. I could have been there for you."

Her heart ached. Living with the consequences had been painful enough, but recalling the gut-wrenching decisions of her youth came with their own set of challenges too. And as of an hour ago, all of it was new to Josh.

Huffing out a breath, she tugged the empty glass from his hands. "Maybe more wine, huh?"

"Oh, ah, yeah, sure."

Squirming free from his lap, she padded back to the kitchen and snagged the wine bottle. Mavis poured, breathing in the soft aromas of nutmeg and cloves as the liquid sloshed in their glasses. *This shit is expensive. Nothing like the house red at Shaker.*

The bottle emptied, and she rinsed it in the sink before

placing it in the recycle bin. Her gaze caught the refrigerator door and another spasm of guilt ricocheted in her chest. Pulling the photo from beneath the magnet, she examined it closer. Josh beamed at the camera, the grin on his sweet lips delectable—boyish, and fun. Her heart melted at his image, her soul calling out to his, the missing half of her whole. But then Austin's baby-blue eyes pierced the comfort and disrupted the safety. The smile on his lips, mischievous, wild, and free. His laughter rang in her ear, and her stomach dipped as she eyed his carefree face.

Mavis lifted the glass of wine to her nose. The scent had changed. *Sandalwood.* Fear gripped her, and she tore her gaze from the photo of the Templeton twins, replacing it on the refrigerator door.

What the hell is wrong with you, Mavis Benson?

She stomped from the room with full wine glasses in hand.

"Everything okay?" Josh accepted the glass as she snuggled back into her former spot on his lap.

"Oh, yeah, just couldn't pull the cork out at first," she lied. Mavis gulped the wine, mimicking Josh's glass swirl. "This is really good."

He nodded. "We got it in Napa a few years ago. But never had a chance to open it."

She tipped her glass to his and a soft clank echoed through the empty room. "Always happy to help," she joked.

He smiled, but the sentiment didn't reach his eyes.

Now what?

"Spill it, Joshua. Say what you want to say."

He shook his head. "No. No... I don't want to badger you."

Her heart flip-flopped in her chest, turmoil holding hands with confusion. "I'll tell you anything you want to know." *Well, not anything...*

"Well maybe then, can you tell me what happened? Were you alone? How far along were you when...?" The questions spiraled from his mouth, vomit from his lips.

You deserve to know everything, don't you?

Mavis released a breath and snuggled back into his chest. Tucking a hand in the pocket of his shorts, she sniffled. "Do you remember my cousin, Angie?"

"Who?"

She nodded. "Yeah, I didn't think so. She was the only person I could think of to ask for help."

"I don't remember you mentioning her at all—ever even. Where did she live?"

"Boston."

His lips disappeared into a thin line. "So, Austin…" he answered with another large gulp of wine.

Ugh, right in the gut. "I was really scared and just really confused after…" she said, closing her eyes as the tears burned behind her lids again. "I… needed someone I trusted, and I knew he was close. Please don't be mad that I went to him."

Josh tightened his grip on her body, and she leaned into his embrace, breathing in the hint of peppermint clinging to his t-shirt.

"No, I understand. I'm not mad. I'm just glad he was there for you—Angie too—since I couldn't…"

"Joshua…"

"I'm sorry. Please keep going."

The tears escaped, running down her face. The little pools of sadness dropped to the cotton of his t-shirt, absorbing into the material like a sponge. Wiping her cheeks, Josh planted a kiss on her head.

"I was in Boston for about three weeks before it happened. I umm, just woke up in a lot of pain. Angie drove me to the hospital. And there wasn't really anything they could do. It was too late." The wine collided with her tongue, and she swallowed the liquid in a large gulp. Reliving the memory forced an image of Casey—and her recent experience in a hospital ER. *Mental note. Call Casey tomorrow and check on her.*

Josh tipped her chin upward. His eyes searched hers, emitting the sadness that had consumed her heart for a decade. "Have you told anyone? Talked about it ever?"

Her stomach churned, twinging her gut. "Are you asking me if I've been to a therapist, or a grief counselor, or something?" She crinkled her nose.

"No!" He shook his head. "I mean, not necessarily, though either aren't bad things. I just meant I hope you haven't had to keep it all to yourself. I imagine it's a hard thing to carry."

The photo from the refrigerator materialized in her mind, Austin's face coming into focus. *Sweet Austin.*

She swallowed. "I've told my best friend, Casey, Doctor Templeton."

Smiling, he squeezed her waist. "I'm sorry. I know I'm pushing too hard." Swallowing the rest of his wine, his tongue circled his lips. A rush of warmth washed over her body, eyeing his mouth.

"It's all right, Joshua. I came here to tell you the truth," she answered, draining her own glass. "And now you know all of it."

Not all of it, missy!

Josh inhaled and set his empty glass on the floor beside them. His eyes sought hers as his fingertips brushed her cheek. "Thank you for telling me, Duchess," he whispered. "Ten years was a long time to wait and wonder."

Sighing, Mavis went back in time, staring into the eyes of the man who had won her heart so many years ago. The boy in the meadow sat beside her, his hand exploring her body—as true as memory. A gasp escaped her as his hand dipped below her dress, running along her thigh.

"God, I missed you, Mavis, so fucking much." His lips rained down on hers, crushing her mouth with intensity.

He tasted of wine, the aromas of the nutmeg and cloves mixing with the saltiness of his lips. The combination fueled her, gripping her groin with a sudden surge of youthful excitement. Her skin tingled, pinpricks of anticipation racing along her limbs. She moved her mouth to nip his ear, and the moan that escaped his lips solidified her choice.

The past be damned.

"Take me upstairs, Joshua. Let me show you how much I missed you too."

JULIE NAVICKAS

CHAPTER FIFTEEN

Josh

Josh kicked the door open. A firestorm of anticipation rippled through his body as he tugged her into the darkened bedroom, backing Mavis to the edge of the mattress.

"Are you sure?" he whispered. "I know today's been kinda…"

Her eyes reflected the display of the neighbor's Christmas lights, a bright speck in a sea of black.

As she pressed her lips to his, her hands wound around his neck, each fingernail raking along his hairline and tickling his sensitive skin. "There's nothing I want more," she whispered.

In the surrounding darkness, Josh lifted his gaze to the photo on the nightstand. Having started the day pleasuring himself to the mere memory of her, the tightening in his groin overtook all willpower as his hands explored her flesh.

Her teeth grazed his earlobe, and a spike of adrenaline blasted through his bloodstream. "Joshua…" she whispered. Her voice echoed in the quiet space, penetrating his heart. "Please, make love to me."

Her request transcended time, biting into his memory

like ten years hadn't been stolen from their time together. His soul stirred, rousing to reclaim the love he'd lost.

Nudged backward, her butt fell to the mattress as a soft giggle left her lips. Her hair spilled across his bed as she lifted her arms to yank the tie constraining the wild mop. Each curl hung loosely, the tendrils meeting the wrinkles of the bedsheets.

Duchess.

Climbing on top of her, Josh pressed his body to hers, the friction and pressure building the arousal—gaining momentum. But his lips stilled as panic ensnared his mind. *Wait.* "Mavis, I don't have any protection," he breathed. "Shit, I never even considered you'd be here tonight, like this."

Her teeth trailed his jawline, her tongue tasting his skin as he spoke. "I've got us covered. That's a mistake I'll make only once," she answered as her fingers tugged at the hem of his shirt.

Josh groaned, her words searing against his heart. Yanking the garment up and over his head, he tossed it to the floor as the cool air kissed his bare skin. Her body lay beneath him, quivering, begging for reconnection, inviting his skin to meet her own. He caved, pushing beyond the past and the mistakes that encased history.

Josh exhaled. "I missed you," he whispered, pressing his lips to hers again. Warmth descended on his body as pleasure ripped through him. He teased her tongue with his until her breath caught in her throat. "It's always been you, Duchess. Always."

His fingers shook, following the zipper's trail on her dress. The fabric loosened, and she pulled herself free of the restriction.

Dizziness took him, disbelief fogging his brain as he contemplated how the nearly naked woman beneath him had returned so suddenly to his life. Her hips arched in a wordless cry, and Josh pushed against her, sliding his hands beneath her thighs. With a thump, her head met his single pillow, and the image freed him from the ropes binding him to unhappiness.

"God, I missed you too," she said in the darkened room. Her hands tugged at his shorts, rubbing against the length of him. His skin tingled, each nerve cell alert and attentive to the stroke of her hands.

With quivering fingers, Josh grasped the clasp of her bra and freed her breasts. She shivered as his hands covered the tender skin, a moan piercing the silence of the bedroom as his mouth lowered to her nipple.

The girl from the meadow wiggled beneath him, her body willing and ready to join souls in love. "Joshua, please…"

His body ached with anticipation, a sheen of sweat forming on his skin as his mouth tasted her, her limbs colliding with his in a race to explore, to refamiliarize. The faint smell of coconuts impaled his nostrils as his lips moved to her neck, sucking at the sensitive skin beneath her ear.

"Don't make me beg," she said with a growl, pushing her hips into his.

Dipping a finger beneath the lace of her panties, Josh paused and breathed out a sigh. The hum of the air conditioner kicked on, mimicking the bees that once stirred in the meadow. Closing his eyes, he yanked his shorts and boxers from his legs and freed her from the confines of the lace—the last bits of clothing from their bodies. She kicked at the sheets, and they tickled his legs like the grass that once grew in their bed of teenage passion.

Dragging his palms along her thighs, he let his weight fall on top of her, appreciating the tingles piercing his body. Pressing his lips to her neck, a delicate—familiar—chain met his lips.

Wait, is that—

"Joshua," she pleaded again, lifting her hips.

"I love you, Duchess." He slid inside her, relishing in the groans of pleasure tumbling from her lips. His brain clouded, struggling to meet her demanding pace as a fire lit in his belly. *This is how it should have always been.* He thrust into her harder, releasing the anger in his heart at the time they lost—at the parting of souls neither asked for.

Love emitted from the moans dripping from her lips, passion spilling from the mounting pleasure building in his groin. Her breath fell ragged against his ear, her small groans purring from the back of her throat. When she cried out—forcing his name from her lips in the culminating moment of passion—he released himself inside of her.

Exhaustion overwhelmed him, the heavy weight of his body testing the muscles in his arms. Pressing a kiss to her forehead, Josh withdrew himself and rolled.

She giggled, and her lips met the skin of his chest for the last time before her eyes closed. Mavis snuggled into him, using his arm as a pillow. Despite the slowly growing numbness creeping into his fingertips, Josh smiled. He inhaled her scent and reveled in the happiness consuming his heart. After a decade of longing for her, she was back. And she was his—mind, body, and soul.

His eyes popped open. Josh's heart slammed into his ribcage as an electrifying jolt rocked his body. Pleasure coursed through him, pressure building wildly in his belly as his brain awakened, playing catch up with his body. Beneath the sheets, her mouth consumed him, the movement of her hands magnifying the rapidly intensifying sensation ripping through his system.

Whoa! Blowing out a breath, he groaned and dragged his hands over his cheeks. Her muffled giggle breached the blankets, and a grin tugged at his lips as he fully registered her playful start to the morning. "Fuck... Mavis..." he whispered, arching his back.

She moved, finding a rhythm that—beyond any doubt—would bring him over the edge before morning dawned.

"Mavs, I—" he sputtered, dropping his hands to her head. He groaned, the release imminent. And with a shockwave of shivers freeing from his gut, he let go. "Holy fuck," he choked out, sucking breath back into his lungs.

She emerged from beneath the sheets with a wide grin and pink cheeks. "Good morning," she whispered, tossing her head to rest beside his. Her warm breath beat against his bare chest, and he tugged her closer.

"Good morning, indeed." His heart raced, the blood pulsating through his body as she giggled. Josh tucked his hand behind her neck, kneading the muscles hidden beneath her dark curls. His finger caught on a thin chain as the memory of last night swirled in his mind. Tracing the silver, his hands slid down until they reached the charm.

My heart is still wrapped around your soul.

"You still have it," he said, his eyes finding hers in the still darkened room.

"Of course, I do. It was the only piece of you I had left."

Josh inhaled, sadness suddenly gripping his heart as his fingers toyed with the charm. He squeezed, rolling it against his fingertips.

"I'm sorry. Maybe I should have taken it off," she whispered. Tugging at the chain, the charm dropped from his grip.

"Why would you say that?"

"Well, it made you sad." Her fingers traced his mouth, hovering over the scar above his top lip. "I was going for happy."

Josh grinned and kissed her fingers. "I haven't been that kind of *happy* in a long time." He pressed his body against hers and smoothed the hair away from her face. "You make me happy."

Rain fell outside, each droplet of water a soft tap on the window. Thunder rumbled, biting into the stillness of the bedroom in the early morning hours. His gaze rested on hers, digging deep into her soul—the doorway to the past. *Nothing's changed. You're still my girl… still my Mavis.*

"Do you remember the Fourth of July?" he asked.

She snicked. "Umm…it's like an annual thing, Josh.

Which one?" She pulled away from his grasp, flopping onto her back.

Josh snorted and tugged at a curl. "Okay, smarty pants… Do you remember the Fourth of July when my dad bought all those fireworks and we lit them off in the backyard?

She pressed her finger to the scar above his lip again, the touch inciting a burning question in his gut.

"Umm yeah… hard to forget the emergency room." Her finger fell, dragging down the length of his cheek. "Why are you asking?"

Lightning flashed behind the curtains, flooding light into the dim bedroom. It reflected in her eyes, each a green pool of curiosity.

"You showed me a story you'd written. I mean, before I set my face on fire." He rolled his eyes and huffed out a breath.

"What're you talking about?" She squinted and smiled.

"It was about a crazy grandmother. And her trip to a grocery store to get cat food. She paid for everything in coins and stacked the cans alphabetically in the bag by flavor."

A belly laugh erupted from her naked body, and she quivered with recall against his chest. "Joshua, why in the world are you asking me about this?" She giggled again, pressing her lips to his.

"Mamelda, right?"

She grinned. "I can't believe you remember that."

"Well, *The Funny Part* is…"

Mavis covered her eyes with her hands and laughed. "There's no fucking way you saw that!"

He pulled her back to his body, his heart coming alive at the sound of her laughter.

"Mitch subscribes. But I'm not kidding! Your story fell open on my lap the moment I told my family I wanted you back." The eerie sense of déjà vu gripped his gut again.

"I published that nonsense under a pen name months ago." She buried her face in the pillow. "I lost a bet to Casey, and she sent it in. I still can't believe they accepted it."

He smiled and stroked her hair, breathing in the natural perfume of her body. "So, Casey is E. Banks?"

Mavis snorted. "E. Banks is Ernie Banks, hall of famer for the Chicago Cubs. Casey's a die-hard fan." She rolled her eyes and tucked her face back into his chest.

The tip of her cold nose triggered goosebumps, and he tugged at the sheets.

"I hoped that you kept writing, Mavs. You were always so good at it." He pressed his lips to the top of her head.

"Umm… I mean, here and there. Hey, are you hungry?" she asked, rolling from the bed. The sheet went with her, dragging along his skin until all that remained was his naked body.

"Duchess, if you wanted to see me naked, all you had to do was ask."

A smirk broke across her lips as he climbed from the bed and pressed his pelvis to her middle. "I won't say no to round three."

She kissed him, sharing the sheet in return.

"Pancakes first, sir."

Oh, fine.

"Pancakes first," he repeated.

Josh flipped a pancake on the griddle. The gushy outer surface sizzled against the hot grill, the smoke wafting upward to scent the kitchen. He swayed to an acoustic playlist and sipped a cup of coffee, blissfully attuning his mind to the woman upstairs in his shower. His stomach growled with hunger. *When did I eat last?* His attention shot to the stairs. *When did you eat last, Duchess?*

With a shrug and sense of guilt bubbling to the surface, he cracked an egg and dumped the pancake onto a warm plate. From across the kitchen, his gaze fell to the balled-up letter, still hiding in the corner of the foyer. From its new home beside the coat rack, it called to him, a relic of their ten-year journey back to each other. Crossing the space with a quick glance up the staircase, Josh rammed her letter back in his pocket and returned to the kitchen.

He opened the door to the pantry and yanked the breakfast-in-bed tray from the back corner. *Never used once.* Wiping off the surface with a paper towel, Josh loaded the tray with pancakes, scrambled eggs, toast, coffee, silverware… and the single, slowly wilting, California poppy he'd snagged from Lauren's vase.

The water shut off above him, and Josh turned to the dining room, ready to lay the spread on the table. But the blue and black swirls on the wall kept his feet moving and he unlocked the screened-in patio instead, the idea of a romantic breakfast in the rain growing in his mind.

Her footsteps padded down the hall. With the last fluff of a cushion, she appeared in the doorway. His heart stopped as his gaze lifted, taking in one of his long-sleeved button-up shirts hanging loosely on her body.

"You're doing this on purpose," he teased, pointing to her bare legs.

"Maybe." She grinned, plopping to the seat beside him. "My suitcase was still downstairs, so I had to raid your closet. I liked this one." Tugging at the collar, she smiled and pressed her nose to the fabric.

Josh swallowed, battling the desire to remove it from her body and throw it to the floor. As he pushed a plate onto her lap instead, her eyes widened.

"Oh, yummy! I'm starving. Thanks, Joshua."

"When's the last time you ate?" Guilt revisited his gut.

She squinted, lifting her gaze to the ceiling. "Umm… a bag of pretzels on the plane."

He squeezed her knee. "I'm sorry. I've been a crappy host."

"Not your responsibility to feed me." She smiled and stuffed a spoonful of scrambled egg into her mouth. "These are really good."

"Glad you like them. They're my mom's recipe."

She nodded. "Thought they tasted familiar." Scooping the last bite of egg into her mouth, she rotated the plate.

There's no way you still eat like that.

"And how is Mrs. Susan Templeton?" She snorted. "And your dad."

"They're good. Retired now, bought a beach house in Clearwater."

"Florida?"

Josh nodded.

Mavis chewed the toast and winced at a sip of hot coffee. "I miss them." She shrugged. "But I can't imagine they feel the same way after…"

Josh sighed and snatched a pillow from the seat, squeezing it against his chest. "They knew how much you meant to me. You—and Mitch—were always part of our family. They missed you too when you left."

Her brow rose as she pushed the last bite of toast into her mouth. Nodding, she rotated her plate and smiled, her eyes darting back and forth.

What're you thinking?

"Umm, hey, Josh?" She cleared her throat. "Do you have to work or something today? I mean, I kind of just showed up at your door…"

He shook his head. "If you didn't show up at mine, I was heading to yours. I'm off through Sunday." Grinning, he pointed to her plate. "You really still eat one thing at a time, don't you?"

Her cheeks tinged pink as she stuffed a pancake in her mouth. "No sense in mixing flavors."

A smile broke free across his lips as he sipped his coffee, eyeing her closely. Her gaze skimmed the backyard as she chewed, mindlessly popping bits of pancake in her mouth. *How are you eating that dry?* He pushed the jar of syrup in her direction, but she shook her head.

"Oh! Ah, well kind of speaking of family. Are you okay with dinner at the manor tonight? Lauren is dying to see you." He scratched the back of his neck. "Even after how he acted, Mitch too. And Austin, I'm sure."

Her mouth froze, the bite of pancake wadded in her mouth. *Mitch was rude yesterday, but he wasn't that bad. Was he?*

She swallowed and set the plate down on the tray. "Umm, yeah, sounds fun."

"Well, it's not until four. We, ah… have the whole day together. What do you want to do?"

She stretched out her legs and dropped her feet on his lap.

"Back to the beach?" he asked with a squeeze of her toes.

Mavis frowned. "I think I had enough of the beach yesterday." She wrapped her arms around her body in a self-hug.

Definitely not the beach. That was a dumb suggestion.

"Right, sorry…" His voice trailed off. "Oh! Hey, I've got an idea, but you'll have to trust me." Josh picked up the poppy from the tray and handed it to Mavis.

She brought the saggy bloom to her nose and inhaled, a contented smile growing on her lips. His insides twisted as her gaze returned to his, peeking over the flower.

With a grin, she nodded.

The flashing lit-up sign for Pacific Park reflected in the windshield.

"Stupid?" He put the Jeep in park and turned to read her expression.

Her gaze circled the Ferris wheel and she grinned, identical to the two small children passing by the car on their way inside.

"Definitely not." She leaned over and pressed her lips to his cheek. "Thank you," she whispered before climbing down from the Jeep.

His heartbeat pounded faster, and a rush of adrenaline raced through his bloodstream, pulsating in tandem with his quick footsteps as he raced to catch up to her.

"The day is yours, Mavs. What's first?" he asked, waving his hand at the carnival.

"Cotton candy and the Ferris wheel—obviously."

You probably haven't experienced either since we were here last, have you?

Josh gripped her hand and led her toward the cotton candy vendor, ordering a pink puff of cloud-like sugar. His fingers stuck to the cone as he passed it off to her. *How do you eat this crap?*

"It's been so many years since I've had this," she said as a large puff of pink entered her mouth. She smirked and closed her eyes.

Josh pressed his lips to her forehead and pulled her away to the Ferris wheel line. She leaned against the weathered fence, her eyes alight with exhilaration at the upcoming ride, mindlessly stuffing bits of pink in her mouth.

"Do you remember the last time we were here?" Her gaze lifted to his.

He nodded and tucked a curl behind her ear. Sighing, he frowned. "Maybe we should have followed the others to the West Coaster after lunch."

The excitement drained from her eyes, the exuberant glow extinguishing. She shook her head, a shy smile meeting the pavement.

The line nudged forward, and the operator waved them into a car. Mavis slid in first and Josh pulled the safety rail downward on their laps. The metal clanked and the rusty screws propelled them forward, gaining height.

"Things would be so different now," he murmured "I should never have suggested we leave. I'm so sorry, Mavs." He brushed her hair behind her shoulder and pulled her body into his.

"Now who's the one always apologizing?" She smirked and pushed a bite of cotton candy into his mouth.

The sugar tingled on his tongue as his stomach dropped, falling from the car to the platform below. The memory of that day bounced around his brain. She blamed herself. But blame lived in his heart just the same. *So many what-ifs…*

"You can still see it," she said, pointing to the Hollywood sign in the distance. Her hand dropped to her lap, and she rubbed her sticky fingers against her jean shorts.

Josh squeezed her knee. "Can I ask you something?"

She nodded.

"Did you finish school?"

Her gaze fell to the floorboards. "Why? It doesn't really matter, does it?"

Josh tipped her chin upward. "It does matter."

What else did my mistake cost you?

She snorted. "Ease up, Josh. You don't need a degree to pour drinks."

He pulled his gaze from hers, raking the back of his hairline with his fingers. The car returned to the platform, and he motioned to the operator for another spin.

"I just meant…" he said hesitantly.

"I know what you meant, Joshua. You're disappointed in me. Embarrassed pro—"

"Stop right there, Duchess. Don't you dare accuse me of that." He yanked his hand from her knee and stared out over the carnival. Her penetrating gaze raked over him, needles piercing into his skin. But when he turned back, her lips resumed in a smile.

"Are we fighting?" she asked, the glow in her eyes returning.

"Yes," he murmured, battling with the muscles in his lips as they forced a grin.

She tugged at his arm, wrapping it around her shoulder. "I didn't finish school. But I would still like to. That's what you want to hear, isn't it?"

"I'd support you. Whatever you needed…"

She nodded before his mouth connected with hers. His lips moved, pressing into her soft flesh, pulling every ounce of feeling from the depths of her soul. His heart hurt. It hurt from his teenage mistakes and the consequences she suffered from his actions. It hurt for *her* and the opportunities she lost. *I'll do whatever it takes to make up for it.*

He pulled his lips from hers and pressed them to her forehead. "I loved you yesterday, I love you today, and I'll love you tomorrow, Mavis," he said with all the sincerity in his heart.

"I love you too, Joshua. That's never changed," she whispered in his ear and snuggled into his chest.

When their ride ended, Mavis rushed to the funnel cake stand. Before chasing her, though, the booth to his right caught his eye. A photo, taken moment ago at the top of the Ferris wheel, stared back. Josh eyed himself, lips connected to Mavis in a kiss of passion.

The photo represented every layer of their conversation: sorrow, blame, guilt, and blinding love. Josh bought a copy. His new photo of her—eyes still bright and a glow radiating from her body—meant to replace the one beside his bedside. New memories created, new memories together, memories that held promise for the future he had planned.

CHAPTER SIXTEEN

Austin

Austin shuffled the mass of papers on his desk into a manilla file folder, the Boyd & Bernstein at Law logo stamped in black ink at the top left corner. Scratching his pen across the surface, he wrote *Tabitha Felton* and dropped it into the left drawer of his desk. His gaze caught the reflection of the afternoon sun, illuminating the thirteen-story view of Los Angeles from his corner office at the law firm.

Boyd, Bernstein & Templeton at Law...

"One day," he murmured to the empty room, dropping his pen on the desk with a grin.

Austin sighed and closed the open tabs on his computer. *The Funny Part*'s website stared back, his eyes skimming the silly cat story once more. "E. Banks," he said with a smirk, contemplating the strange pen name. *It has to be you, Mavis. It's your story. I know it.*

Closing the laptop, he leaned back, resigning himself to ask her about it this evening. The chair creaked beneath his weight, and he swiveled his body left to right, right to left. Shaking his head, Austin stuffed down the rising bout of affection bubbling to the surface. Forbidden love bloomed in his heart as his mind returned to the Chicago hotel room six years ago.

Her hands raced along his skin, her fingernails digging into his flesh. Ragged breath sounded in his ear, moans turning to cries of mounting passion. She'd been wild that night, bending to every will his body desired.

Austin brushed the back of his hand across his forehead, sweat coating his skin. *You felt something for me that night, that's for sure.*

He willed the memory away. Guilt soured his empty stomach, and he reluctantly stood from his desk and collected his things, dreading the impending dinner party. Mitch was still mad at him, Josh he hid secrets from, Mavis he secretly loved… and Lauren. *The only safe place this evening.* With a sigh, he tapped the light switch and left the office, sneaking down the back stairwell.

His shoes squeaked across the tile as he crossed through the main lobby of City Hall and entered the parking garage. The engine of his black Corvette purred to life, and he inched out of his parking space, pulling into the line of stop-and-go traffic. His foot alternated—right petal, go—left petal, stop. Anxiety gripped him, recognizing the parallel it drew. *Tell her you love her. Stuff your feelings down. Tell her you love her. Stuff your feelings down.*

Within minutes, his tires met the interstate and he sped along faster than the speed limit allowed, ready to leave the stop-and-go traffic and indecisiveness behind him in the endless line of cars. The city view disappeared, and the rolling hills of Rosewood met his gaze. He turned into the manor's driveway, parking behind Mitch's truck. *Ready or not…*

"You're early."

Exiting the car, Austin spun, his attention landing on his brother-in-law. Mitch tugged a piece of plywood from the garage and attempted to heave it over the bed of his truck.

"I wanted the first crack at Lauren's chip dip," answered

Austin, grabbing the sagging side of the board and boosting it over the truck bed. It thumped against the plastic.

Mitch smirked. "She's in there stirring something. You might be in luck." He stepped away, his feet aiming for the garage. Austin followed, watching as he began sorting a pile of tools on the work bench.

Apologize. Do it now.

"Mitch, I'm sorry," he said, handing him a drill. "I should never have kept Mavis from you. I was wrong, and I should have told you the truth a long time ago. It was your decision to make, not mine... and I'm sorry." The words tumbled from his lips as his elbow upended a box of nails. They scattered across the workbench, and Austin mindlessly picked at them, tossing them one by one back into the box.

Mitch waved his hand as if pushing the apology aside. "I know why you did what you did, and to be honest..." A screwdriver clanged to the floor at Austin's touch, hiding beneath the tool chest. Mitch sighed. "I don't know that I would have done anything even if I knew where she was."

Austin bent to the floor and retrieved the screwdriver, returning it to its home on the bench. He picked up an Allen wrench set next and looped the ring around his finger, spinning the tool without care. "Really?" he asked, furrowing his brow. The wrench met the workbench with a clang.

"Yes. Really," said Mitch, pulling the tool from Austin's grasp with an eye roll. "Come on. Chip dip, remember?"

He followed his brother-in-law into the house and down the hallway to the kitchen, Lauren's head appearing from behind a mixing bowl.

"Shit, is it four already?" she asked, panic in her eyes as she glanced at the clock.

"No, I'm early." Pulling out the barstool from beneath the counter, he dropped his weight into the seat. "Can I help with anything?"

She shook her head, placing the bowl on the surface. "Umm... not that I can think of. Mitch?"

He pushed a bottle of gin and a shot glass down the counter under Lauren's nose.

Austin untwisted the cap and grinned. "Now this I can help with."

Lauren rolled her eyes. "Seriously, guys? You can't face Mavis and Josh without hard liquor?"

"Cheers," answered Austin, raising his full shot glass to his sister's face. *If you only knew the truth.* The liquid burned his throat on the way down and he choked out a dry cough.

"How about Long Islands tonight?" Mitch stuffed his head in the corner cabinet. Pulling out bottles of vodka and tequila, he tapped them together.

"Works for me," he said as he poured himself another shot of gin.

Lauren huffed out a breath and dumped her chip dip onto a platter. She pushed a bag of chips in Austin's direction. "Here. Before you can't think straight. Taste test."

He dipped a chip and grinned when his mom's secret cream cheese recipe met his tongue. "Pairs well with gin."

She snorted and moved to the sink to wash her hands.

"I'm joking, Lauren." He tilted his head to the side. "It's good. It always is."

Mitch pushed a mason jar of a Long Island iced tea in his direction. "Does this pair well with gin too?" he asked, sampling from his own cup.

Austin raised the glass to his lips and swallowed, the instant euphoria clouding his brain. He tugged at his tie and cast it aside on the counter, popping a few buttons at his collar for good measure.

"When you boys are done *taste testing*, can you please open the umbrella and make sure the cushions are clean out there?" She gestured to the patio.

Austin held up a finger. "One more before you put me to work." He emptied his Long Island and pushed the empty glass back at Mitch. "Ready?"

Mitch nodded and gulped down his cup. Following in Austin's footsteps, he snagged the bottle of gin on the way out the door.

The afternoon sun warmed his face as he stepped outdoors, the gentle ocean breeze tickling his skin. Austin bent to fluff a red cushion and brushed a bug from the seat. Straightening, he turned his gaze to Mitch as he switched on the twinkle lights and cranked open the umbrella.

"Can I ask you something?" he asked, mid-cushion-fluff. Mitch nodded. "You saw Mavis yesterday, right?"

"Yeah…"

"How was she?"

"What do you mean?"

"Was she like… *into* Josh? Do you think they're back together? Like, still in love?"

Mitch wrinkled his nose. "Well, yeah. I mean, I guess? They seemed into each other." He shrugged. "Austin, she's my sister. I don't really know how to answer this." He pulled his gaze away, focusing his attention on the one twinkle light that didn't turn on. "Why do you care?" he asked, untwisting the bulb.

"No reason. Just curious." Austin plopped into a seat at the patio table, deflating the cushion he just fluffed.

"What's your deal with her, man? All these secrets and keeping in touch with her all this time behind our backs. What gives?" Mitch's eyes tore into his soul as Austin's heart stilled.

He hiccupped, the taste of gin revisiting his mouth. "It's nothing." *Lies. Lies. Lies.* His cheeks reddened, anxiety fueling his bloodstream.

Mitch rolled his eyes and raised a brow. "Okay, sure." He pushed the gin across the table and Austin snagged it, twisting the cap. "Whatever." He huffed out a breath. "But Austin… if there is something between you two, just be careful. Josh isn't going to appreciate you being in the middle."

"Well, he should have considered that ten years ago before he…" Defensiveness gripped his heart.

"Before he what?" Mitch's knee bumped the table as he

sat down. He rubbed at it but kept his eyes on Austin. "What the hell happened? What do you know?"

Austin shook his head. "It's not my secret to tell."

And God knows I have too many secrets to keep.

CHAPTER SEVENTEEN

Mavis

"How are you?"

Casey exhaled, her breath crackling through the speaker of the phone. "All good, Mavs. But I'm not the one who hopped a red-eye out of O'Hare. What the hell happened? I came home from Shaker to a post-it note on the fridge."

Mavis cringed, her hasty decision churning in her gut. "I'm sorry, Case." Her gaze drifted to the floor, zeroing in on a tiny bubble-gum-pink stain beside Josh's nightstand. "Umm... really spur of the moment decision." *Is that nail polish?*

"I mean, yeah, girl! But tell me everything! What's happening? Where are you? Have you seen Josh? What about Austin?" Casey sucked in a breath as the questions tumbled from her lips, like lava spewing from a volcano.

Mavis snickered, imagining Casey's flailing arms back in their Chicago apartment, each question punctuated by a body part sailing through the air. As she fell backward onto Josh's bed, his scent touched her nose, a sense of calm encasing her soul.

"Where do I even start?" she murmured, her gaze

meeting the pillow. It still held the indent from their resting heads. "But Casey, you first. Please. Are you feeling okay?"

Casey cleared her throat. "Umm... yeah... for sure. Like I said before, it's just really weird to talk about it. Embarrassing..." Her voice trailed off.

"I know. And really, I'm not trying to pry. I just want to make sure you're okay. Did you make an appointment to see your doctor?"

"Well, I mean, not yet."

Mavis rolled her eyes and exhaled.

"But I will. I promise."

No, you won't.

"I'll go with you," she offered, pulling her body back to a sitting position. She squinted, her gaze landing on the corners of a crumpled envelope on the nightstand. She reached for it, her fingertips numbing at the touch as her loopy handwriting greeted her again. Her chest ached, stilling the beat of her heart, frozen in place. *You saved it, Josh?*

"No way. Like you need to sit with me in another room with no pants on."

Mavis uncrumpled the envelope as the letter dropped to her lap. *My dearest Joshua* may as well have been tattooed to her thigh, the words branding her skin, burning with the fire of Hell itself. With a quick flip of her wrist, she brushed the offending note to the floor.

"Mavs, are you there?" Casey's voice wafted through the airway, pulling at the shreds of sanity still clinging to her brain.

"Sorry, Casey! I, umm... dropped my phone for a second," she lied.

"All good. But seriously, I'm dying to know, have you seen Josh yet?"

Josh's soulful eyes awoke in her mind, his sweet smile tugging at her heartstrings. She grinned and ran her fingers over his pillow.

"Yeah, I have."

"Mavis! Oh, my God! Tell me everything! What did he say? Did he like forgive you and stuff?" Her voice rose an octave, and Mavis held the phone away from her ear.

Forgive me? Uncertainty stirred in her stomach, confusion mixing with the carnival food. Josh had been unrelenting with his admission of love and willingness to move forward within the last twenty-four hours, a whirlwind of second chances. Her brain fogged, trying to grasp at the shreds of truth. *But he doesn't know the full story.*

"Case, hey umm, maybe we can talk about everything when I get back on Sunday, okay?"

"It's Austin, isn't it? Did he tell Josh what you guys did or something?"

The air left her lungs as if a vacuum had been jammed down her throat, sucking her body dry of oxygen. Casey's words—even though unintended— were a sucker punch to the gut. The mere mention of Austin's name sparked fireworks in her stomach. *And now I'm an hour away from sitting in between them both, in the same room, at the same party.*

From the bottom of the stairs, Josh called her name. *Shit. Less than an hour.*

"Umm… no he didn't say anything, but Casey, I actually do have to go. I promise, I'll fill you in on the details when I get home, okay?" Mavis bent to the floor and picked up the letter, ramming it back into the crinkled envelope. She rested it against the lamp where she found it and frowned. *Why didn't you throw it away?*

"Oh, fine. Leave me hanging."

"I love you. I'll talk to you soon."

"Love you back." Casey ended the call, and Mavis dropped the phone on the bed. With her next inhale, the fireworks in her stomach exploded.

The dread and anxiety burning beneath her skin's surface sizzled, a layer of sweat glistening across her brow. Mavis angled the vents in her direction, allowing the cool air to fan her frying skin.

"You're really pale. Do you feel okay?" asked Josh. His gaze left the road as he reached for a bottle of water in the middle console. He stretched it out in her direction.

"Just nervous, I guess." She accepted the water and twisted the cap, the cool liquid sliding down her throat.

"Don't be. Everyone just wants to see you. It's not just me who missed you, Mavs." He flipped on the turn signal and pulled into the Templeton Manor driveway.

Mavis stared out the window, the familiar path pulling forth the memories of her youth. The Victorian mansion emerged—unchanged and unwavering—standing tall before her eyes. Time may have passed, but the same willow trees dropped their long leaves, waving to her in the gentle breeze with a welcome home.

Josh parked and cut the engine, the cool air from the vents falling away as the breath escaped her lungs. *Please let there be alcohol.*

"We're a little early. Do you want to take a walk first?" His fingers squeezed her knee as pink tinged his cheeks.

The meadow.

The uncertainty returned, descending on her body like a sudden summer rainstorm—cold pelts of water dropping from the sky to meet her skin. *First the beach, then Pacific Park… and now the meadow.*

Fear gripped her heart as Josh leaned in to press his lips against her cheek.

"I mean, unless you don't want to. We could go grab a coffee or something instead. It's still early."

My sweet Joshua. You're trying so hard.

"No, it's okay, a walk sounds really nice. Let's go." She opened the door and hopped down from the Jeep. Her gaze caught sight of a black Corvette with a license plate that read LAW4YOU parked on the opposite side of the driveway. Slamming the Jeep's door, she rolled her eyes.

Geez, Austin, a bit pretentious?

Josh rested his hand on her back, guiding her forward

until the trees crept closer, the wild forest coming into view. Her feet sank into the damp earth as they ducked into the brush along the familiar path. Time may have moved forward, but the worn path lived on as they trudged forward.

"Have you gone back at all?"

The image of him standing alone in the meadow squeezed her heart. She breathed in, circulating the moist air through her lungs.

"To the Lonely Mountain?"

She grinned. "You know what I mean."

"Just once," he answered, a shy smile appearing on his lips. "Like two weeks ago." Josh stopped walking and bent to scratch his ankle, tugging a stray piece of grass from his shoe.

Behind him, the meadow called. Searching for the orange blossoms in the distance, her stomach dropped on the mid-December day. *No wild poppies.*

Cupping the back of his neck, Josh rubbed at the muscle on his left shoulder before tugging her further into the forest. "It doesn't look the same, but it feels..." He grabbed her hand and pulled her forward until their toes met the line drawn by the forest floor. "Well, you'll see."

A knife pierced her heart. The truth was written among the trees, infused in the earth. Each breath of wind whispered, pressing the memories of their past into the depths of their souls. Tears pooled in her eyes as the crows in the treetops welcomed them back to their meadow, to the place of dreams that started the nightmare.

Our meadow.

The tips of her toes pressed into the mud, the precipice before her. One step would carry her body over the threshold and into the brittle grass and overgrown bed of nature.

Josh stilled beside her as heartache consumed her chest. The air in her lungs caught in her throat, confined to an internal prison. She swallowed. *I can't do it.*

The tears pooling in her eyes crashed the floodgates, and she lifted her hands to cover her face, wrestling internally with her inability to take Josh's hand and dance in the meadow again.

His arms consumed her, drawing her body into his—each muscle working to bring their souls together. Mavis pressed her nose to his chest, inhaling the faint scent of funnel cake still clinging to his t-shirt.

"Mavis… Mavis… Mavis…" Josh cooed in her ear.

With each sympathetic whisper from the man beside her, guilt set up a permanent residence in her heart, nail by nail. Guilt over running away. Guilt over losing their child. Guilt over her betrayal with Austin.

Guilt.

Just guilt.

"I gotta get out of here, Joshua," she whispered, pulling herself away from his warm embrace. She marched away, stumbling through the brush without a look back.

She wasn't ready.

The meadow wasn't ready.

Mavis rounded the corner of the manor, her feet meeting the pavement again. Opening the door to Josh's Jeep, she snagged her purse and rummaged through the contents for a tissue. Josh silently loomed, each hand rammed deep in his pockets. He hadn't said a word on the walk back. *I've ruined this, haven't I?* She dabbed at her eyes. *What is wrong with me?*

"I'm sorry, Duchess," he whispered. "I shouldn't have suggested we go back there." His feet shuffled beneath him, kicking a stray stone into the tulip beds. "I should have realized what feelings that would stir up…"

You have no idea, but guilt tops my list.

Mavis sucked in a deep breath and stepped toward him. Folding her body back into his, she released a sigh.

"Please don't apologize." She slipped her fingers into the

belt loops of his shorts. "I'm... I don't know... it's just weird being back here. It's harder than I thought."

"Do you want me to cancel tonight?"

"No." Mavis shook her head and pulled away, patting her cheeks dry. "I'm good, I swear. No more tears."

Josh pecked her on the lips and nodded, clasping his hand in hers as their feet stepped forward. The front porch came into view. *Nothing's changed.* Each tulip in place, the faded wood on the porch swing, even the rose bushes pruned to perfection.

Don't cry again. Don't cry again.

They climbed the short staircase, the wooden steps creaking beneath their weight. A breeze rocked the swing—back and forth, back and forth—each rusted screw squeaking with age.

Josh's arms wrapped around her, his warmth descending on her skin as she leaned into his inviting embrace. Her mind played tricks on her, blending the past with the present as she recalled the last memory they shared together in this place, another moment in time.

The ghost of her feet springing from the wooden steps crashed into the stillness of the air, and Mavis rammed her eyes closed, forcing back the tears burning behind her eyelids.

His grip tightened. "If I had known, I would have held on to you this tight that day too," he murmured, pressing his lips to her forehead.

Well, that'll do it. The dam burst and the well-traveled path of tears on her cheeks glistened again. She pressed her face into his chest, willing his arms to never drop from her body.

The screen door whined behind them, biting into the still moment of the memory.

"I feel like I time-traveled," Lauren said as she held the door open.

"Lauren." Mavis forced her feet to move, pulling away from Josh. Falling into the outstretched arms of her long-lost friend, Mavis closed her eyes and squeezed. Her hair smelled of banana bread, the aroma gripping her nose as she clung to the sister-like girl from her youth.

"I can't believe you're home! Damn, Mavs... we missed you!"

From over Lauren's shoulder, Mavis eyed the growing grin on Josh's lips. He dipped his hands back in his pockets and rocked backward on his heels. "*See!*" he mouthed.

Swaying back and forth in a tight bear hug, Lauren whispered, "I think my brother really missed you."

The black Corvette in the driveway glistened in the afternoon sun directly behind Josh. The sight of it poked pins in her skin as goosebumps erupted on her forearms. *Which brother?*

Mavis pulled away and wrapped her body into a self-hug as the question soured her stomach. She forced a polite smile on her lips as her gaze returned to Lauren.

A squeeze on her shoulder jolted her heart. Gasping for breath, she turned, meeting the identical shade of green eyes as her own.

"Welcome home." Mitch tugged her into his arms with a gentle squeeze. Her nose pressed into his shirt, inhaling the soft scent of pine—and gin. "I'm sorry. I came on too strong yesterday," he continued, hanging his head until his dark hair fell into his eyes. "Forgive me?"

A new form of guilt settled in her chest, pressing against her heart as Mitch released her body. The image of a laundry basket flitted across her mind, stirring the regret and sadness swelling in her stomach.

"Mitch... I, umm..." *That hug wasn't nearly enough.* Gripping him around the middle, she leaned back into his arms, the presence of protection encasing her soul as the streak of independence she'd been forced to live behind sank deep into her skin. "I'm the one who's sorry," she muttered as his arms tightened around her.

Her eyes closed, and she released a breath into his chest until the tingle on her elbow detonated a bomb in her gut.

The mystery fingertips on her skin turned to knives, carving and digging into her flesh. The combination scent of sandalwood and gin engulfed her, and the sense of calm resting on her heart evaporated.

His warm palm grasped her bicep, tugging her from Mitch's body. A net encased her, and an unexplainable force jerked her soul until it tumbled into the very vault of secrets she'd sealed a decade ago. Falling into Austin's arms, her heart incinerated at his touch. Fire blazed through her blood until his icy blue eyes smothered the flames.

His gin-soaked breath tickled her ear. "Mmm…" he purred. Gripping her neck, his fingers discreetly tugged at the silver chain beneath her hair. "So fragile," he whispered. Winking, his smattering of white eyelashes caught in the sun as he released her.

Her head swam; fog crept into her mind and blanketed her brain. The sounds around her diminished, each noise muffled against the thick cover coating her body. The ring in her ears intensified as the blood rushed from her head.

"Gin and tonic, Princess?" he called over his shoulder, stepping inside.

Mavis shuddered. Sweat glistened on her brow, each heartbeat in her chest growing louder and banging against her ribcage. She swallowed, gulping down a deep breath as the air cleared around her, the alcohol fumes disappearing.

A squeeze on her waist coaxed her back to life, the sounds around her rising to the forefront of her mind. The fog lifted, wafting away like the tide rolling back into the sea.

Josh's voice grounded her. "What did he just say to you?" His nose crinkled as his gaze followed his twin deeper into the house. Clasping his fingers around the heart charm of her necklace, he frowned.

"Oh, umm… he just said the necklace looked familiar or something." She pulled a hand through her hair and brushed her palm against her forehead. "Is it hot in here?" she asked, fanning herself.

Mitch stepped forward and nudged Lauren in the back.

"Come on, let's head out to the patio. It's cooler back there, and I made some Long Islands." He snagged his wife's hand and pulled. "And Peaches made chip dip."

They walked the length of the memory-laden manor and exited through the back door. A full-page spread plucked from *Better Homes & Gardens* greeted Mavis as she stepped outside and dropped into a red cushioned chair. Appetizers filled the table before her, twinkle lights glittered above her head, and a stocked bar cart rested to her left. *Jackpot.*

"Are you okay?" Josh murmured in her ear as he sat in the chair to her right, squeezing her knee.

"Oh, yeah... sorry, guess I'm not used to the heat," she answered, reaching forward to accept the Long Island Mitch pushed in her direction. The ice clanked against the glass as she brought it to her lips.

Austin snorted. "Heat?" His butt sank to the yellow cushion on her left. *Literally caught in the middle.* "It's like seventy-five degrees."

Mavis gulped, sucking down the brown liquid. "And blizzarding in Chicago, I'm sure." She set her glass down and leaned back. The ocean air filtered through her lungs, a taste of salt lingering on her tongue.

Austin pushed a bowl in her direction. "Chip dip?" A mischievous grin grew along his lips as he dipped a chip and inserted it into his mouth, his tongue catching a stray bit of cream cheese.

Her skin tingled, the tips of her fingers numbing. She shook her head and lifted her gaze from his mouth, hurling aside the memories the flick of his tongue incited. Her body warmed over again, and she lifted the hair from the nape of her neck, twisting it into a braid. *Don't look at him. Don't look at him. Don't look at him. Find something else...*

"Lauren, umm... this food looks amazing. Josh tells me you own a restaurant now, right?"

"Yeah, I do! Pier Ninety-two." She beamed and sliced the banana bread. "It's been my baby for a few years now."

"What does Pier Ninety-two mean?"

Lauren nodded, a smile cracking her lips as she chewed. "Well… it's not too far from the Santa Monica Pier, so that part was easy to name. And the ninety-two…" She giggled. "Austin, you tell her. You named it."

Begrudgingly, Mavis spun her head, heat washing over her body again at Austin's playful grin. "Ninety-two?"

Austin dunked another chip and tossed it in his mouth. "It's the average amount of hours you sit in traffic each year in L.A."

Her eyes widened. "Oh, shit… I mean, Chicago is cold, but…" She shrugged and drained her cup, crunching the ice at the bottom. "I can at least walk to work."

Mitch snagged her glass and refilled it. "So… Chicago," he said, leaning back into his seat. "What do you do there?"

"Like my job?"

Mitch nodded.

"I bartend, just a restaurant in Wrigleyville called The Broken Shaker." She dropped her gaze, examining the contents of her glass, embarrassed of the words spilling from her lips as she sat surrounded by success. "I mean, it's not much, but it pays the bills."

Josh squeezed her knee, but the willpower to lift her gaze to his sympathetic smile lacked.

"But that's not all you do, is it, E. Banks?" asked Austin, leaning forward to rest his elbows on the table. His knee knocked into her own beneath the table, and an electric jolt shocked her heart like a bolt of lightning striking metal. *How do you know that?*

Mavis shook her head as her cheeks reddened in the late afternoon sun. "I… umm… lost a bet. My roommate Casey published that story. Not me," she admitted.

Austin cocked his head. "The blonde?"

"Umm, yeah…" *How the hell do you remember that? You met her for like two seconds!*

"What're you guys talking about?" asked Lauren.

"Oh! The cat story!" Mitch slapped his knee and snorted. "Damn, I knew it was familiar! That was you?"

Mavis giggled. "Just something dumb from high school. But, umm… my roommate, Casey found it and submitted it to her favorite magazine. I still can't believe they published it." The glass met her lips again as the tea slid down her throat, each gulp offering a dizzying freedom from the conversation.

"What was the bet?" asked Josh, reaching over to snag her hand.

She grinned. "Crosstown Classic. The Cubs pulled out a win in the ninth and Mamelda got submitted to *The Funny Part.*"

"The Cubs… so E. Banks…" Austin scratched his chin and smirked. "Is Ernie Banks."

Mavis nodded. "Mr. Cub."

Their eyes connected, an invisible game of tug-of-war pulling at her heartstrings. Her stomach dipped, sloshing the tea in her gut, and she forcefully tore her eyes away before his tongue raked his lips again. *Pull yourself together, Mavis!*

Austin chuckled and pushed his glass across the table to Mitch. "Well hell, bartending skills run in the family."

"Austin, you really might want to slow down," cooed Lauren, swatting at a mosquito near her ear.

Mitch waved her off and refilled the glass. "Oh, lay off. Let him do what he wants, *mom.*"

"Come on, Lauren! Tonight's a celebration. Mavs came home." He swallowed a gulp of tea, dropping the cup to the table with a bang. "And by the look of it…" Austin pointed to Josh's hand wrapped around her own. "The *full* truth is out in the open. Welcome back to Rosewood, Princess."

He winked, and the bottom of her stomach dropped to the patio floor.

Fuck. Fuck. Fuck.

Mitch placed another empty pitcher of Long Islands on the bar cart, the glass bottom scratching the surface. He winced at the screech. "Sorry," he muttered.

"How many is that?" asked Lauren with a chip on the way to her mouth. She rubbed her eyes and stretched her arms upward.

"Lost count." Mitch chuckled and pulled the hair back from his face.

The air cooled as darkness crept along the patio. The twinkle lights glittered above, and the lightning bugs glowed beneath the setting sun.

Mavis's head swirled with a cloud of fog, her brother's magical tea toying with her brain. *Damn, I have to pee!* Rising from her seat, she swayed on the spot.

Josh gripped her around the middle. "Whoa! Are you okay?" He snickered and leaned forward in his seat to steady her.

"Umm… yeah, I'm good," she slurred with a giggle. "Just have to pee." Forcing her feet to move, she shuffled across the patio.

The quiet and calm of the house quelled the anxiety racing through her bloodstream. Her fingers danced along the walls of the hallway as she headed for the powder room. With a click of the lock and a flip of a switch, her reflection stared back in the small space. At first, her smudged eyeliner and messy hair drew her attention, but then her gaze deepened. An independent woman looked back—a force to be reckoned with—no longer the girl that Rosewood remembered. *There you are.*

She sighed and splashed water on her face, the momentary streak of confidence vanishing as quickly as the tap turned off. *What're you even thinking? You've had way too much to drink.*

After relieving herself, she returned to the sink and washed her hands. The soap smelled of jasmine, the floral scent filling the room with an unparalleled potency as the last forty-eight hours raged through her mind—and her heart—the soothing fragrance wrapping around her soul. A sense of calm enveloped her at the thought of Joshua, his sweet smile and unwavering sense of comfort and safety bending her mind and swallowing her heart whole. The love of her life returned with a giant red bow, eager to sweep her off her feet.

But then there was his brother, the blond with the pretentious grin and wild streak of excitement. The keeper of her dirty secrets and the link to home she never knew she needed. His blue eyes carved a knife into the comfort and sliced into the safety.

Mavis shuddered and willed away the confusion surfacing at the thought. *Just get through this party. That's all you have to do right now. Just get through tonight.*

Her fingers clicked the lock and twisted the door handle. With a flip of the light switch, her toes touched the hallway floor as her heart lodged in her throat. The icy blue eyes from her mind pierced the darkness.

"Fuck, Austin!" She clutched her heart, each beat pounding with rapid fire. "You scared the shit out of me!" Her hands grazed his chest with a gentle push. "What're you doing?" Scanning the dark hallway, only the soft murmur of voices from the patio filtered back. *Alone. Completely alone.*

His hand covered hers, pressing her fingertips into the beat of his heart. "Do you feel that?" he whispered. *Thump. Thump. Thump.* His breath tickled her neck, each exhale tinged with gin. *Bump. Bump. Bump.* A squeeze on her waist sent her body falling forward, crashing into Austin's arms like the inevitable way day falls into night.

His mouth collided with hers, and the grip on her body tightened. Her back hit the wall as Austin pinned her in place, left powerless to move nothing more than her lips. A devilish desire erupted in her gut, the warmth cascading around her body as fire flared beneath her skin.

What am I doing? Make this stop! Her brain screamed what her body refused to obey. Austin's hands cradled the back of her head, tugging at her curls as his lips moved against her own.

Abruptly, he pulled away, his mouth falling from hers. "Don't deny it, Mavs. There's something here and you know it," he whispered.

The gleam in his eyes jarred her, the drunken memories from their Chicago hotel room slamming into her brain as they awoke from their six-year slumber.

*

"Do you ever think about that night in my dorm room?"

Austin stood at the mini bar, mixing another round of gin and tonics. His untucked shirt hung loosely at his waist, the knot on his tie looping around his neck by a thread.

The empty cups on the table outnumbered the ones left back at the bar; the early evening hours had flown by in a nostalgic whirl. The city of Chicago awoke beneath them as they stared out from the twelfth floor of the Palmer House Hilton.

With her legs curled beneath her, Mavis tucked her feet into the cracks of the couch cushions. Her brain swirled in a haze of gin as Austin's weight sank into the seat beside her. As he handed her a drink, his gaze settled on hers.

"Yeah, I do. Not really my best moment," she answered, the tip of her glass meeting her lips. She winced. Damn, you make strong drinks!

His hand, cold from the glass, rested on her bare thigh, and he squeezed her skin, sympathy softening his face. Mavis followed the trail of his fingers as they roamed, tracing the freckles that marked her skin. She shivered at his gentle touch, denying the tightening his actions stirred in her groin.

"I think about it a lot, but not for the same reasons you might."

Setting his drink on the table, his attention turned to the bold movements of his fingers as they journeyed up her leg. The tip of his thumb traced circles in her skin, sending waves of heat racing up and down her spine. She breathed in deeply, and Austin took her drink, placing it alongside his on the table.

He leaned into her body. "I think about what it felt like to have you beneath me," he purred. His lips met the delicate skin on her neck. "And I think about how it felt to have your lips on mine…" His mouth met hers as he playfully nipped her bottom lip. "But mostly, I think about what it felt like to be inside you."

Her eyes popped open, met with an icy blue stare. His piercing gaze played with her heart, stirring unexplored desires in the depths of her soul.

"Austin…"

His lips crashed into hers, longing spilling from her core as his hands squeezed her hips and pulled her into his lap. Numbness crept into her toes as her skin tingled. What are we doing? Yanking the tie from his neck, Mavis tore at his shirt until his bare torso greeted her needy fingers. The masculine scent of his skin impaled her nose, mixing with the alcohol fumes suffocating the stale hotel air.

With a tug of her skirt, the material dropped to the floor and his fingers dipped below her panties. A carnal desire awakened at his touch, the buttons to her blouse bursting from the fabric in his quest to remove the remaining barriers to her naked body.

"What're we doing?" she sputtered between ragged breaths. Her hands glided over his body, the sheen of his sweat mixing with her own. Her fingertips shook as she tugged at the zipper on his pants.

He grinned and yanked the material away, pressing his newly naked arousal into her belly. "Having another sleepover," he whispered.

Mavis giggled as he scooped her body up and carried her across the room. Dropping her to the mattress, he nudged her backward until her head hit the pillow. "Spread your legs, Princess."

In the dim lighting, his voracious gaze raked over her. Releasing a breath, he slid inside of her as a wicked grin consumed his face. Relishing the moans spilling from her lips, he moved in and out.

Blood pounded in her ears, a tightening sensation pulling at her insides—pinpricks of pleasure. Playfully biting her lower lip, Austin sighed.

"I've always wanted you," he breathed. "Always…" And then his pace increased.

She climaxed as his silky voice dissolved into her soul.

Somehow, maybe I always have, too.

*

"Don't lie to yourself, Mavis. I know you think you want Josh, but you want me just as badly." He tucked a curl behind her ear. "You remember us in Chicago. What it felt like to be together... you remember the passion and the excitement. Consider this my intent to play—and win."

Austin leaned forward and cupped her chin. His teeth nibbled her bottom lip like they had so many years ago before his lips fully met hers. A flurry of confusion rippled through her body. *This shouldn't feel good! This isn't right!*

Clarity beat at her brain, overriding the physical arousal he'd awakened. *What the fuck am I doing?*

Her hands pushed at his chest, and he stumbled backward.

"Back off, Austin. Back off now! You can pocket your ego because I have no interest in this. Our past means nothing. Chicago meant nothing. It was a drunken mistake. Just like this is!" She dragged her hands across her cheeks and wiped her mouth. "I'm in love with Joshua, and that won't ever change—ever."

She brushed past him, anger fueling each step until a faint whisper touched her ear. "Keep telling yourself that, Princess, but the wetness between your legs says otherwise."

"Fucking asshole," she spit back before rounding the corner.

But you're not wrong.

JULIE NAVICKAS

CHAPTER EIGHTEEN

Josh

His head throbbed with an angry ache as consciousness called. The Long Islands of last evening drilled into his skull, a jackhammer to his brain. Josh squinted in the brilliant sunshine flooding the bedroom.

He rolled, shielding his eyes, and met Mavis nose to nose on the pillow they shared. Still in yesterday's clothing, she didn't stir, but the tips of her dark curls tickled his cheeks as he brushed them away. Behind her, the clock on the nightstand read 11:27AM, and the momentary dip in his gut at the late hour had him considering a sprint to the bathroom to upend last night's liquid diet. *Is it that late already?*

Josh rubbed his forehead, kneading his temples to release the built-up tension. He struggled recalling the return ride home. Yawning with the air of a twenty-one-year-old who partied too hard the night before, his gaze fell to the woman beside him.

Her chest rose and fell with each breath—rhythmic and predictable. And the pink on her cheeks filled his body with warmth, the rosy glow speeding the rate of his heart.

"I still can't believe you're back, Mavs," he whispered to her sleeping form. His fingers pinched the charm on her necklace and then dropped it from his grasp. It tumbled away, resting on her rising and falling chest.

Contentment encased his soul, the last ten years of his life slowly dripping away from the ache long surrounding his heart. In every way, the woman beside him completed his very existence—two halves of one whole—united in love on the path of second chances.

With a smile, Josh stumbled from the bed and padded softly to the bathroom. He eased on the shower and stepped into the warmth as the hot water pelted his skin. It soothed his aching temples and brought life back to his exhausted body.

Last night's reunion danced through his mind. As expected, Lauren had been a gracious host, welcoming Mavis home as if the last ten years hadn't happened. While he'd had his initial reservations about Mitch, he'd behaved himself and refrained from prodding questions. *I'm not ready for everyone to know the details just yet.*

The bar of soap slipped from his fingers. As he bent down to retrieve it, his twin swam to the forefront of his mind. Josh's chest tightened, a tingle of unease rippling along his spine for reasons unable to put into words. *Something's off…*

Twisting the faucet, he stepped from the shower and toweled off, considering the disquiet. Resolving to call Austin to sift through the unease further, Josh left the bathroom and tossed on clean shorts. With a click of the bedroom door, he left Mavis behind.

His feet tiptoed across the wooden floor of the foyer, the cold tile of the kitchen piercing his skin before he slid onto a barstool. Josh picked up his phone and sighed; seven missed calls, two voicemails, and eight unread text messages. *Tess.*

"Why the fuck?" he muttered to the empty room with an eye roll. The nausea his stomach awakened to returned with vigor, and he swallowed the taste of disgust rising in his throat. *What can you possibly want?*

The doorbell bit into the silence of the house. "Please don't let it be her…" Josh groaned and slumped from his seat, the high likelihood of his ex-wife standing on the opposite side of the door gripping his gut. "Please don't let it be her…" he repeated as his hand touched the doorknob. With a twist of his wrist, Tess's teary face looked back.

"Josh!" Her arms encircled his middle, pressing her damp face into his chest.

Resentment built in his heart as he breathed out the sickening scent of her perfume. With an exhale, he unraveled her arms and stepped backward.

"Tess, I don't know why you're here, but I have an intense hangover, and any conversation we share is guaranteed to make it worse." He pressed his fingers to his temples.

Tears pooled in her eyes, thick black streaks of mascara traveling down her face. With the back of her hand, she wiped her nose.

"Dalton left me."

A swell of amusement crashed through his body as her words fell from her pink lips. *Oh, Karma's a bitch, isn't it?* A grin tugged at the corner of his mouth, each muscle in his face working to hold back the bubble of laughter threatening escape. "That is absolutely not my problem."

She nodded and hung her head. "I made a terrible mistake, Josh. Can we please talk?"

Her perfectly manicured fingernails tapped the mahogany door, and a hot pink Barbie-like heel crossed the threshold into the foyer. The click of her heel on the wood scraped against his ears like nails on a chalkboard.

"No way. I have absolutely no interest in speaking to you or learning about Dalton Sheppard's wisest decision to date."

The breath caught in her throat. "But Joshua," she whined, pulling her blonde hair away from her face and tucking it behind her ears.

"First, don't call me that. And second, you can't be serious right now!" Josh furrowed his brow and dragged his palms across his cheeks with a snicker. *You're crazier than I thought!*

"Please! I just want to talk."

He snorted, swallowing a belly of hilarity.

"Tess, when I wanted to talk, you were naked in our neighbor's bed. We're divorced. It's over. There's not one thing left in the world that you and I need to talk about."

"But there is, Josh!" Her hand stretched outward, grazing the skin on the back of his hand. "I was wrong. All of it is my fault." She sniffled. "But... I think there's a way you and I could be happy again. Just give me a ch—"

"Fuck no." His head throbbed between each word of her weak apology.

Her lips pursed, the thin line of pink disappearing into her mouth entirely. "But we've been through so much together!" Her hands balanced on her hips.

"Past tense, Tess. It's all in the past. Every part of it."

"What if it's not though? I know we had a few rough years but think of the way we started." Her nails trailed along his chest as she fully stepped inside the house. "*I* picked up the pieces of your heart when *she* destroyed you." Her gaze lifted to the second floor.

Josh pushed her hands away, scoffing at the sickening thought of her proposal. "I know what you did for me, and I know what we shared. But even after all this time, I don't know if any of it was truly real." He raked his hands through his hair, each finger threading through the short dark strands. His gaze lifted to the staircase, a creak in the floor catching his ear. "I've moved on. I know the truth, and I don't fault Mavis for anything. She's the woman I love."

"So, that's it then? You just forgive her, and she's back in your bed." Her eyes widened as she readjusted the strap of her purse on her shoulder. "You may know *why* it all happened, Josh, but I swear to you, there's more. She wouldn't be upstairs under the sheets right now if you knew." Tears spilled from her eyes, and she swiped at them furiously.

With a shift of his weight, he stepped forward and squeezed her shoulders. "You're dead wrong. Mavis isn't withholding anything from me," he answered, nudging her out the door. "You have to leave."

"Just hear me out!" she pleaded as her feet left the foyer and clicked against the porch.

Josh rolled his eyes. "Come on, Tess. You're smarter than this. You cheated on me. You had a secret affair for like a year. Then you divorced me. Say what you want about Mavis, but those are all things she's never done." Josh pushed the door until it nearly closed. "Please stop calling me."

She laughed, her shrill cackle grating against his ears. "You have no idea, do you, Joshua?" she asked, stepping down the staircase. "That promiscuous bitch upstairs in our bed is *still* hiding something. And I'll prove it to you."

Is that a fucking threat?

"Whatever you say, Tess," he added before slamming the door behind her retreating figure.

He exhaled, leaning his forehead against the door. Josh breathed in for clarity, and out for insanity.

Wow, she's nuts.

"I can't imagine why you divorced her." Mavis's voice called from the second floor.

A smile crossed his lips as he moved to the bottom of the staircase. She sat on the topmost step, arms folded around her legs, chin resting on her knees.

"You heard that, huh?" he asked, climbing the stairs. She scooted to the right as he parked himself beside her.

"Sorry. I couldn't resist eavesdropping." She grinned. "But this promiscuous bitch couldn't help herself. I suppose she never did like me, even in high school."

Josh snorted. "She wasn't always this..." His fingers picked at the carpet as his voice trailed off.

"Always this?" Mavis leaned her head against his shoulder.

"Crazy maybe? I don't know… she seems to think she's got something on you." He dropped his cheek to rest against the top of her head.

Her body stilled, an intake of breath catching in her throat.

"Nonsense, right?" he asked, pushing away the unease gripping his heart.

Pulling her head from his shoulder, she stood and wiggled her toes into the carpet.

"Complete nonsense. I literally haven't seen her in ten years. What could she possibly think she has on me?" She twisted the strands of her hair into a braid. "Unless of course you care that I cheated off of Bobby Stillman on a geometry final my freshmen year? She did see me do that."

Josh laughed. "Deal breaker, Duchess. Pack your bags."

She smiled and tiptoed back to the bedroom. "Well, at least let me try to make it up to you first. Come with me."

Josh followed, his eyes readjusting to the darkened room as she pulled the curtains closed, banishing the blinding rays of light to the outdoors.

Mavis pointed to the bed. "Pacific Park may have been your idea, but it was me who dragged you on eight rollercoasters."

A spasm of excitement ricocheted through his body as he fell face-first back into bed. The gentle scent of her shampoo clung to the pillowcase, and Josh smushed his face deeper into the material. He inhaled, and a hint of coconuts invaded his nose as her fingertips pressed into his shoulder blades. The ache in his muscles melted, fizzling away with the press of her hand as she kneaded, each connection a release of pressure and tension.

"Mmmm," he murmured, searching his mind for the last time he enjoyed a back rub. *No clue.*

She giggled as she climbed on top of him. "Do you forgive me for cheating in geometry now?" she purred, using his butt as a seat cushion.

"Bobby who?" he asked, his consciousness drowning in a pool of pleasure.

She leaned forward, her teeth nipping at his ear as a twinge of desire stirred in his groin, battling with the steady throb in his head. But with each caress of her fingers, the pain in his brain lessened, and the ache of his sore muscles relaxed into contentment.

"You're really good at this," he whispered.

Her ragged breath caught in his ear as she pressed her lips to his hairline. "You've always been my muse, Joshua."

The blood in his veins ran rampant, bouts of adrenaline surging through his body. A warmth crept along his skin, sizzling with the heat of Hell as she rocked her body back and forth atop his own.

"Don't move," he instructed, rolling his body to face hers.

Her smile stole his heart, the flush on her cheeks framing the smirk on her lips. With a tug, her t-shirt lifted from her body and fell to the floor.

His blood rerouted, pulling the ache from his head completely as a swell of desire mounted within him. Her fingernails dragged along his chest, a mischievous grin consuming her lips as the trail caught his nipple.

Euphoria gripped him, waves of longing building arousal as her naked body moved on top of him, inciting friction and fantasy to intertwine.

Her fingers tugged at his shorts, pulling the material lower on his legs. She shifted and giggled; his clothing disappearing as quickly as the gleam in his brown eyes ignited.

"Hop on then, Duchess," he quipped, resting his head on the pillow with a wide, anticipatory grin.

A bubble of laughter tumbled from her mouth, each cheek tinging pink as she climbed back on top of him. "This doesn't look like a piggyback ride."

He steadied himself and bathed in the sensation rippling

through his body as she slid on top of him. "Different kind of ride," he groaned, gripping her hips with fervor.

She grinned, and then she moved, her body finding a steady pace that tightened the building internal pressure. Where her heart thumped, his heart bumped, matching the rhythm of her heartbeat. Two hearts beating as one as their souls collided, interlacing and fusing together, stitch for stitch of each heartstring.

Her breath caught before her body shivered, the heart charm of her necklace stilling as passion blazed through her. The glow of her soft, satiated eyes penetrated his body—his cue to follow. Bliss thundered through him, erupting in mounting passion as he released himself inside her.

Gasping for breath, she tumbled to his side and snuggled into the crook of his arm. A sheen of sweat coated her skin, and Josh pressed his lips to her forehead.

"All backrubs should end like that," he murmured, threading his fingers through her wild hair, the braid long gone. Her lips tickled his chest.

"Agreed."

The silence of the room rested on Josh's ears, the distant hum of the air conditioner kicking on. His heart rate slowed, and exhaustion threatened his eyelids. With a yank of the sheet, the material floated, kissing their skin as it covered their bodies.

"I love you, Mavs," he whispered, tightening his embrace around her. The threat of Sunday loomed, the hours ticking by until her plane departed for the Windy City.

"I love you too, Joshua." She exhaled and nuzzled into his chest. "I always have."

"Then stay in Rosewood with me. Move home." His own plea rang in his ear. *Wow, way to not sound pathetic, Josh.*

Her head lifted, and she propped her body up on an elbow with a crinkled nose.

"I know your brain moves quick, Josh, but what about the State of California?" She snorted. "I mean, is the ink even dry on your divorce papers?"

He rolled his eyes. "All right, I earned that one," he admitted, tugging her body back into his. Her head rested on his chest, each breath warming his skin. She blinked, and her eyelashes fluttered against him, sending a shiver racing through his body.

"She's so stupid..." said Mavis.

"Hmm?"

The air conditioner turned off, leaving the room in silence until a plane roared overhead.

"I just don't understand how Tess gave you up."

Josh reached for the charm on the necklace, pinching it between his fingers. "To be fair, she knew she was always runner-up." The charm dropped as he shifted. "That wasn't her fault. It was mine."

Mavis scrunched her nose again and flopped backward, tugging the sheet up to her neck. "Always the gentleman, Joshua."

He leaned on his side to face her. "What's that supposed to mean?" he asked, brushing her hair behind her ear.

"Austin told me you blamed yourself for the divorce."

Josh rolled his eyes. "Don't listen to my brother."

"I mean, he's not wrong, is he?" Her fingers tugged at the sheet, rubbing the soft material between her thumb and index finger.

"I'm not defending, Tess..."

"But you do blame yourself." Her gaze bore into his, pressing for the truth. "Austin isn't wrong."

His stomach dropped, falling through the mattress to ooze onto the carpet below. The way his brother's name dripped from her lips boiled his blood in an unexplained, irrational way. Jealousy sizzled along his spine. *Why did you stay so close to him all these years? What's the connection you have?*

He grinned, zeroing his eyes in on her. "Why are you defending *him?*"

The light left her eyes, the glow diminishing in the dim bedroom as she blinked. Running a hand through her hair, she sighed. "I'm not." Her feet hit the ground as she tugged her body from the bed. "I need to shower," she murmured.

The bathroom door closed, and seconds later, the water turned on. The monotonous drizzle of the water through the wall grated against his brain, each drip a prick of a needle to his gut. His brother pushed against his soul, brushing up against the happiness consuming his heart. An inkling of doubt and a return attack of unease blossomed in his body. Austin had never let go of Mavis—at least, not the way he had to. He'd held her hand and kept her close for ten years. His brother's voice caught in his memory, the pen name *E. Banks* breathing life into the doubt surfacing in his mind. *He recognized her story—her writing too. Why would he have paid that close of attention?*

"What aren't you telling me, Mavs?" he whispered to the empty bedroom. His eyes sought the nightstand as his eyes pierced the photo of teenage Mavis. Her timeless green gaze met his own. *Is Tess right? Just how many secrets do you have?*

The hangover nausea fueled him, and Josh stomped from the bed, cracking the bathroom door open. Steam filled the room, a gust of hot, damp air greeting his face. The walls of the shower stall fogged over, her body hidden behind the smeary glass.

"Mavis?"

Her blurred body stilled behind the glass. "Yeah?"

Just ask.

"Is there something between you and my brother?" The silence pounded in his ear, each passing second a heavy brick crushing his heart.

"No."

Her voice competed with the crashing water, but Josh exhaled, breathing a sigh of instant relief from his lungs.

"Okay," he answered, tugging the door closed. But steam escaped, the billows of warm air wafting into the bedroom like a trail of doubt following him down the stairs.

Why don't I believe you?

CHAPTER NINETEEN

Austin

What did I do?

The guilt crept through his veins, stemming from the ache in his heart. Austin heaved out a sigh and pressed his eyes closed, burying his face in the pillow. His head spun, a dizzying sensation gripping his brain as his mind wrestled with the memories of the night before.

With a roll, the floral bedspread of a Templeton guest room tangled around his legs. He kicked at the bedding, ridding his body of the cheerful sunflower print. Their brilliant yellow faces stared back with far too much merriment for the bile churning in his gut.

"Ugh, I'm so sorry, Princess," he whispered to the empty room. Her face swirled in his mind, her last words, *fucking asshole,* ringing in his ear. "I'm so stupid," he groaned, dragging his hands across his face.

His fingertips lingered on his lips, the memory of her mouth moving against his own flooding his brain. She'd responded to him, her body pressing into his own with the same level of intensity. His passion and desire had been met, kiss for kiss, and groan for groan. *You'll never admit it, but you wanted me, too.*

A smile grew as warmth prickled his skin. Mavis had been intertwined in his life for so long, always the girl next door and an arm's length away. But for a decade, he'd held her hand, kept her secrets, and stashed her away in his heart for safekeeping. *But maybe I don't have to anymore?*

He pictured her and the impulsive spirit she carried paving the way for their future. Chicago manifested in his mind, an image of the Magnificent Mile brought to life by the city lights. Their relationship had blossomed there, and with a bit of convincing at the law firm, he could relocate. He could be the man to start the new branch in the Windy City he'd heard rumblings about. And he could do it all with her by his side. *An easy fit.*

Sunlight streaked through the window above his head, jarring his mind from the Midwestern fantasy. The guilt he woke with grew, coating the inside of his stomach. He could dream all he wanted, but reality stung. He'd forced his kiss on her last night, drunken desire getting the best of him. While her body had responded, the name that fell from her lips when they broke apart wasn't his.

Josh.

Austin tugged at the covers, giving in to the happy sunflowers. He blanketed his body, tucking his head firmly beneath the pillow, wallowing in a pool of self-pity, confusion, and deep confliction.

A knock on the door lifted the fog and he choked out, "Come in," swallowing the invisible cotton ball of dehydration in his mouth. The smell of the cheesy sandwich preceded her, its buttery aroma inducing instant nausea.

"You have to get up. It's almost one in the afternoon," Lauren scolded.

She dropped to the foot of the bed, and the mattress bounced, shaking the only bit of stability beneath him. Yesterday's liquor sloshed in his belly, and Austin inhaled, ramming his eyes shut.

"Stop moving."

Lauren swatted his feet. "You can't say I didn't warn you." She sighed and took a bite of the sandwich. "You're just as a big of an idiot as Mitch."

He snorted. "I... can't argue with that." Unburying his head from beneath the pillow, he begrudgingly hauled his body to a sitting position, cursing his brother-in-law as the room spun. *I'm never drinking again.*

"Here." She tossed a bottle of water onto his lap and rolled her eyes. "Maybe next time you'll listen to me."

With a smirk, he unscrewed the cap and brought the plastic to his lips. The cool liquid slid down his throat, quelling the emotions bubbling in his gut.

"I'll consider it." He grinned and scratched the tip of his ear as the flush on his cheeks spread.

"Do you want this?" she asked, holding up the sandwich. The cheese dripped to the plate.

"All yours, kid," he answered, pressing the water to his forehead.

She nodded and stuffed a bite in her mouth, chewing thoughtfully. "Kinda weird seeing Mavis again last night, right?" She took another bite and rested her gaze on Austin. "I mean, it was sweet to see her back with Josh, you know? I'm happy for him. Well, happy for *them* after so long."

The pit in his stomach deepened, distaste rising in the back of his throat. A snake of jealousy wound around his spine, hissing and spitting at his sister's words.

"What the hell is your problem?" She crinkled her nose.

Austin shook his head, hurling the angst of her question away. "I don't know what you mean."

"Your face just now. You looked like someone just stole your lunch money or something." She grinned.

"Stole *something*," he muttered, tugging the blanket up to cover his chest.

"What're you talking about?" Lauren dropped the sandwich to the plate and wiped her hands on her pants. She squinted, her gaze boring into him.

"It's nothing. I didn't mean anything," he answered,

slumping further into the bed. "Look, give me a minute and I'll get out of he—"

"Oh, my God!" Her body twisted. "You have feelings for her, don't you?" She gripped his ankle and shook his foot, her eyes wide with disbelief.

Fuck. Fuck. Fuck.

A false smile tugged at his lips as he shook his head, dropping his gaze to the bedroom floor. A dust bunny hid in the corner beneath the nightstand. Longing to switch places with the ball of fluff, he dragged a hand over the stubble on his chin.

She shook his foot again.

"That's crazy, and so not true." He jabbed her in the thigh with his toes.

Am I that obvious?

"No way! I see it. It's all over your face!" Lauren gaped, her mouth falling open as an understanding beat at her brain.

"Lauren, you're wrong, okay? Whatever you think you see—"

"Wait a minute… she likes you back, doesn't she?" She stood, the paper plate with melted cheese floating to the floor. "She could hardly even look at you last night," she muttered, clapping her hands to her forehead with sudden realization. "Oh, my God. Does Josh know?"

Fuck no!

Austin hopped from the bed, his feet meeting the cold wood flooring. A wave of nausea washed over his body, and he swallowed the urge to upend his stomach. He tugged at his sister's hands, willing her to stop connecting the dots so easily.

"Tell me the truth, Austin," she demanded.

He rolled his eyes and huffed out a sigh. *Trapped.* The truth stared him in the face, resting resolutely in his sister's eyes, the same brown hue of his twin reflecting back. The acid churning in his stomach stilled, and the sweat on his brow grew cold. Of all the secrets lodged deep in his heart, the one resting on the tip of his tongue held the weight of the world—a crushing blow of honesty.

He sighed. "Fuck. I'm in love with her, Lauren." His gaze fell to the floor. An invisible force squeezed his heart, the admission of love weighing heavily on his chest. Having hardly admitted the truth to himself, the words tumbling from his lips held a realism unparalleled beyond anything else.

She gasped, her hands covering her mouth. "You can't be serious."

The tenor of her voice broke the small glimmer of hope clinging to his soul. His arms dropped to his sides, slumping in defeat, like a puppy, scolded for having chewed on a rug.

"I can't help it," he groaned with a shrug. "I've loved her for years."

"How did—" She blinked. "Wait. How long—" Her head bobbed, processing the truth. "Geez, Austin. So that's why you knew where she lived? You guys have had like… a thing going on?"

Austin moaned. "Ugh, Lauren, you can't tell anyone any of this, okay?" His hands gripped her shoulders. "Please?" he begged. "I'm still sorting through it all myself. *We're* still sorting through it all."

"Damn it, Austin! What are you thinking? It's Mavis Benson, for fuck's sake!" She pulled away from him, frustration rising in her voice. "Josh is your brother! And *she* is like his freaking Duchess or whatever the hell he calls her!"

Yeah well, she's my Princess.

Rage sizzled beneath his skin, a fountain of fury bursting forth from his heart. "You think I don't know that?" he yelled. He dragged his fingers through his hair, his fingertips resting at the nape of his neck. He squeezed, cupping the back of his head. "What do you want me to do, Lauren? I've been fighting my feelings for her my entire life! For fucking *years!*"

Her eyes glossed over, each muscle in her face softening.

The anger dripping from her lips moments ago reined in. She stepped forward, her hand outstretched until her fingers collided with his arm. She fell into his chest, wrapping her arms around his middle.

"I'm sorry, Austin. I had no idea you felt this way."

He returned her embrace, leaning into her support and newfound understanding. "I know it's wrong," he whispered. "I've tried to shake her. I really have, but even after six years apart, I can't help myself."

"And Josh has no idea," she whispered. Pulling away, her gaze traveled upward to meet his own. "But you can't hide this from him."

"The truth unravels by the day," he admitted. His body sank back onto the bed, resting his weight against his palms. "But Mavs has to admit her feelings in all of this too. It's not just me here."

Her eyes widened. "You mean…"

"I kissed her last night." He nodded. "And she kissed me back. Big time."

Lauren gasped, a hand lifting to cover her mouth. "Austin, this is *bad*. You have to talk to Mavis. You have to figure this out. Josh is…" Her voice trailed off as her body dropped to the bed beside him.

Austin sank further onto the mattress, his back meeting the sunflowers. His hands buried his face as his soul seeped into the growing pit in his stomach.

"I know."

"Austin, I love Mavis like a sister. I really do. But her feelings are not what I'm worried about here. Josh is—"

"I get it, all right?" Anger punctuated each word. *It's always about Josh…*

Lauren stood and tiptoed to the door, twisting the knob. "All I'm saying is that he's been through a lot," she mumbled, one foot leaving the bedroom. "Think this through carefully, Austin. There's so much at stake here. You know their history."

"*Believe me*. I know it better than anyone," he grumbled.

Her brow furrowed as she tugged the door closed. The latch clicked, and her footsteps disappeared down the hall. And his truth went with her.

Austin rolled from the bed and snagged his phone from the nightstand, mulling over Lauren's last words. *You know their history.* The blinking cursor stared back on a new text message, unsure if he should text Josh or Mavis. His body stilled as he searched for a decision.

History is just going to have to be rewritten.

He typed *M*.

CHAPTER TWENTY

Mavis

For the last ten years, guilt had been a routine part of life—always there, always present—a fraction of her heart, wedged between other steadfast emotions like uncertainty and anxiety.

But the guilt had doubled in her time since returning to Rosewood, splitting her heart down the middle—shoving both uncertainty and anxiety aside like cast-off clothing in a donation pile.

What did I do?

Her phone pinged as Josh flipped a piece of French toast. It crackled in the hot pan as he sprinkled cinnamon and sugar on its surface.

Each letter of Austin's name punctuated the splintered pieces of her screen. She frowned, a twinge in her gut forcing the air from her lungs.

"Everything okay?" Josh lifted his gaze from the delicacy.

Plastering a smile on her lips, Mavis nodded. "Yep. It's just Casey asking about my flight tomorrow. She's picking me up from the airport."

Josh's grin faded. "Maybe you should stay a few more days. We can talk through…" He pulled the piece of crispy toast from the pan and dropped it on the plate in front of him. "Some stuff," he added, pushing the plate in her direction.

The maple syrup drizzle clung to the perfectly sizzled bit of toast. The steam tickled her face as she leaned across the counter and pecked Josh on the lips.

"I think I might stay just for the food." She smirked, stabbing her fork into the gooey treat. It broke apart with ease, and she brought the afternoon breakfast to her lips. The sugar melted onto her tongue, the syrup sticking to her lips. "But Josh, if I don't work, I don't get paid."

Unease—mixed with the freestanding guilt—rippled through her. *I haven't been at Shaker since the dinner rush on Monday night. How am I going to make rent this month?*

Josh nodded, bringing a mug of fresh coffee to his mouth. His gaze darted back and forth as he stepped away, ready to drop another piece of bread in the pan.

"I'm not trying to sound like a total ass here." He grinned and sprinkled his secret mixture. "But, I mean, I can help…"

She giggled and rolled her eyes. "I know you can, *Doctor* Templeton." The flush on his cheeks warmed her soul, the hint of embarrassment at his words infringing on her independence. "Speaking of which, don't you need to get back to work too?"

Josh frowned, dropping a spoonful of butter into the pan. It hissed against the heat, and he adjusted the flame on the burner. "I can prob—"

"Joshua." She pushed the empty plate away and tapped her belly playfully. "We can figure this out, but I have to fly home tomorrow. And *you* have patients who need you, I'm sure."

He nodded, flipping the bread to the opposite side. "I know you're right." The toast crackled against the heat as he shuffled it around in the pan. "But I, umm… just got you back. I don't want you to leave so soon," he added, pulling his gaze from the pan.

Her heart melted, caving in on itself. Joshua—the other half of her whole stood before her, spatula in hand and heart on his sleeve—begging her to stay by his side. And in her palm, she held a text message from his twin brother. The only line she could read started with, *Princess, you and I...*

Like the syrup Josh poured from the bottle, guilt drizzled over her body, coating her in a sticky, inescapable mess. The longer she waited, the further it spread, soaking into her core, oozing and consuming what lay beneath.

Her phone pinged again, the shattered screen lighting up with Mitch's name. Her already soggy heart disintegrated.

Josh leaned over the counter and tapped Mitch's name on her broken phone. "And I'm not the only one who wants you to stay," he whispered.

Mavis nodded as a wave of warmth bloomed in her chest. She'd come home for Joshua, but the prospect of rekindling a relationship with her brother appealed more and more with each passing day. Her fingers tapped open the text, her eyes reading over the words. *Lauren told me you leave tomorrow. Can I steal you from Josh this afternoon? Ten years gone and two days back ain't gonna work for me, sis.*

She grinned, the promise of repaired love tugging at her frail heartstrings. "Mitch wants to see me."

"Well, that's a one-eighty for him," he answered with another sip of coffee. A smile consumed his face as he rested the cup on the counter. "You should go." He pushed his car keys in her direction.

Mavis eyed the keys in front of her and smiled. "I drive a manual."

Laughter bubbled from his mouth, his fingers tugging the keys backward. "Of course, you do." He stepped from behind the counter and pressed his lips to her forehead. "You never did do anything the easy way."

Truth.

Her feet carried her through the door of Highside as Josh's Jeep left the parking lot. Sports memorabilia cluttered the walls, each big screen TV broadcasting a different sport. Mitch waved from across the bar, and she shrugged into the booth's seat opposite him, her butt meeting the red faux leather.

"I can't believe you wanted to meet at a bar after last night," she murmured, catching the beer he slid across the table. Her stomach groaned with the after-effects of a hangover.

"Aren't you a bartender?" He squinted and took a sip. "The Navy taught me the best hangover cure is a beer the morning after."

She grinned. "It's like four in the afternoon." Mavis clinked her bottle to his and tipped it against her lips until the golden liquid greeted her tongue. Her gut tightened, ready to gag.

He shrugged. "Morning to me. I got up an hour ago."

The waitress approached their table, dropping sticky menus in front of them. "What'll it be, ya'll?" she asked in a Southern drawl, smacking her gum to the roof of her mouth. Mavis tilted her head, the out-of-place accent capturing her attention.

"Did you eat?" Mitch asked, his eyes scanning the menu.

"Josh made me French toast." Her gaze lingered on the appetizer menu, the basket of fried cheese calling her name. She pointed to it with a smile. "But I can't pass this up."

Mitch smirked. "Make it two." He passed the menus back to the waitress. Her flip-flops slapped against the floor, each step competing with the squeak of the shoes in the televised basketball game above their heads.

"I like this place." Mavis pointed to the huge TV screen above her. "I don't even need to wear contacts to see this one."

"It's our favorite.' Mitch leaned back into the booth. "We usually grab a beer here once a week." He pointed to the TV she just referenced. "Great for us Lakers fans."

"I like the Bulls." A smile played across her lips as she sipped her beer.

"Then I guess you like to lose?"

She giggled, pulling her phone from the depths of her purse as it pinged again. "I mean, you can probably just chalk my whole life up to one in the loss column." Her eyes sought the screen, Austin's name reflecting back. *You can't avoid me forever, Princess.* With a bubble of unease rising in her throat, she gulped her beer and tossed the phone aside.

"You never struck me as a defeatist." He leaned back as the waitress laid their baskets of fried cheese on the table.

"No, I guess not. But maybe now… just a realist." She popped a cheeseball in her mouth and grinned. The hot cheddar melted across her tongue, complementing the taste of light beer.

"Answer me this then. How *realistic* is it that you're actually here to stay?" He tossed a cheeseball into his mouth and chewed. "Because I'll be honest, Mavs. I didn't want a damn thing to do with you until about two days ago. And if you're gonna get up and walk out of here again, just tell me now and save me that bit of heartache."

Ouch. I earned that one.

She dropped her gaze to her lap, toying with the bracelets on her wrist. Her brain twisted his question, sorting through the varying levels of answers she could give. *Start at the surface.*

"What do you do for a living, Mitch?" she asked, lifting her gaze back to her brother.

"Huh?" A cheeseball froze midair on the way to his mouth.

"What do you do? How do you earn money?"

"I'm a carpenter. I flip houses." He popped the fried bite in his mouth and chewed.

She nodded. "So, there's probably some good money in that, right?"

"It's not bad…" He crinkled his nose and leaned

forward. "Why aren't you answering my question?"

"You're answering it for me."

His eyes widened with confusion. "I'm really not."

Mavis sighed and slumped back into the booth. Embarrassment tinged her cheeks pink, and a warmth sizzled along her skin.

"I'm trying," she said, shoving her purse away from her leg as it pinged again. "Look, Mitch, the simple answer here is if I don't work, I don't get paid. I've been back here for two days, and already, I'm not going to make rent this month unless I pull double shifts through next Friday. I have to fly home tomorrow."

Mitch shifted in his seat and tucked his hair behind his ears. The basketball game above her head reflected in the green of his eyes.

"I can't stay here. At least not yet." Her head hung, a flood of humiliation resting in her belly next to the French toast and fried cheese. She shivered. "I've tried my hardest, but bartending at a mediocre restaurant isn't exactly a lucrative career."

His hand reached across the table. Squeezing her fingers, an unspoken understanding quelled her nerves.

"I mean, we'd help you—"

"Now you sound like Josh," she answered, rolling her eyes. She tugged her hand away and dropped back into the booth with a thud, all confidence dissolving into the seat cushion beneath her.

Mitch blew out a deep breath and nodded. "I get it," he admitted, pushing up the sleeves on his sweatshirt.

"You do?"

He nodded. "Yeah. When I came back here after my tours were over with the Navy, I had next to nothing. I moved in with Lauren because of it."

Mavis dropped her gaze to the floor. "The Templetons to the rescue," she joked.

"No shit." He pulled his hands up to cup the back of his head. His gaze lifted to the basketball game on the TV, and

Mavis followed it. The players zoomed across the screen with squeaking shoes.

Eyeing the exhibition game, the team in blue played with intensity. Sweat dripped from their exhausted faces, their muscles testing their limits as they zipped back and forth across the court. But no matter the amount of heart they put in, the scoreboard betrayed them, and the buzzer sounded with finality.

"Sometimes it doesn't really matter how much you try." Mitch upended his beer and placed the empty bottle gently on the table. "Loss is inevitable…"

Her phone rang, the cheery ringtone competing with the announcer of the broadcast. Austin's name glared back at her on the screen, and she tapped the button to accept the call, bringing the phone to her ear.

"Meet me at Java Jane's in twenty minutes, Princess." He ended the call.

Mavis sighed and stared at her brother as he peeled the label from the empty bottle.

"Especially as a Benson," she answered.

"Especially as a Benson," he repeated, tipping his bottle in her direction. "Who was that?"

She shook her head, resting her chin in her palms. "Will you take me to Java Jane's in twenty minutes?"

"Yeah. Why?"

Mavis considered her brother. Having not studied him too closely since her return, her gaze raked over him. He'd acquired laugh lines on his forehead, and his hair had darkened from the memories she held. But the green gaze mirroring her own hadn't changed.

"Mitch, can I tell you a secret?"

He nodded and leaned forward, resting his elbows against the table. The tattoo on his forearm caught her interest, its inky black writing stirring memories from childhood. Her fingertips traced the cursive as her eyes read, *not all those who wander are lost.*

Her heart clenched. They may have led lives apart from

one another for the last decade, but to their core, they shared a bond—both lost souls at sea, floating in the depths of the ocean until they drifted to shore.

"I think it's about damn time you did." He gripped her fingers and squeezed.

She breathed, the rush of oxygen fueling her brain. "The money thing is true." Her head bobbed. "But it's not the only reason I can't stick around Rosewood right now."

Mitch inhaled, his body stilling as his lungs expanded. "Then what is?"

"I might need a lawyer present for this…"

He stared at her, his gaze glossing over her face. Mitch blinked, his pupils expanding as understanding seemingly touched his heart.

"Fucking Austin Templeton," he murmured, slumping back into his seat.

"Fucking Austin Templeton," she repeated and scooted out of the booth.

He waited for her, his legs crossed casually, seated at a small four-person table on the outdoor patio. His sunglasses covered his baby-blue eyes as he scrolled through his phone, sipping coffee.

Mavis stepped forward, one foot crossing the threshold of Java Jane's. Unease surged through her body from the tip of her sandaled toe to the last curl of her long dark hair. Every nerve shook in her system. Her palms tingled as she marched forward, weaving between the tables, each step bringing her closer to the forbidden fruit in the Garden of Eden.

He rose from his seat as she neared, pulling her chair out like a gentleman. "Thanks for coming," he said, pushing the chair in as she sat.

The metal chair clung to the back of her thighs, cooling her body from the heat boiling inside her.

"You didn't give me a choice, Austin," she murmured,

accepting the iced coffee he pushed in her direction. "I—"

"Wait. Before you say anything, please let me apologize." He reached across the table and squeezed her hands, his warm fingers interlacing with her own. "I was wrong—*so wrong*—to have forced myself on you like that last night. It was stupid, and I have no excuse for my poor behavior."

Her cheeks flushed as he tugged his sunglasses from his face, his piercing gaze digging into her soul with his usual blazing intensity. A *V* shape formed across his forehead as his apology dropped from his lips.

"I'm sorry, Mavs. I got too caught up in the memory of us." The remorse in his voice penetrated her, digging into her heart with a spade, scoop by scoop. "And if I'm being completely honest… it pissed me off seeing you with my brother again."

She bit her bottom lip, sifting through his words of apology-turned-confession. His grasp on her fingers tightened, and he shifted his chair to move closer to her own.

"I don't know what to say, Aus—"

"Then let me keep going," he pleaded. His fingers threaded through the curl escaping her ponytail, and he tucked it behind her ear. "I'm sorry for what I did, but I can't be sorry for what I said. At least, not all of it." His gaze softened, searching hers.

She pulled away and dropped back in her seat in defeat. "Damn it, Austin!" She sighed and sucked on the straw of her coffee, tasting the creamy goodness of the beverage. "What am I supposed to do here, huh?" Tossing her arms up, each palm met the sky. "You're putting me in an impossible situation." Anger flared at his honesty, his willingness to suddenly label the growing feelings between them.

He grinned and leaned back as well, his hands cupping the nape of his neck. "This isn't one-sided, Princess. You kissed me back. Big time."

She rolled her eyes. "I drank too much!" she yelled,

drawing the attention of their neighbors. "That's always my problem around you!"

He chuckled and waved to the older man at his right reading a newspaper. "Do you want to keep your voice down or just broadcast to the entire coffeehouse that we're troubled alcoholics?"

"I'm not a troubled alcoholic," she quipped, pulling her body back into the table. "And neither are you. We just do stupid shit together when we drink."

His knee bounced beneath the table, rattling the contents on the surface. Each packet of sugar jiggled in the plastic container, an earthquake on a miniature scale. He held one finger up. "First, sure, that's kind of the truth." He nodded and held up another finger. "Second, though, have you ever considered what our stupid shit *means?*"

She scoffed, ripping her gaze from his hands. "It doesn't mean anything. If it did, you wouldn't have let *six years* go by."

A bark of laughter escaped his mouth. "Princess, you left *me* naked in a hotel bed, not the other way around."

The man reading the newspaper snorted.

"Would you keep your voice down?" She adjusted her chair, moving closer until their knees bumped beneath the table.

"Oh, now an audience matters to you?" He leaned forward, his face nearing her own until the coffee on his breath caught in her nose. His thumb grazed her bottom lip, his eyes challenging her to pull away.

Her body froze, stilling the flurry of thoughts racing through her mind—all rational thinking out the window. "What is it you want, Austin? Do you want me to admit that I have feelings for you?" she asked, her gaze lingering on his lips. "Because I do. You fucking know I do! But *you* called me that night, asking me to come home for *Joshua*—not you." She swatted his hand away and leaned back in her seat. "This little game we're playing is stupid." She folded her arms across her chest. "And I'm over it."

Austin gripped the arm of her chair and tugged. The metal grated against the cement, squelching the calm conversation of their neighboring coffee drinkers.

Her heart skipped a beat, each nerve cell electrifying with shock. She gripped the armrest, balancing her body as she skidded in his direction with a muscled tug.

"What're you do—"

His mouth crushed hers, his lips moving against her own. The coffeehouse disappeared. All chatter subsided and passing traffic calmed to a stop. Nothing existed beyond his lips and the warmth of his breath as his mouth collided with hers. His hands grasped her neck, locking her in place, the arms of the chair a makeshift prison.

Austin pulled back, his breathing heavy. The cologne on the collar of his shirt intertwined with the scent of coffee—sandalwood and Columbian coffee beans fusing in her nostrils.

Mavis opened her eyes, meeting his icy blue gaze six inches away. She stared, finding more in his eyes than she'd ever witnessed before—more than the passion that fueled their relationship.

"My brother sees you as the same girl he loved back in high school," he whispered. "He wants you to move home, into his house, and ready to bake cookies with a ring on your finger. He'll pretend the last ten years never happened."

She pressed a hand over his chest, pushing to increase the distance, but his hold held firm. "Austin…"

"I see *you*, Princess, the *new* you. The you that survived. That's the woman I want, the one who hops on a plane in the middle of the night. The one who loses bets and puts herself out into the world. The one who solves problems, and figures shit out, never one to admit defeat. I want the woman who *thrives*." His hand pressed hers into the beat of his heart. "That's the woman I want, the one I fell in love with in a hotel room in Chicago."

Her lungs didn't want to work, each breath held captive in her throat. The love spell he'd cast dizzied her brain, fogging her ability to think. She blinked, staring blankly at the profession of love tumbling from his lips—from the lips of her *friend* turned... *lover?*

"You don't love me, Austin," she mumbled, pushing away from the hold he held over her.

His eyes closed, releasing her from the challenge. "The hell I don't, Mavs." He slumped in his seat, his fingers kneading his forehead. "You let Josh love you because he loves the memory of you, a girl you used to like." He snorted. "But me? You can't even fathom my feelings for you because you don't love yourself as you are today." He pointed to her, his finger shaking. "And until you realize how fucking incredible you are..."

His voice trailed off as he stood and shook his head, ramming his hands into his wallet. He dropped a twenty-dollar bill to the table. "Safe flight back to Chicago."

He stepped away, leaving the bomb he just ignited to detonate around her.

Mavis trudged up the front stairs and gripped the doorknob. She stared; the beautiful brass of the knob held tightly in her hand. Her brain instructed her wrist to twist, but her heart steadied her hand. She breathed, allowing the memory of Josh to fill her soul, the way his arms had clung to her in this very spot not more than forty-eight hours ago. The ten years they'd spent apart culminated on the very stair beneath her feet.

Austin's admission of love interrupted the recall, separating her soul from the deep-seated feelings stirring in her core. An echo of his voice whispered in her ear, his own revelation of truth twisting a knife in her heart.

"You're a complete fuckup, Mavis Benson," she whispered to herself.

How can you have feelings for them both? She pictured a box filled to the brim with her guilty conscience and dumped it into the dungeon at the back of her brain. Pushing the mahogany door open, she stepped inside.

"There you are," said Josh as he twisted his body to peer over his shoulder. His laptop rested on the arm of the chair, and he quickly snapped it shut and placed it on the floor. "How'd it go?"

Mavis kicked off her flip-flops. His sweet brown eyes, hidden behind a pair of reading glasses, peeked over the back of the chair like a child cheating in a game of hide-and-seek.

A bulldozer plowed into her heart, shattering the illusion of a second chance at love. *I have to tell him. I can't keep hiding this.*

"I have to tell you something," she said, stepping further into the house until her toes met the living room carpet.

He snorted. "That bad, huh?" He reached for her, and she plopped her body down beside him.

"Hmm?"

"Mitch. What did he say?"

Oh. Right...

"Oh, umm, Mitch was fine." She picked at a snagged string on the oversized chair's seat. "He..." She ping-ponged her index finger between herself and Josh. "Just wanted to see if all of this was real. See if I was staying in Rosewood."

He smiled and enveloped her body, pulling her into his chest until her ear rested atop his heart. *Thump. Thump. Thump.*

"I keep asking myself the same thing, Duchess," he whispered, brushing the hair from her face. "Having you back here again, it feels like I'll be walking you to chemistry class in the morning or something."

Austin's voice rang in her mind. *He'll pretend the last ten years never existed.*

Her gut clenched, the truth in Austin's words ringing in her ears as Josh's words about the past fell from his lips.

"God, that sounds terrible," she joked, squashing the sickening feeling blanketing her body. "I didn't understand atomic structure then, and I really could care less about the periodic table now."

Josh snickered. "Oh, come on, that's need-to-know information!" He trailed a finger across her stomach, and she clenched at the tickle. "Principle quantum shells determine the period of the element. Tell me how that's not useful."

She rolled her eyes and sat up with a grin. "Tell me how that *is* useful."

He smiled and squeezed her hand, the laughter sparking their conversation suddenly dying before them. "I took so much from you," he mumbled.

Mavis scrunched her nose. "Josh, I've never been upset that I didn't get to learn about the periodic table." She dragged a finger across his cheek and cupped his chin.

His gaze lingered on hers before he tugged her hand away. "It's not just the periodic table, Mavs. It's all of it. You never got to finish school because of me."

She shook her head. "No, I didn't… but that doesn't mean—"

Josh's phone interrupted at the same moment the timer went off in the kitchen. He frowned, reading the screen. "It's the hospital. Can you pull the cookies out of the oven for me?" he asked, bringing the phone to his ear.

Cookies? Seriously?

She tiptoed out of the room, Josh's voice fading in the background as Austin consumed her mind. With a touch of a button, she silenced the timer and rammed the oven mitts on the counter over her hands. Mavis yanked open the oven door and stared at the perfect chocolate chip cookies on the top rack, baked to perfection.

"All I need now is the ring…" she muttered, turning to look at the photo on the fridge. The Templeton twins smiled back, Austin's glossy paper-version eyes piercing her soul.

With a sigh, she reached for the cookie sheet, letting it fall to the counter with an angry clank. *Fuck you, Austin. Why do you have to be right?*

The doorbell interrupted her internal musings. Josh's feet shuffled in the distance, his voice still echoing on the phone. Mavis searched for a spatula and separated the cookies from the hot pan, tossing them to the cool counter one by one.

Not one cookie had burned, each perfect circle melted with warm chocolate as if baked by a professional. She snorted, recalling the attempt Casey once made with a premade roll of sugar cookies. All she had to do was slice, bake, and enjoy. A smile tugged at her lips remembering the smoke that suffocated their apartment.

Tess's voice shrieked at the front door. "Where is she, Josh?" her voice demanded.

What the hell?

Mavis dropped the spatula with two cookies left on the pan. She rounded the corner, each oven mitt still resting on her hands.

The most sinister, devilish grin she'd ever seen rested on Tess's face, her usual Barbie-like appearance falling short with a misplaced maniacal expression.

"*There you are,*" she mouthed. Her finger rose, a hot-pink manicured nail pointing at her heart.

"I can be there in about twenty minutes," said Josh into the phone. He tapped the screen and scowled, shoving the phone in his pocket. "Damn it, Tess. Why are you back here again?" He swatted at her raised finger.

"I came for the show." Her heels clicked against the wood flooring as each calculated step she took brought her further into the house. *Clickity-clack.* Her toes stopped as her gaze lifted, locking Mavis into a petrified state of confusion. Tess winked. "Ready?" she whispered.

"What show?" Josh asked with a roll of his eyes. "Look, Tess, I don't have time—"

"You have time for this," she snapped and tossed her phone in his direction. He caught it, tipping his head to glare at the screen.

Tess turned her body to face Mavis head-on, a half-smile playing faintly across her lips. "In case you're wondering. This is the moment Josh learns you've been fucking his brother behind his back."

The world stilled, each particle hanging, suspended in time. Her heart stalled, the crushing weight of a ten-year secret burying her body alive. The small glimmer of light at the top of her grave closed in, and a sickening black pit swallowed up the last fraction of her existence.

Josh gulped, his eyes sweeping the phone. A bubble of laughter burst from his lips as he hunched over, his hands resting his weight against his knees. He coughed, air sputtering from his lungs as he tipped the phone back up to meet his eyes.

"Something you wanted to tell me, Duchess?" he asked, dragging his body back upright. Josh raked a hand through his hair and tugged the glasses from his nose. "Something you want to fucking admit to?" he yelled. The glasses sailed through the air, smashing into the banister. The lenses shattered, bits of fragmented glass streaking across the floor.

Josh stepped forward, his eyes glossy with threatening tears. His hands reached outward, tugging the oven mitts from her fingers. They fell to the floor with a thud as he dropped Tess's phone into her palms.

The image imprinted on her mind—razor-sharp—each pixel branded into her brain. She stared, transfixed by the proof of her betrayal. Austin's lips pressed onto her own at the little coffeehouse down the street.

His voice shook, wavering into the silent air. "I asked you point-blank just this morning if anything existed between you and my brother. And you told me no," he whispered.

Mavis swallowed the lie in her throat, the ugly truth confined to her heart for eternity. Tears burned the back of her eyelids, the ring in her ears clouding the chorus of voices battling in her brain.

"Joshua…" she choked.

Tess rested her hands on Josh's forearm, rubbing the skin with a gentle graze of her nails. "I didn't want to be right, but you had to know the truth."

He shook his arm, breaking his contact with her. "How?" He stepped backward until his back met the wall. He tipped his head, the connection jarring the tears loose from his eyes. "How do you even know any of this, Tess?"

She stepped forward, cutting their distance in half. "Do you remember that girl's weekend getaway I went on to Chicago?" she asked, her eyes blazing.

Josh nodded.

"Does the Palmer House Hilton ring a bell, Mavs?" she asked, tilting her head to the side. Tess's gaze raked over her slumped form. "Actually, probably not. I don't think either of you remember anything but the alcohol, am I right?" She laughed.

Mavis shook her head, tears streaming down her cheeks, recall flashing through her mind at Tess's words. The truth hurt, her past intoxicated choices, shooting arrows through her heart.

"It was a drunken mistake," she spit out, her head still shaking side to side.

Josh snorted and pointed to the phone still clutched in her hands. "Were you drunk at the coffeehouse too?"

Her knees gave out, her body dropping to the floor in a pool of mush. A shiver shot through her, the chill of her skin inciting a cold sweat to glisten across her forehead. She wound her arms around herself in a self-hug, the only layer of protection left available.

Josh stepped forward, each footfall a nail in her coffin. He bent down, his face hovering before her own. With his fingertips, he tucked a stray curl behind her ear before picking up the heart charm. He toyed with it, eyeing the necklace—the only surviving symbol of their past relationship.

"I loved you yesterday, Mavis Benson. I really did." He

dropped the necklace and sighed, rising to his feet. "Give my best to Chicago."

The last nail of her coffin pounded in. Josh's words the hammer that shattered her heart for good.

CHAPTER TWENTY-ONE

Austin

Austin sighed, snuggling deeper into the lounge chair. His computer balanced on his lap, unread emails having piled high in his inbox since he last left the office on Friday afternoon. He clicked mindlessly, scanning messages and creating client to-do lists for the week ahead. The subject line in one of the emails referenced the plans for the new Chicago office, and he clicked fervently, glossing over the details.

That job has to be for me.

If there was ever a chance to move to the Windy City to be with Mavis, this job was his first-class ticket.

Austin reached for the coffee on the side table, the steam from the roast tickling his upper lip as he sipped. He stretched, ready to hop in the shower before heading to the manor for the usual Sunday morning brunch with the family. Guilt settled in his gut, battling with the caffeine. It sloshed around with fury as Austin shuffled back to the kitchen to toss the cup in the dishwasher.

With an inhale, he folded his body over the counter, his bare chest meeting the cold quartz. A shiver sizzled along his spine at the cool shift in temperature.

How am I supposed to sit next to Josh and eat a stupid muffin?

"This is all so fucked up," he whispered.

He laid his cheek on the countertop, allowing the ache in his heart to spread. His soul called to hers, the longstanding friendship between them blossoming into something so much more. The passion on her lips calling forth the yearning in his heart to name her his own.

Austin flipped his head, his opposite cheek meeting the surface. Josh, his brother, his best friend. *How can I steal the love of your life?*

"I can't," he murmured to the empty kitchen.

Austin scrunched his eyes closed and heaved out a breath, willing away the conflict stirring in his soul. But the battle of desire versus loyalty raged on with no end in sight.

There's just no good answer here.

His phone pinged in his pocket, and Austin fumbled to retrieve it without moving his body from the counter. Tess's name lit up the screen, and he cringed. Not once had a text message from her been a pleasant experience. He inhaled and accepted the text, rolling his eyes as the image downloaded.

His body tingled, a sudden coldness creeping along his skin. Every muscle in his body tensed, his grasp on the phone tightening until pain radiated from his fingertips. The photo on his screen dug the grave for the relationship he shared with his brother. He swallowed and tapped the text she wrote below. *I've been dying to tell Josh for years, but I never had the proof. I owe Jerry one for this. He was the old dude with a newspaper.*

Austin choked out a breath, forcing his body to stand. "Fucking bitch!" he yelled to the empty kitchen, jamming his phone back in his pocket. Anger flared in his heart as he paced the tile floor, raking his fingers through his hair. "God damn it, what do I do now?" he whined.

The doorbell rang. "Open up, Austin! I need to talk to you," yelled Mitch.

"Does everyone already know?" He released the last breath held in his lungs and shuffled to the front door, his bare feet thudding against the wood floor of the foyer.

Mitch's shadowy figure stood behind the exterior glass, his impatient form shifting his weight from side to side. "Damn it, Austin! Open the door," he yelled again.

Austin cringed, his nose scrunching with unease. "Do you know?" he asked, pressing down on the handle.

"Know what?"

Austin tugged the door open, and his brother-in-law stepped inside. The robust smells of cedar and pine entered with him, each earthy scent wafting from his clothes. White paint coated his hands and dirt lived beneath his fingernails.

"Know what?" he repeated, raising his shoulders.

"Josh." Austin's eyes widened, his brow raising to meet his hairline.

"What about him?"

"Why're you here?" Austin tipped his head in curiosity, his eyes penetrating Mitch's gaze. *You don't know yet, do you?* The ripples of fear lessened, his blood flow slowing in his veins.

"What's wrong with you? I'm so confused," admitted Mitch.

Austin hung his head, ramming his hands in his pockets. "I'm... in trouble."

Mitch nodded. "Yeah, I think you are, but I don't know exactly why." He stepped into the living room. His butt met the sofa, and his body leaned back, hands cupping the base of his neck. "Talk, dude." He pointed to the chair opposite him.

Austin groaned and slumped into the seat, dropping his head into his palms. He opened his eyes, peeking through the cracks of his fingers.

"Do you know where she is?"

Mitch shrugged. "I assume you mean my sister, and I'm guessing she's on a plane back to Chicago, right?"

Austin nodded. "Yeah, right..." He smashed his hand to

his forehead, kneading the tension. "Have you talked to Josh?"

"Spit it out, man. Whatever it is, just say it." He leaned forward, his elbows resting against his knees, meeting the holes in his paint-slopped jeans.

The beat of Austin's heart stilled as he lifted his gaze from the safety of his palms. His brother-in-law's familiar green gaze stared back, an exact replica of the eyes he knew so well—the eyes he longed for in his dreams. Austin inhaled, drawing in a breath that filled his lungs to capacity.

"I love your sister," he said, spilling the secret words from his lips. His confession oozed from his mouth, the clandestine truth of his soul on the way to Mitch's ears. "I'm *in love* with Mavis," he clarified.

Mitch stared back, expressionless, eyes vacant. "That adds up," he murmured.

"And now Josh knows. I'm fucked, Mitch," he said, disbelief dripping from his confession.

Mitch snorted and reined in a laugh. "Yeah, you are, man." He shook his head. "What the hell are you thinking?"

Austin rammed his eyes shut and slumped back in the chair, pressing the palms of his hands to cover his eyes once again. "I can't help it!" he yelled. "I didn't choose this!"

"None of us do," Mitch answered with a shrug. "But it doesn't mean we get free rein to act on those feelings."

He snorted. "Where was that advice ten years ago?" Austin rolled his eyes.

"Tell me what happened."

"Fucking Tess," he answered, tossing his phone into Mitch's lap.

Mitch typed in his passcode, his eyes widening as the offending image appeared. A low whistle blew from his lips. "Was this yesterday?" He crinkled his nose.

Austin nodded.

"Damn it, Austin! I drove her to that stupid coffeehouse! I drove her into this mess—into *your* mess!" he yelled, chucking the phone into the cushion beside him.

Austin held up his hand. "Hang on. You don't know all the details. Mavis isn't blameless here."

"She rarely is." Mitch stood, his feet wearing a pattern into the living room carpet as he paced. Bits of wood and dried paint flaked from his pants as he moved, and Austin scrunched his nose, eyeing the foreign and unwelcomed objects on his carpet. "You better start from the beginning, man. Tell me everything."

Austin raised his arms and let them drop to the chair with a thud. "I *can't!* I can't, okay?" he pleaded.

"Why does it matter anymore? The truth is out there. You've got some sick love triangle going on…" Mitch waved his hand, swatting at the air in Austin's direction. "Ugh, with my sister!"

"You fuck *my* sister," he murmured into the cushion.

Mitch shook his head and smashed his eyes closed. "I'm *married* to your sister. Big difference here, dude!"

Austin tugged a throw pillow into his lap, squeezing the square of soft fluff to his chest. He toyed with the button in the middle, spinning the plastic between his fingers.

"Look… buddy…" Mitch sighed and plopped down on the sofa again, reclaiming his seat. "You can't do this. Josh…"

"What?" he tossed the pillow from his lap. "He just has a claim on her for life?" Austin snapped his knuckles and leaned forward. "Ten years. He literally hasn't seen her for ten years. Hasn't been a part of her life in a decade." He pointed toward his heart. "But I *have.*"

Mitch nodded but pursed his lips. "That still doesn't make it right." He exhaled and tossed Austin's phone back to his lap. "It's wrong and you know it."

The incriminating image stared up at him, his lips pressed sweetly to hers in an admission of love in its purest form. His kiss, an invitation for a future together.

"I can't help the way I feel about her."

Mitch shook his head. "No, but you *can* control what you do with those feelings."

"It's not fair," he shot back.

Mitch snorted. "When has life ever been fair?" He picked at a paint splotch on his forearm covering his tattoo.

Austin's heart sank, Mitch's words seeping into the core of his existence. His whiny plea rang in his ears, listening to his childish reasons that he should have a turn with his brother's toy.

"She's had a shitty life, Austin. You know that…" He grinned and huffed out a breath. "And I guess you know more than I do about it…"

"Mitch—"

He raised his hand, silencing the interruption. "Hear me out, okay?"

Austin slumped back into his seat, defeated.

"You might *think* you love Mavis."

"Oh, come on—"

"And I don't dismiss that you feel *something* for her," Mitch continued. "But you don't love her. If you did, you wouldn't be doing this. You wouldn't be messing with her chance to come home." Mitch sighed and stood, resuming his steps throughout the living room. "It's not lost on me that you've helped her. I don't know all the details, but I know you've been there."

Austin nodded. "Yeah."

"But she's not yours, dude."

The simple words struck him—a freight train to the chest, barreling into his heart at full speed. The love growing in his soul fractured; each shard of affection splintered.

She's not yours.

Austin slumped, a breath of defeat expelling from his lungs.

"But I love her," he murmured. "I always have."

"I don't doubt it. And I know she's not blameless here either. But Austin, you gotta step aside. You'll kill Josh over this. You'll kill Mavis, too. Don't split her heart into any more pieces."

Austin pictured the stupid heart charm around her neck,

her fingers always looped around it, always fiddling with the aged silver. Its once shining finish rubbed into dull gray, compounded over time with desire and longing. *It isn't me she thinks of. It isn't me her soul calls for… and it never will be.*

"You know, for the guy who wanted nothing to do with her two days ago, you're overly protective of her heart." He rolled his eyes.

"You've protected her heart for the last ten years. Let someone else take a turn." He smiled.

Tears burned the back of Austin's eyes as the truth settled in his gut. He swallowed, fighting the conclusion to the conversation—fighting the conclusion to his deep-seated feelings. Love wasn't enough, and it would never be enough.

He stood, stuffing his hands in his pockets. His head hung, all fight deflating from the depths of his soul.

Much like the games they played as children, inevitably, the dragon would always be slayed. The princess would always be rescued, and Josh reigned as the hero.

"The treasure is likely to be your death, though the dragon is no more," he quoted.

Mitch grinned. "Come on, Smaug. Let's go fix this."

I am fire. I am death.

JULIE NAVICKAS

CHAPTER TWENTY-TWO

Josh

The waves crashed onto the beach.

Josh stared, the white caps spilling over—endless, expected, and predictable. Beauty unfolded before him, the cycles of the waves rotating with grace, swirling the sand and seaweed. He saw none of it. Each grain of sand was a shattered piece of his heart, and each wave of the ocean a pool of his blood as it seeped from his still-beating heart.

Thunder rumbled overhead as lightning threatened in the distance. Josh sank to the picnic table, his eyes glossing over the blinking sign of Sandy's Surf. The holiday lights sparkled in the darkening sky, a small bit of cheer splashing across the backdrop of the damp beach. Wind rustled through his hair as the impending storm sought power.

He tugged his legs to his chest and rested his chin on his knees, closing his eyes until the ocean faded to black. *How could you do this to us, Duchess?*

"Josh?"

His muscles tensed. Austin's voice grated against his ear, the hopeful tenor stirring rage in his gut. Fury rolled through his body, a tidal wave building momentum before the inevitable collision.

Josh twisted, peering over his shoulder. He snorted as Mitch stepped forward first.

"You brought a bodyguard?" he scoffed, returning his chin to his knees.

Mitch sat on the bench beneath him, the rickety table swaying beneath their combined weight. "Can my title be peacekeeper instead?" he asked, elbowing Josh in the shin.

"That implies I'm going to speak to my brother, so no." Josh snorted and closed his eyes.

The picnic table shook again as Austin sat behind him.

"Josh... can I at least try to ex—"

A burst of manic laughter escaped his lips, giggles tumbling uncontrollably from his mouth as his body trembled, expelling the hilarity of his twin's request. "There is literally not one thing you can say that can explain what you did." The laughter ceased as he turned to survey his brother.

Austin's head hung, dropping into his palms as he leaned forward. He swallowed, his pale complexion blending into the sand behind him.

"I'm sorry, Josh," he murmured, shaking his head. "I never meant to fall in love with her."

Josh pulled his head upright, his brother's admission crashing into his heart as jealousy boiled, billowing from his body in an invisible cloud.

"She isn't *yours to love*." His teeth ground together, the muscles in his cheeks restricting as his jaw clenched. "How dare you... You're my fucking *brother*."

Austin exhaled and slumped in his seat. "I know, and I'm sorry. I never should have acted on it—any of it." His gaze lifted from the sand, colliding with Josh's for the first time since arriving. "But there are things you don't know, reasons for the way I feel. You need the *truth*."

"The truth?" Josh snorted. "A decade of deception..." He slapped the table. "But hey, if today's the day you choose to unload, let's have it," he quipped.

"Josh..." Austin pulled a hand through his hair and rested his palms against the back of his neck, each finger pressing into the muscle.

"I'll get you going." Josh angled his body to face him. He smiled, sarcastic excitement coating his words. "Let's start with my ex-wife, okay?"

Austin groaned.

"Tell me. How did she snap a photo of your lips on my ex-girlfriend?" He propped his elbows against his knees and dropped his chin to his palms. "Go on, start with that."

Austin shook his head. "Look, I... kissed her, all right?" His shoulders rose.

"Not the first time, was it?" Josh grinned.

"I mean, no..." Austin stood, pulling his body from the picnic table. His feet shuffled in the sand, each footfall pressing into the beach, marking the moment in time the truth revealed itself. "But it's not me she wants. She'll choose you, Josh. She'll always choose you." His face lifted to the sky as the first drop of rain fell. "But after all this time, I needed her to know that I love her too. I love the person she's become."

Raindrops penetrated the wood of the picnic table, and Josh ran his hand along the dampening surface. "How long have you been hanging on to that little secret?"

"Yeah, Austin," piped in Mitch. "Why now?" He cleared his throat. "If—whatever all of this was between you two—happened like six years ago, where'd all this come from?"

Austin sighed and wiped the rain from his cheeks. "It was never supposed to matter! That night in Chicago was just a dumb, drunken mistake, a sore spot in our past soaked with gin." He stuffed his hands in his pockets. "But then Josh got all interested in her again, dragging her back here." Austin kicked the sand. "I guess there was just more there than I ever realized."

"Wow. We're just learning so fucking much about you this week, aren't we?" asked Josh, his fist pounding the table's surface. "Kissing the love of my life in

237

coffeehouses… drunk screwing her in hotel rooms… oh, and my personal favorite… keeping her pregnancy a fucking secret!" Josh buried his face in his hands, the truth of his words tearing holes in the relationship with his brother.

Like it's not bad enough losing Mavis, now I get to lose you too.

"Pregnancy?"

The word stung, the knowledge still raw. A fresh rip in his heart tore, the truth a jagged razor cutting along the inner workings of his soul. Josh cringed, his gaze flying to his brother. Austin mouthed, "*It wasn't my secret to tell.*"

Tears stung, welling in the corners of his eyes. He shook his head, dragging his hands through his damp hair until the tears that fell blended into the rain on his cheeks.

"I'm sorry, Mitch," he whispered. "It was an accident."

"You got my sister pregnant? That's why she left?" Mitch scrunched his nose, his fingers mindlessly tracing the gouge on the picnic table bench. "It's called a fucking condom, you idiot!" he barked, swatting at Josh's legs. "What the hell happened?"

Josh exhaled, the regret tumbling from his body at his careless teenage mistake. "I didn't know anything about it until two days ago. I had absolutely no idea," he murmured, returning his face to the safety of his palms. "But I'm sure Austin can fill in the gaps for us." He tilted his head in his direction. "He's known the whole time."

"And I made a promise to Mavis to keep it a secret," he said, each year of serving as her vault punctuating the words falling from his lips.

"Are you saying she told *you*?" asked Mitch, hurt infusing his question.

Austin dropped back to his seat at the picnic table, folding his arms across the surface. He rested his cheek against his forearm, tears of his own leaking onto his arm. "She showed up at my door a couple of weeks after she miscarried," he whispered, burying his face into the crook of his elbow. "I swear to God, Josh. I never meant to do anything more than comfort her."

Josh lifted his head, Austin's last words hammering into his brain. *Do anything more?* Nausea gripped him, an internal pressure squeezing his empty stomach, wringing it like a saturated sponge.

"Don't you dare stop," he threatened as dread poured from the sky above him, coating his body in an unbearable wet blanket.

Austin shook his head. His voice quivered. "I... I... made love to her."

A crack of lightning lit up the sky, a streak of gold meeting the ocean, separating the sky with a slice of a sword. The rain poured from above, soaking the beach with tears, each admission and truth revealed seeping into the sand for eternity.

Josh rose from his seat and stumbled away, each step carrying him further from the picnic table, further from the truth, and further from his best friend.

Storms were temporary, but the damage left in their wake wasn't.

Josh faceplanted into his mattress, his head meeting the pillow with a sigh. Her scent clung to the material—coconuts settling into his nose like a tropical vacation. He breathed deeply, inhaling the memory of her, digging into the brief moments they'd been given before the earth collapsed around them, upending the steady ground beneath their feet.

He closed his eyes, running his hands along the sheets. The bed was empty, void of her presence. Her reentry into his life had been brief. Like a cruel joke, he'd been granted entry into his dreams, only to have the key tugged away and thrown into the abyss. Never to be explored, never to be permitted again. His world had shattered, each edge to her memory sharp as glass, ready to cut and razor into his heart.

Josh groaned, and his lungs suffocated as he held his breath, forcing the pain in his soul to tolerate his new reality.

Mavis had gone as quickly as she'd come home.

"Duchess…" he called into the pillow.

The silent room held no response, her name fading into the air, lost to the solitude. Exhaustion overwhelmed him, and the land of dreams called to his psyche. His eyes closed, and darkness took him.

In his dreams, she danced among the poppies, each bubble of laughter falling from her lips, careless and free. Weightless and swirling, her youth and innocence clung to his soul, each heartbeat an echo of his own.

She called his name, love stitching a thread through her words, woven with strings of passion and profound connection. The gentle breeze ruffled her dress as she fell into his arms, caught in his grasp for each day they'd been afforded life together, until the day mortality would separate them.

As the flowers of the meadow wilted with age, her edges faded too, her body translucent, falling from his arms as her soul left the earth—and left him alone in the dying grass. Her voice sang to him as she drifted away, the last words on her lips his very name.

Cold sweat coated his skin, dampening the sheets as his name called forth his waking consciousness. His heart pounded, and his eyes shot open. Josh pulled his body from the bed, desperate to leave the nightmare. He staggered to the bathroom and splashed water on his pale face, the water dripping from his cheeks to the sink. Ragged breaths fell from his mouth as his heart worked to regain a steady rhythm.

"I can't lose you." *It can't be over. I won't let it be over. You're my forever, Mavs, no matter what's happened.*

His reflection stared back in the mirror, his empty eyes haunted by his dream. He breathed deeply, in to calm his racing heart and out to push the ghost far from his troubled mind.

Josh's feet carried him back to bed, and he dropped to the mattress. Pulling from within his wallet, his gaze lingered over the new photo of the amusement park, his lips pressed to Mavis's in a moment of promise.

Austin's voice drifted to the forefront of his mind. *"She'll choose you. She'll always choose you."*

"It was my fault I lost you to begin with. How can I be angry with you, Mavs?" Josh dragged his fingers through his hair and dropped his hands to the mattress. "No. We're not over because I'll never be over you."

His gaze darted to his desk, a blank notebook resting on the surface. He crossed the bedroom to ease into the desk chair.

Mavis always had a way with words, her imagination a minefield for stories and the pen in her hand a dance of poetry as her words blossomed from the tip.

The blank paper stared back at him.

It all started with a letter.

"But it's not going to end with a letter." Josh picked up the pen.

CHAPTER TWENTY-THREE

Mavis

Her feet trudged through the snow, the bitter cold sneaking through the hole in her boot's toe. The eerie silence of the city echoed around her, 3AM offering nothing more than scattered flurries and the occasional cab sloshing through the iced-over streets.

Mavis stopped at the crosswalk, the red hand of the pedestrian signal glaring back through the snow. Wind lashed at her body, the only lone soul on the street corner. The ice-cold blasts of air froze the tears on her raw cheeks, overflowing from the hours held back behind her eyelids.

She'd stepped into The Broken Shaker yesterday for the lunch hour, pulling a double shift to help compensate for the cost of her California-adventure-turned-disaster. For sixteen straight hours, customers had barked in her face over undercooked burgers, liquor bottles had tipped, sloshing sticky liquid over her shoes, and she'd been stiffed on a tip more times than she could count on a single hand.

Her eyes glossed over, fog rippling through her brain. An invisible dark cloud hovered above her head, its dreary sadness a constant presence, an ache in her existence from dawn until dusk.

The light changed, and she stepped from the curb, slipping on a patch of black ice. Her butt met the pavement, and dirty slush coated her leggings, soaking into the material with all the quick absorbency of Casey's go-to roll of paper towels. A dull pain careened through her body, the impact of the holiday-infested city street colliding with the exhaustion of her muscles and cold, aching bones.

"W-h-y?" she whined to the silent night. Her sob caught in the gusty wind, carried off into the ether, with not one other person in the world to witness her sorrow.

She pressed her gloved hand to the pavement and pushed her body upright. Mavis staggered across the street, blinded by her tears of agony. Each step forward drilled a new hole in her heart, the unrelenting sense of misery setting up base camp in her gut.

She stumbled through a snowdrift as she turned the corner, her apartment coming into view. Mavis dragged her hand along the brick wall of a neighboring building, seeking the steady support of its foundation. Not one moment in life compared to the bitter haze engulfing her soul, her existence fading into a pit of black with nothing to cling to—all hope blinded by shadow.

Warmth enveloped her as the door to her building closed behind her, banishing the wind to the outdoors. She banged her snow-covered boots off on the lowermost stair and started the climb. Her breathing labored, each step a test of her will to persist. Mavis tugged off her wet gloves on the third floor and grasped the doorknob, twisting and pushing until it heaved open with a squeak.

Damn it, Casey, lock the damn door!

Her roommate stretched, the thin blanket dropping to the floor from her shoulders. Casey pushed herself upright from the couch, a yawn gripping her words. "What time is it?"

"Late. Go back to sleep, Case—"

"What happened to you?" She pointed.

Mavis snorted. "Ice is slippery." Her eyes widened as she dropped her bag to the dining room table, knocking askew a pile of mail. She scooped up the stack and shuffled through an overdue water bill, a tiny royalty check from *The Funny Part*, a flyer for professional carpet cleaning, and a letter addressed to *Duchess*.

The breath caught in her throat, the familiar handwriting on the envelope snaking around her heart.

"When did this mail come?"

"Umm… I think I grabbed it this morning. Or umm, yesterday now, I guess?" Casey tugged her hair into a ponytail and stepped toward the dining room table. "Why? Another overdue bill?" She giggled and wrapped her arms around Mavis, resting her chin on her shoulder. "You okay?"

"I guess that depends on what's in this." She twisted the letter in her hands.

"Who's the duchess?" She grinned and plucked the letter from Mavis's grasp, examining the envelope.

"It's what Josh calls me…" Her eyes narrowed. The now-familiar squeeze of her heart gripped her, his name the source of all guilt.

Casey scrunched her nose and handed the letter back. "I thought it was Princess?"

Her stomach dropped like a dip on a rollercoaster. "Umm, that's what Austin calls me," she admitted, pulling her body from Casey's embrace as her cheeks reddened.

"A *Lifetime* movie in the making…" She stepped toward the kitchen and dragged the coffeepot forward.

"I thought it was the *Hallmark* channel. But either way, it's a box office flop," Mavis mumbled, kicking off her wet boots.

Casey dumped coffee grounds in the machine and filled the reservoir with water from the faucet. "Maybe not. Depends on what's in that, right?" She pointed to the letter and clicked the start button, the orange glow lighting up her index finger. "Oh, and before I forget, you left your phone on the counter. I think your brother called you like seven times today." She scrunched her nose and watched the brown liquid drip into a Chicago Cubs mug.

Mavis swallowed the guilt rising in her throat before dropping her gaze to the envelope. She flipped it, inserting a finger beneath the lip and tearing the paper until a letter peeked out. Her butt dropped to the chair, the cold damp of her leggings pressing into her skin.

She tipped the envelope and a photo fell... the Ferris wheel at Pacific Park. Tears burned behind her eyes, the frozen moment preserved in front of her a distant memory, no longer attainable.

Mavis pushed the photo aside and unfolded the letter, preparing her heart for the final farewell—the words that would release her from Josh's lifelong grasp.

She inhaled, holding the breath in her lungs.

Duchess,

In our decade apart, I learned to wait. I learned to wait for someone who challenges me—someone who will always keep my life interesting. I learned to wait for someone who takes their time to understand me in a way no one else does. I learned to wait for someone who wants to be a part of my world and wants me to be a part of theirs. I learned to wait for someone who lets me know I'm on their mind, someone who checks in on me, who wants me to know that they care. I learned to wait for someone who makes love feel easy, like you can pick up where time left off. I learned to wait for someone who strives to protect my heart at all costs. But most of all, I learned to wait for someone who will choose me over and over and over again. I learned to wait for someone who reminds me that love was always meant to be.

In short, I learned to wait for you.

I didn't understand it at first, but I do now. Life has hardened us both, and while we shared a love of innocence and youth, it doesn't mean nothing has changed. Because everything has changed. And if it takes me the rest of forever, I'd like to prove to you that I understand, and I respect and admire the woman you've become.

There is no one to blame here but myself.

I love you, Mavis Benson. Because your soul is my soul, no matter how many years have passed. I do not fault you for anything—past, present, or future—because it was my error that cost you the life you knew. You waited for me for a decade, and your love too is worth waiting for. And I'd wait another lifetime if it means I can call you mine again.

Joshua

Her heart stalled, each tear blurring her vision until the paper in her hands disappeared from her grasp entirely. The ache of her body lessened—each breath a release of guilt consuming her core. The weights pressing down on her body lifted, filling her lungs with fresh air for the first time in four days. She smiled through the tears, life stirring in her soul from the blackened pit.

"Well?" Casey's gaze lifted from the counter, brown liquid spilling across the surface.

"He still wants me, Case," she whispered, pressing the letter to her chest.

"Josh?" she asked, grabbing a roll of paper towels. "You never did tell me what happened."

"I… umm…" she hedged, pulling her body from the chair. "I have to call Austin."

Casey mopped up the spilled coffee and scrunched her nose. "I thought that letter was from Josh?"

The smile on Mavis's lips faded, the task ahead slicing through the elation kickstarting her heart moments ago. "It is." She dragged a hand through her wet hair. "I should have done this ten years ago," she murmured, tiptoeing across the tile. "I see it now," she added, padding down the hall.

"Do you want this coffee?"

"Sorry, Case. I need a minute."

She closed the door to her bedroom, dumping her purse and Josh's letter on the bed. Her hands tore at her wet bottoms, tugging the soggy fabric from her legs. The damp material clung to her cold skin as she hopped on one foot, yanking them from her body until they fell to the floor in a cold lump.

Her eyes caught sight of the bloody smear on the wall as she pulled on dry pants. The familiar sensation of a rug being pulled from beneath her feet gripped her stomach, all the hope blooming in her heart from Josh's letter dissolving as the momentary happiness softened back into conflicted reality.

My sweet Austin.

"Where does that leave you?" she asked, dragging her hand across the stain. His grin flashed in her mind, his tender embrace folding around her like a comforting blanket. From the moment the world crashed in around her, he'd stood by her side, a lone friend in the dark.

Nothing made sense. Nothing aligned, each half of her heart tugged in opposite directions. Forever conflicted, forever in turmoil until the moment the motion ceased, and the silence echoed until just one name could fall from her lips. *Just one.*

Her fingers sought the charm around her neck. She squeezed, collapsing the heart into the palm of her hand. In the deafening silence, she listened. And her soul spoke, calling forth the truth that lived beyond the physical means of the world. With each beat in her chest, her heart answered. Her soul had found its other half as a child, fusing together in a bond unparalleled to anything more than the universe offered. The truth belonged to her heart, and no matter the pain and agony it had endured over time, the answer lived on, buried amidst the rubble and scattered tears. Josh's love existed—persisted—beyond time and space.

She'd grown, she'd crawled and clawed her way through life. While Austin had held her hand and tugged her from the wreckage, the bond they'd ignited had been fueled by a flame of vulnerability. Their relationship had blossomed in a bed of weeds. At first glance, beautiful with bulbs of color, but on closer inspection, nothing more, never a true flower. Never a true poppy.

With a groan, she pulled her phone from the depths of her bag, each shaking finger grasping the device until the screen reflected his name in an open text message. She typed, *Are you awake?* Like a needle, each letter punctured the relationship that could never be—that would never be.

Mavis tapped *send*, and for the first time, clarity settled in her heart. A line had been drawn in the sand… and her toe stepped over the division. Final. And sure, but riddled with heartache.

Her ringtone bit into the silence of the room, and she brought the phone to her ear like a death sentence. His voice crashed into her, an echo, a song of the past. Her savior, her friend, her source of all comfort all pooled in the pit of her stomach.

I've done difficult things before, but this, oh this…

"Can't sleep either?" he asked with a ragged breath.

"I can't close my eyes," she whispered, tears beginning to trickle down her face.

He sighed. "Then let me help you rest, Princess," he whispered.

She swallowed the sob, choking on the air as it stopped in her throat. The oxygen pulled from the room, a suffocating blanket of words earmarked for *the end*.

"I'm sorry," he said.

"It's me that should apologiz—"

"Shhh, please don't. Before you say anything, I need you to hear something first, okay?"

Mavis exhaled, forcing the breath from her body as the sensation of tiny pins stabbed holes in her heart. She nodded, choking on the words that wouldn't come.

"I know it's over for us, but Mavis Benson, I need you to know that I've loved you since we were kids—"

"Austin…" she squeaked. Her hand clutched her heart, tears cascading down her face at his words. Pressure built in her ears, the sound of his voice thick and distant.

"And it's my own damn fault for not realizing it sooner." His words caught in his throat. "But maybe letting go of you won't be all that different from actually loving you… because I know now that I never really had you to begin with."

His words—his admission—hung in the airways. The truth fell from his lips, releasing her from the ten-year journey they'd started together. Over the last week, each secret they shared had unraveled like a spool of thread, spiraling apart with unrelenting speed, leaving nothing but a frail, frayed end.

A sob bubbled over, and Mavis covered her mouth with her hand. Her cold fingertips touched her cheeks, brushing the trail of tears from her skin.

"You belong with Josh, not me. We both know it. I was wrong to think otherwise. And, Princess…" He exhaled. "I'm sorry for hurting you. It's the last thing in the world I ever wanted to do."

His apology sliced through her heart, ripping the very strings he once stitched together.

"Damn it, Austin!" she screeched. "I fucking hate this! None of this is fair!"

"No, Mavs… it isn't. But whoever said it should be?"

Tell him you love him. Tell him what he means to you! Tell him that he carried you, that he pulled you from a blackened pit when no one else would. Tell him that love exists, that love burns bright and beautiful. Tell him that he's loved, that he's worthy of love still…

The words settled in her heart, finding their final resting place beneath the wreckage and shattered armor. Swallowed by the finality of her soul's decision, peace bloomed eternal on the grave of unjust love.

Her mouth opened, ready to relay the emotion, ready to relay the feelings. But all that would tumble out was, "I love you."

And maybe… somehow… that's enough…

"I love you, too, Princess. But you love my brother more," he answered. "And it's okay that you do. Josh knows the truth, all of it now," he said. "And it's only a matter of time before…" His words trailed off, catching in his throat.

"He'll want you back. I'm sure he already does."

The savage pain radiating from her chest brought a cold sweat to her brow as she stared at the letter on the bed beside her. Her heart ached to know the hurt Austin suffered stemmed from her hand. But her soul recognized the truth, wading through the momentary heartbreak of love to find the dry shore on the other side in Josh's arms.

"I'm so broken, Austin," she whispered, squeezing her eyes shut.

He sighed. "I've seen you broken before. And I've also seen you put yourself back together. You're more than your past mistakes. Put your pen to the paper, Mavis, and write yourself a happy ending for once."

She swallowed, pushing away the sorrow, pushing away the anger. A smile spread across her lips at his parting words—his last expression of love.

"Goodbye, Princess," he whispered and ended the call.

Her phone dropped to the bed, bouncing across the mattress with a thud. Mavis collapsed onto her pillow, the tears leaking into the soft material as they trickled from her tired eyes. The ache in her heart lessened with each heavy breath she drew, each inhale and exhale bringing with it a sense of closure.

She reached for the handle on the nightstand and tugged it open until an empty notebook looked back. And with shaking hands, she pressed the tip of her pen to the pages. *I am more than my past mistakes. I am more than my past mistakes. I am more than my past mistakes.*

Near her toes, her phone vibrated, and she pulled the device to her lap to read a text from Josh. *Duchess—it's been four days. And I can't go another four without hearing your voice. I'm coming for you. I'm coming for us.*

She inhaled, staring at his words, every letter reiterating the truth he penned in his letter.

Exhaustion swirled in her brain, the haze of emotions rippling through her body with the undercurrent of Poseidon's wrath. Sleep took her, and in the dizzying swirl of dreams running through her unconscious mind, a pounding on a distant door brought her back to the waking world.

CHAPTER TWENTY-FOUR

Josh

Josh stared at the radar on his phone, his eyes transfixed on the Christmas snowstorm hampering the Midwest. His flight had been delayed for over twenty-four hours and no matter how many times he refreshed the weather app, the blur of red covering Chicago wouldn't dissipate.

He shifted in his seat, crossing one numb leg over the other. His palms gripped the armrests of the chair as his eyes glazed over the flashing *delayed* sign above the check-in counter. A tired flight attendant tapped away at the computer as the clock turned to 1:33AM.

I should already be in Chicago by now. I should already have you back, Mavs!

His phone vibrated as Austin's name lit up the tiny screen. The betrayal, the lies, the secrets, all of it had his stomach in knots. He opened the message and swallowed the distaste settling in his mouth. *She was never mine to love. But I fell for her anyway. And I'm sorry for the mess it caused. But Josh, I need you to know that it was always you she wanted. And it still is.*

His grip on the chair tightened, the metal in his hands warming to the touch. Josh heaved out a sigh and raked his hands through his hair, clenching his jaw.

"Damn fucking right," he muttered under his breath.

He dropped his phone to the seat beside him and wiped his sweaty palms across his jeans. The grime on his hands soured his stomach, and he dug for his hand sanitizer, seeking the nearly empty bottle from the bottom of his backpack.

His heart ached. It ached from the wedge that had been driven into the relationship with his brother. It ached from the truth that had been spilled, and the fallout of his past mistakes. But mostly, it ached for the other half of his missing soul. *Did you get my letter, Duchess?*

Josh pressed his fingers to his temples and reopened the text he'd sent to her moments ago. She hadn't responded, not to his text or his letter. He groaned, tucking the phone into his pocket.

If I can just get to Chicago, I can fix this whole fucking mess! His voice roared in his head, the frustration spewing from his psyche. And as if God himself heard his cry, the intercom clicked on above.

"Ladies and gentlemen, we apologize for the lengthy delay. We will now begin boarding our flight to Chicago. At this time, we invite Group A passengers to prepare to board. Please have your ticket and identification in hand when you approach the gate."

Josh smiled, his heart hammering wildly in his chest. "Well, Duchess, if you're not going to answer your phone, you're damn well going to answer your door."

He stood and approached the gate.

The same ugly brown suitcase circled the carousel for the hundredth time. A frayed yellow ribbon clung to the handle, dragging across the conveyor belt with all the stamina Josh felt in his core.

Sleep hadn't come on the flight over. Every time his eyes had closed, turbulence rocked the aircraft, followed by muffled cries from a small child two rows behind him. Josh rubbed his eyes and inhaled the scent of airport coffee from the woman to his right. Her lips had left a big red smear on the lid.

A gust of cold air and snow flurries burst through the doors behind him as a pack of security guards marched outside in heavy parkas. Josh tugged his thin jacket closer and furrowed his brow.

"I'd follow you anywhere, sand or snow," he muttered into his collar. He snorted, recalling the moment he'd committed to her snowy desires. The memory brought a smile to his lips as the bell sounded and red lights flashed on the carousel. And like a herd of cattle, every passenger moved forward at once, careening to see if the first bag would be theirs.

His gaze circled the endless rotation of luggage until his bag appeared amidst a taped-up car seat and a guitar case. With a muscled tug, he wrestled it free and shuffled through the crowd toward the exit. A blast of icy air impaled his body as he stepped outside the terminal. Josh drew in a breath, the cold biting into his lungs with the same intensity as the harsh wind lashing at his face.

"Where to?" the cab driver barked as he opened the door.

Josh chucked his bag in the trunk and dove into the warmth of the cabin. "Wrigleyville," he answered, digging for the address in his back pocket.

The driver nodded and put the car in gear, maneuvering out into the airport traffic. Bumper to bumper, the cab jerked forward until the heavy wet snow pummeled the windshield on I-90.

Josh squeezed his last bit of hand sanitizer onto his palms before pulling out his phone. Mavis still hadn't responded, and Austin's 1:33AM text had gone unanswered. Unease grew in his gut as the TV screen in front of him ran a prerecorded roll of advertisements. His tired brain took the bait, his attention floundering into air-fryer heaven.

"Yummy!" the happy man on the infomercial exclaimed while rubbing his belly. He licked his lips and wiggled his hips.

Josh snorted and pulled his gaze back to the road, ready to pay the makers of the miraculous air-fryer two installments of $99.99 to just make the nonsense stop.

The cab scooted forward, plowing through the wet slush coating the streets until the city skyline materialized behind the cloud of gray.

"Are we close to Wrigleyville?"

"About fifteen minutes, give or take in this weather."

Josh nodded, his heart hammering against his ribcage. He looked back at his phone and settled on the best quote his weary brain could muster for his brother. He tapped out, *So comes snow after fire, and even dragons have their endings.*

The cab stopped in a line of traffic at a red light. Out his window, a crooked sign stared back; etched into the wood read The Broken Shaker. The air caught in his lungs as the phone in his grasp pinged. Josh read, *Consider Smaug defeated, Bilbo.*

A grin tugged at his lips as the cab rolled two more city blocks, pulled to the side of the street, and parked.

"Your stop, buddy."

A tall brick building loomed through the window, its snow-covered exterior lacking invitation. Josh paid the fare and collected his bag before sloshing through the thick slush to the building's entrance.

Cigarette smoke pierced the cold air and Josh scrunched his nose and frowned. His gaze lifted to the petite curly-haired blonde standing between him and the front door. Hidden beneath a parka and winter hat, her light-blue gaze raked over him with curiosity as smoke blew from her glossy lips.

"Umm... excuse me," said Josh, distracted by her contradictory bare legs and flip-flops. *What the hell?* "Aren't you cold?" he asked with a grin. *Do you even know what frostbite is?*

She glanced down and wiggled her royal blue-painted toes. "I guess." She smiled and dropped the cigarette to the concrete, smashing the butt with her shoe. "Did you need something?"

Josh grinned and stepped forward, holding out his phone. A photo of Mavis lit up the screen. "Mavis Benson. Does she live here?" He gestured to the building.

She squinted at the image and rammed her hands in her pocket. "Who are you?"

"Oh, umm... Josh Templeton." He extended his hand in her direction and smiled. "Her kinda... sorta... ex—no, boyfriend?" He snorted and shook his head. "I don't even know anymore."

"Oh my, God! You're *the* Josh!" She lunged forward and grabbed his hand, leading him up the snow-covered steps and through the building's door.

Warmth collided with his skin as his vision adjusted to the dim entryway. He stumbled on the first step, following the quirky flip-flop-clad blonde. Her rubber soles slapped against the concrete with each step upward. *Flip. Flop. Flip. Flop.*

"I'm Casey, her roommate," she called over her shoulder. She stopped at the first-floor landing and grinned. "Mavs didn't tell me you were coming."

"She doesn't know I'm here," he answered, propping his suitcase against his leg.

"Wait. What?" Her eyes narrowed. "She doesn't know you're here?"

"No." His shoulders fell, the air deflating from his lungs. The last few days of heartache caught up with him, squeezing his soul with the ugly truth—gripping his gut with the possibility that even though he'd made it to Chicago, she could refuse him. His suitcase tipped, landing in a pool of wet slush from their feet. "I don't know how much you know, Casey..." His gaze bore into hers as he willed the truth in his heart to radiate outward. "But I love her. And I need the chance to speak to her. I have to fix this—I have to fix *us*."

Her face softened into a grin. "She hides everything. She always has, but if there's one thing I *do* know about her, it's that she loves you too." Casey bent forward and picked up the handle of his bag, placing the plastic in Josh's hand. "So come on, Prince Charming. She's in the tallest tower."

She winked and started to climb, leaving hope in her wake. Josh followed, each step forward bringing him closer to his soul's missing half.

I'm coming for you, Duchess. I'm coming for us.

Casey reached the third floor and twisted the handle of the door on the right. But nothing happened.

"Shit…" she murmured, twisting with more force. "Damn it, I always do this!" She rammed her shoulder into the door. "Mavs!"

Josh grinned as her tiny fists pummeled the door, one lousy lock preventing him from the happy ending he'd come to secure.

CHAPTER TWENTY-FIVE

Mavis

Her feet hit the floor, the cold of the kitchen tile radiating upward through her body as she stumbled through the apartment. Mavis dragged a hand through her unkempt hair, rubbing her eyes free of yesterday's makeup.

Casey's fists beat into her brain as they rapped on the opposite side of the door.

"I'm gonna nail your keys to your forehead, Casey McDaniels!" she yelled, gripping the doorknob and twisting with angst.

Warmth flooded through her chest as Josh appeared. His heart called to hers, the depths of his soul snaking around the remnants of rubble, rousing her existence from the crumbling ache of the last four days.

"Duchess," he whispered, sidestepping Casey. "I'm so sorry," he muttered, tugging her body into his.

His damp jacket met her face, smelling of cigarette smoke and a stale cab. She swallowed, breathing in the stench, willing to endure every breath as long as his arms held her. His lips pressed onto the top of her head and whispers fell from his mouth, the word *sorry* tangling in her wild curls until the apologies penetrated her ear.

"Let me grab some pants and I'll give you guys some privacy," said Casey, sliding into the apartment behind them.

A giggle escaped Mavis, a true bubble of laughter erupting from within as Casey flip-flopped beside her and into her bedroom.

"You've met Casey," she said, her face still pressed into Josh's chest.

A thud in the back bedroom echoed through the dining room and Casey returned with covered legs.

"It was nice to meet you, Casey," cooed Josh, his arms still wrapped around Mavis.

Casey winked and scooped up her purse and keys, stepping to the doorway. "Mavs, he's even hotter in person. Maybe don't let him go this time?" she called over her shoulder as the door closed behind her.

Josh laughed. "I like her," he joked.

Mavis snorted and pulled away. "I love her, but her smoke is all over your jacket."

He scrunched his nose and slipped the coat from his arms, draping it over a dining room table chair.

"I can't believe you're here," she whispered, wrapping her body in a self-hug. "You should hate me after what I did." She frowned and dropped her gaze to the floor, the familiar blankets of guilt and embarrassment suffocating her.

Josh sighed and rested his hands behind his head. His gaze bore into her, the hurt in his soul penetrating his stare. "It's my fault that it happened." Pain radiated from his lips, the admission of fault ringing in the air.

Mavis snorted, rolling her eyes while stepping into the living room. Her butt dropped to the sofa as she tucked her legs beneath her. "Joshua, I can blame the gin. I can blame my poor decision-making. I can even blame my own insecurities. But I really can't blame *you* for anything I did with Austin."

He stuffed his hands in his pockets and grimaced. "Mavis Benson. I want to scratch my eyes out every time I think about it." He swallowed and shuffled his feet, shifting his weight. "I *hate* that it happened. But I know *why* it did. I've had four days of *your* silence to think about it." He exhaled and stepped forward. "And that's why I can't fault you for it... geez, and maybe not even him." He sank to his knees, scooping her hands up in his own. "If it wasn't for me—and my mistake—you never would have been in a position to need my brother, to need *anyone* else but me."

Tears welled in her eyes as his hands trailed up her arms. He tugged at her necklace, the small heart charm falling between his fingers.

"Joshua..." She inhaled, allowing his words to consume her.

"There's a part—a very small part—that's thankful that you had him all these years. I'm grateful you had each other," he whispered, dropping the charm as he sank backward to the floor.

The wind whistled through the gaps in the window, chilling the air with the breath of winter. A dog howled on the snowy streets below as shovels scraped at buried cars. The silence of the apartment caved in, compounding the pressure building in her chest to admit the truth.

"Josh," she whispered, burying her face in her hands. "I have to confess something to you..." She gulped, swallowing a sob.

He nodded, pressing his lips together. "I think I already know..."

Adrenaline coursed through her veins, a heightened pressure building around her heart and pushing the truth, forcing the words to leave her lips.

"I... I love him," she sputtered. Her chest tightened, all blood draining from the source of guilt. "And that's officially the last secret I have."

Josh's face fell, her words seemingly deflating the air from his lungs. He slumped, dragging his hands across the carpet.

"A knife to my heart, Mavs," he muttered.

She dropped from the couch, her knees meeting the carpet in front of him. Her palm reached out, resting atop his chest, and he covered her hand with his own. His fingers squeezed, pressing their connection into his heart.

"I do love him. But it's not the love I have for you. My heart is *your* heart, Joshua Templeton. I know it in my soul. I've always known it," she said, squeezing the charm around her neck. "Your heart—wrapped around mine forever…"

His gaze drifted to the necklace. "You know, as kids, you were so easy to love, so easy to be with, and Austin saw it too." His fingers trailed along her cheek, wiping a tear away. "But Mavis?"

"Yeah?"

"He can't have you. Because you're not his to love." He pressed his lips to hers. "You're mine. I loved you yesterday, I love you today, and damn it, I'll love you tomorrow too."

She grinned and pressed a kiss to his lips, their two souls melding together as one. The way it was always meant to be.

EPILOGUE

Casey

Four Months Later

"Ouch!"

Her toe throbbed, pain radiating through her body as she hopped on one foot. Casey shoved the offending box across the apartment floor, pushing more than just pain away. *Damn it, Mavis! How can you leave me?* She rubbed her foot, soothing the sure-to-come bruise.

Giggles drifted down the hallway, laughter filtering from Mavis's bedroom.

"Not much packing getting done…" She scrunched her nose and moved to the kitchen, opening the cabinet holding the supply of random coffee mugs and glassware. She tugged down a shot glass, the words *The Broken Shaker* etched into the side. Casey cradled the glass, the memories of the last eight years of their friendship settling in her heart. "I'm gonna miss you, Mavs."

She packed the box with odds and ends of kitchen supplies, taking care to wrap the glassware with extra paper towel.

"Dimo's for dinner, Case?" asked Mavis, stepping from her bedroom. The diamond on her finger caught the light as she sat at the barstool.

Casey giggled. "Umm, it's like two in the afternoon."

"Can't help it. I'm gonna miss it." She grinned and poked her head in the box. "You know I bought bubble wrap, right?"

"Oh, lay off." Casey smirked, shoving the box in her direction. The glasses clanked together.

"Who packed that?" asked Josh, joining the girls in the kitchen. He set two boxes by the door, taped closed and packed with perfection.

"Casey." Mavis giggled and hopped from her barstool, pulling Casey into a bear hug. "Who else would pack with a roll of paper towels?"

Casey's cheeks reddened as heat bathed her body. "Cheaper than bubble wrap," she muttered. Her sour mood spread, poisoning her body from the top of her head down to her bruised toe. "Oh, umm… I left your sunglasses in the car." She stepped toward the door and shoved her feet into flip-flops.

"Keep them. The car is yours, so it's no big deal," answered Mavis, snaking her arms around Josh's middle.

"No. No… I'll go grab them." Casey tugged the door open and stepped out, releasing a pent-up sigh of unease. Her gaze dropped to the floor as she trudged down the steps, grasping the railing with the frustration building in her heart.

She swung her body around the second-floor landing, her right flip-flop slipping from her toes. *Thud.* Her face smashed into his chest as his arms encircled her, breaking her fall. The scent of sandalwood clung to his t-shirt, the rugged smell meeting her nose in a dizzy haze. A soft snicker met her ear, his warm breath tickling her neck.

"Shit! I'm so sorry!" Casey pulled herself upward, hopping on one foot. "My damn shoe…"

"You okay there, Cinderella?" he asked, bending

forward to scoop up the lost flip-flop. He handed her the shoe and grinned.

"Thank you." She smiled. "Now that's an embarrassing way to say hello to a stranger." Her stomach dipped as their eyes met, the ache in her heart rapidly replaced by intrigue.

"Austin." He held his hand out, squeezing her fingers, numbing her body at the touch.

"Casey," she murmured. "Your resident walking accident."

He snorted. "Well, Casey... the resident walking accident. Now we're not strangers anymore."

He grinned, and the earth fell from her feet.

No, Austin, we're sure not.

JULIE NAVICKAS

ACKNOWLEGEMENTS

First and foremost, thank you for reading *I Loved You Yesterday!* The inklings of this story took shape while enrolled in a script writing course. For over ten years the characters of this trilogy have begged me to breathe life into their stories in novel format. And thanks to Melissa Keir at Inkspell Publishing, the Templeton siblings and all those they love will share the printed page forever. Melissa, from the bottom of my heart, thank you for giving me a chance.

Along this journey to becoming a published author I have learned that it takes a village to bring a story to life. And I never would have had that opportunity without Lauren Eckhardt. Lauren, thank you for allowing me a spot beside you. Your passion for storytelling and talent for writing has filled a void in my heart, and I am eternally grateful to you for helping me to find this path.

Speaking of a village, I would be remiss if I did not thank Marcia Bufalo Juarez and Shelby Holt, my two incredible critique partners, who read through every terrible draft (and there were a lot of them!) and provided me with incredible insight, feedback, and guidance. *The Trading Heartbeats Trilogy* would not be what it is today without your help. Additionally, I am forever grateful to my faithful beta readers, Elizabeth Chupp and Kate Boutilier. Thank you for the many happy-hour brainstorms and unfailing support (in literally every aspect of my life, not just writing!)

I'd also like to thank my two editors who have poured their hearts into *I Loved You Yesterday.* Emma O'Connell, without your developmental edits, I shudder to think where this story would be today. And Audrey Bobak, I'll never look at the words "pull" or "eyes" the same way ever again! Thank you for your incredible attention to detail.

Have you looked at the gorgeous cover of this book?

Because the astoundingly talented Shel with Fantasia Frog Designs is responsible. Shel, I am blown away by your creative talent and cannot thank you enough for taking my vision and delivering on a simply gorgeous book cover.

To my colleagues in the School of Communication at Illinois State University, you all will forever hold my heart. When I first started my journey as a Redbird, you took me under your wing and helped me appreciate and develop a skillset in writing. I am grateful to your teaching, your unwavering support, and your belief in me. Dr. John McHale, I am indebted to you for asking me to write a full-length film script in COM 351. This assignment inspired *The Trading Heartbeats Trilogy.*

I once thought that writing a book was the hardest part of the process. As it turns out, that's the easy part! Thank you, Claire Coffey, for your marketing strategy genius. Thank you to my incredible launch team. And thank you, Itsy Bitsy Book Bits and Silver Dagger Book Tours for helping me put *I Loved You Yesterday* into the hands of romance readers everywhere. I'm also quite thankful for the talented Lyndsie Schlink and her photography skills (special shoutout to Toni Tucker at Ewing Manor) for helping me "look" like a true author in all my promotional tools.

Lastly, I'm grateful to my immediate support system. Lillian, Colton, and Brady, I hope you know how much I love you! All I want is for you to be proud of me and tell your friends, "My mom is an author!" And to my mom, Tracey Boyd, you instilled in me a love for reading romance novels, and your faith in me has never faltered. Thank you for making sure I know what it feels like to be loved and supported when others couldn't do so. You're the strongest person I know. And then there's you, Tommy, my forever best friend, and life partner. When I told you, "I want to write a book," you nodded and encouraged me to chase the dream. You didn't laugh. You didn't tell me I was stupid. Like everything else in our lives together, you supported me through every page.

Sneak Peek at I LOVE YOU TODAY

CHAPTER ONE

Austin

Austin dumped the last box in the moving truck. The kitchen glassware inside rattled, clanking together with the force of a tiny earthquake. *Who the hell packed this?* He scrunched his nose as his feet hammered down the ramp and returned to the city sidewalk.

"So long, Chicago." He rammed the heavy metal back into its home beneath the floor of the truck. *Well, I guess that's it, Mavs…*

His gaze lifted to the brick building beside him, meeting the third story window. Mavis—the girl who stole his heart, and princess at the top of the tallest tower—was now the soon-to-be bride of his twin brother, Josh. From the day her feet fled Rosewood over ten years ago, she'd been his brother's missing puzzle piece. And for a decade Austin had held her close and kept her safe in his heart for protection. But now… her edges melted back into Josh's with the ease of love, two halves meeting to form one whole. And Austin… the piece that got lumped into the wrong box and cast aside.

His stomach plummeted, the sinking feeling of defeat and heartache gripping his soul. *How the hell am I supposed to just let you go, Princess?* He slammed the back of the moving truck closed and maneuvered the lever to lock it in place. *And worse, watch you move on with my brother?* He grumbled, the soft whine escaping his lips into the damp air.

"She's really leaving, isn't she?"

Austin turned, seeking the voice interrupting his pity party.

Casey's bouncy blonde curls fell in her face as her pink lips smashed together in a thin line. Her arms, laden with a giant pizza box, two plastic grocery bags, and a purse, lowered with a shrug.

A tingle along his spine shivered its way to his fingertips, complementing the gust of spring air chilling his skin. *Cinderella returned from the ball... err—or the pizza place.* "Umm... yeah... back to California." He gestured to her full hands. "Can I help you with that?"

"Oh, yeah, thanks." She stepped forward and handed over the two grocery bags, the glass bottles inside clanking against each other.

Austin peeked inside and cracked a grin at the bottles of gin.

"Is Mavs not back yet? Or are you really out here packing her crap by yourself?"

He rolled his eyes as she started toward the building. "Yeah, umm... Josh said something about dropping off the last rent check to the landlord. They took off about a half an hour ago. I figured I'd just finish the boxes for her."

Casey nodded as they approached the entrance. "Awfully nice of you, considering..." She set the pizza on the concrete stoop, sinking to her knees to rummage in her bag.

"Considering?" He scrunched his nose.

"I'm sorry. It's none of my business." She shook her head as a blue lighter tumbled from her purse to the concrete at his toes.

"You're fine. You can say it." Austin bent down and retrieved it, resting it in Casey's outstretched palm. "Considering she picked my brother."

Her eyes widened. "Oh, ah... well..."

Austin sighed, swallowing hard. The pit in his stomach deepened, the black hole in his heart filling with despair. The truth lived inside him, but speaking the words... sliced new holes in his broken soul.

The glass bottles in the bags clanked together as he held

a hand out to her. Casey's fingers squeezed his palm as she pulled her body upward. "Leave it to me to make things awkward." The right side of her mouth tugged upward in a small smile as the sun poked out from behind a cloud. The light danced across her face as her eyes found his.

A wave of warmth flooded his body as he adjusted the ball cap on his head, tugging it down to shadow his face. *What the hell is wrong with me?* "No, I think that one's on me." He grinned. "Oh, but hey… glad you turned up when you did though." He pointed to the brick he'd used to keep the door ajar, cast-off in a bed of weeds. "I couldn't get back in."

She sighed and rolled her eyes. "The people in this building are super weird." Casey rammed the key in the lock, tugging the door open. "Like our new neighbor. He moved in about two weeks ago. Reeks like pot—and he's super loud and kinda creepy."

"Are you gonna stay living here?" Austin shuffled the grocery bags to free his right hand. He held the door open for Casey as she picked up the pizza and stepped inside. Her foot caught on the lowermost step and she staggered. "You okay?"

She giggled but started the climb to the third floor. "My dad always used to call me Klutzy Casey."

Grinning, Austin followed, his eyes catching the wiggle of her butt as she moved upward.

"Are you staying for dinner?" she asked over her shoulder.

JULIE NAVICKAS

ABOUT THE AUTHOR

Julie Navickas is an award-winning nationally recognized contemporary romance novelist, known for her keen ability to tell heart-wrenching, second-chance love stories through relatable characters with humility, humor, and heroism. She is also an award-winning university instructor and serves as the executive director of The Writing Champions Project. Julie earned master's degrees in both organizational communication and English studies with an emphasis in book history, as well as a bachelor's degree in public relations, graduating cum laude from Illinois State University.

Website: https://authorjulienavickas.com/

Facebook:
https://www.facebook.com/AuthorJulieNavickas
Twitter: https://twitter.com/JulieNavickas
Instagram: https://www.instagram.com/julienavickas/
LinkedIn: https://www.linkedin.com/in/julienavickas/
Tik Tok: https://www.tiktok.com/@julienavickas
YouTube:
https://www.youtube.com/channel/UCNUW07fs9AmSR
N2o-yAjISg
Email: julienavickasauthor@gmail.com
Goodreads:
https://www.goodreads.com/user/show/134518278-julie-navickas